STRAYS

BY JUSTIN KASSAB

KAYLIE JONES BOOKS

Published by Akashic Books
©2016 Justin Kassab

ISBN: 978-1-61775-501-9
e-ISBN: 978-1-61775-524-8
Library of Congress Control Number: 2016939318

First printing

Kaylie Jones Books
Twitter: @KaylieJonesBook, @JustinKassab
Websites: www.kayliejonesbooks.com, www.JustinKassab.com

Akashic Books
Twitter: @AkashicBooks
Facebook: AkashicBooks
E-mail: info@akashicbooks.com
Website: www.akashicbooks.com

To Kaylie Jones for seeing what others couldn't
and the
(e)ST

CHAPTER I

ALL THE PRESIDENT'S MEN

It was an ambush, pure and simple. Kade knew it the moment he saw Mick and Jem coming through the door to the roof of Lambian Hall. His longtime friends, now his end-of-the-world family, had been wearing him down for months. They wanted his permission to journey to a location where there were other survivors.

The two men stood side by side, shooting looks at each other and waiting for the other to lead the attack. Mick stood to the left, still wearing his navy blue police uniform from his Old World life. The dark blue of the uniform made his fire-red hair stand out even more. Jem was on the right, also wearing a uniform, but his was Pennsylvania National Guard. Kade knew he wouldn't be able to stop them when Jem's ice-blue eyes locked on his. Sooner or later they would leave, whether they had his permission or not.

Jem stepped forward, and Kade braced for what was coming.

"I understand why you don't want to worry about people outside of Houghton, but it's not fair to the rest of us. You have your sister, brother, and lover. What do the rest of us have?" Jem said.

The night went silent, as if even the creatures were in on their plan. Kade squatted down and petted the large black dog, Fenris, who was sleeping at his feet. He responded by giving his friends a nod, then turned his back to them and looked out over the campus he was responsible for protecting. His eyes followed the stream that made up the west boundary of the college campus, over the half-dozen buildings that used to be dorms or classrooms. It was a small patch of land, but it was his.

* * *

Mick watched the trees go by as they drove south from Houghton, New York, toward Washington, DC. Jem's National Guard unit had been called to defend DC before the Primal Age had settled upon mankind, and now he felt duty-bound to return to those he'd left behind in the fall. From what Jem had told Mick, Mick found it hard to believe Jem was still alive. The former president of the United States had, upon the release of the Feline Flu vaccine, ordered all soldiers vaccinated. The casualties had been catastrophic. The vaccine had caused far greater losses than had the following weeklong battle against the former civilians of the area, who had been defending themselves against the Hitler-like actions of the president.

Mick was deeply relieved that they were going to seek the survivors Jem had promised to return to in DC. But he wasn't looking forward to this trip. Jem had fallen asleep early into the drive, and Mick found some solace in the silence. They were approaching the spot on the highway where he and his group of friends had been ambushed in the first days of the Primal Age. The first thing their attackers had done was ram his cop car, knocking him unconscious. Not realizing they were under assault, his friend Lucas had sacrificed his life to save Mick. Mick's grip tightened on the steering wheel, wishing it was the neck of the gunman.

There hadn't been a single generation of Mick's family that didn't have at least one cop. His father had been a police officer, as well as a sports-loving, beer-drinking homophobe. From a young age Mick knew he was different from the other men in his family, but he didn't realize how different until high school. When all his friends had been worried about losing their virginity, he had been worried someone would find out how he felt about Lucas. He didn't know how his friends would take that information, and he knew his family wouldn't have stood for it.

Jem tapped the window, drawing Mick back to reality. The former soldier was leaning heavily against the door. Jem had never been out of shape, but the past few months he had been training alongside Kade and had sculpted himself into a statue of muscle.

"Sorry I'm not more talkative. I just have a lot on my mind," Jem said.

"I'm in the same boat. Anything you want to talk about?" Mick asked.

"Talking won't do me any good."

"Yeah. Me eith—" Mick caught sight of his overturned police cruiser on the side of the road and slowed the Humvee to a stop. Without another word, he put it in park and got out. He scrambled over the bank and ran his hand along the burned out skeleton of the vehicle. A sharp piece of the frame sliced his hand, a painful reminder of the world that was. At one point in his life Mick had spent twelve hours a day in this cruiser. Those days were only a few months in the past, but he had as much trouble remembering them as if they had been a lifetime ago.

Mick circled around the car. He stopped by a patch of dirt marked with a cross made of arrows, and dropped to his knees at his friend's grave.

"Lucas, we're getting by. We'd be doing better with you, but we're keeping on as you would have wanted. I never had a chance to thank you for saving my life, though I wish you hadn't traded yours for mine." Mick stopped a tear from falling from the corner of his eye with a sweep of his hand. "We miss you. I miss you. I need to tell you that I love you, and I'm sorry I never had the courage to tell you. I hope you're resting well. Keep an eye on the rest of us."

Jem put a hand on Mick's shoulder, causing him to jump. Mick hadn't noticed him come down the bank and was now terrified at how much he had heard. If Jem knew, it would only be a matter of time before everyone knew. His heart felt like it was sinking into an abyss. Each second of silence increased the pressure in his chest.

The world had grown quiet—not a bird chirping or the slightest of breezes.

As his heart clenched tighter, he hoped it might just explode. It would be easier than letting the secret out and having to face the fall-out. The world had already ended, but this would be the undoing of his life.

He kept his eyes locked on Lucas's grave. Lucas, who would never know his secret, who would never know how he felt. The rest of the cohort would know, but not Lucas. Not Lucas.

Lucas could have known if Mick hadn't been so afraid. Maybe if Lucas hadn't died, Mick would have found the courage to tell him. Then Lucas could have known his secret.

The possibilities of that world released the pressure in Mick's chest. Mick took a deep breath and reminded himself that he was with friends, not his family. Still, he feared what the news would do to his friends' perceptions of him.

Leaning forward, he lifted himself to his feet and stood beside Jem. Mick felt Lucas's spirit giving him a swell of strength.

"I'm gay," Mick blurted out.

"Cool," Jem said, then turned and headed toward the Humvee.

"Cool? That's it?" Mick said as he rushed after Jem.

"Yeah. I'll take a turn at the wheel."

Mick climbed into the passenger side of the Humvee and slammed the door. For years he had been holding on to that secret, and when he finally had the courage to tell someone, his response was *cool*. That was it. No questions, no thoughts, no response.

Jem looked at Mick as he drove. "You okay?"

"No. I'm pissed," Mick said, crossing his arms.

"You're pissed 'cause I'm okay with you being gay?"

"Shouldn't you have questions? How long have I known? Why did I keep it to myself?"

"I've known since your junior year. I figured you kept it to yourself because you weren't ready to face it. If you want me to act homophobic about it, I can."

Even Mick hadn't been sure of things his junior year. "I screwed Vanessa P. that year. She told the whole school."

Jem laughed. "It was the night we lost and ruined our chance of a perfect season in soccer. We had a drown-your-sorrows party. Why don't you tell the rest of the story?"

"Vanessa was all over me. I told her to meet me in the guest room in ten minutes so I could tell my ride not to wait. Then I met her in the room and screwed her until morning."

"Any foreplay, or just sex? What positions did you use? Was it your first time?" Jem paused, letting the silence settle. "I was passed out in that guest room when Vanessa P. got there. Lights were off. I didn't realize until an hour in to it that she thought I was you. I'd have been in trouble 'cause I was dating what's-her-name—the one who became a stripper? So I let Vanessa think it was you."

Mick's body shook as he clenched his hands into fists. "You never thought to talk to me about it?"

Jem shrugged. "I'm not about to ask one of my friends if he's into dudes."

Mick took a deep breath to compose himself. "Do you think the others will be okay with this?"

"X is sleeping with Kade's little sister. I think you'll be fine."

For the first time in years, Mick didn't feel like he had a thorn under his skin.

Drew was tired. Not like a long-day-at-work tired. He was beat. Exhausted. Sore. Worn-out. Hurt to the bone. Bloodied. Battered. He was *tired.*

As he dropped onto the leather couch in his luxury apartment, he could feel his mind already drifting toward sleep, but the patter of the children's footsteps brought him back to reality. They weren't his kids, but for the last few months they had become his responsibility. Drew was only twenty, and before the world had fallen he hadn't wanted kids for at least ten more years.

The three kids had once been members of his swim team. Due mostly to bad luck and a brave man, they had ended up in his care.

They now lived in the few blocks surrounding DC's National Mall, where the National Guard had established themselves as the Residence of Power. The city immediately surrounding the Mall had been burned down during a brief civil war. Sadly, Drew was not a member of the National Guard, which meant that to get a daily ration for himself and his kids he'd been forced to join the Civilian Corp, which meant manual labor ten to twelve hours a day. Today's duty had been burying the dead, which had also been yesterday's duty, as it would be tomorrow's.

And what was his big prize at the end of the day? A backpack filled with enough water and food to keep him and his kids alive until tomorrow. Three things kept him from packing up and leaving. The first was that he doubted his ability to keep the kids alive out in the wild. The second was that James Masters, the soldier who had saved them, had promised to come back. Last was security. With all the rabids, resistance, and rambos running around, nothing was safe.

Drew opened his eyes and watched the three kids search through the backpack. He didn't have the energy to lift his head, but smiled as the tallest, yet youngest, of the three got excited over a Pop-Tart. The rations varied by day, but Drew knew Scott had a soft spot for Pop-Tarts, so he always did his best to try to snag at least one pack.

Before the Primal Age, Scott had been such a cute ten-year-old that he'd done some catalog modeling. Even if magazines had still existed, Scott's career as a child model would have been terminated. Scott had set off a shotgun trip wire during their trip through the metro tunnels to safety, which had scarred the right side of his body as badly as the face of Mars. The worst part of his injury was the loss of his right eye, and even with medical attention—which had saved his life—the eye socket sat empty, like a cave in a mountainside, and was surrounded by mangled flesh and scars. Scott took to wearing sunglasses to cover the damage.

Beside him was the lone girl, Meredith, who had also been wounded when the trap had sprung. The damage was far less noticeable, and the marks from the bird shot could easily be mistaken for chicken pox scars. Her eyes lit up as she pulled a soda from the bag, popped the tab, and chugged a few gulps. Drew knew soda wasn't good for her and that anything that wasn't water wasn't helping, but there were so few things to get excited about that he didn't want to deny her that joy.

The third child, Franklin, was the oldest of the three at eleven, but he was also the smallest. He wore his glasses awkwardly down his nose and had a bad habit of looking over them. Drew didn't need to watch him to know what he would go for first. The kid had managed to tame a cheetah cub from the DC Zoo, which made Drew's life much more difficult. Animal food was not included in the rations, so he had to go through barter channels to get cat food. This generally came at the price of part of his own ration. As always, before ever taking something for himself, Franklin pulled out the can of cat food and disappeared into one of the rooms to feed his pet.

Drew smiled to himself as he let his weary body rest. As his thoughts faded to dreams, he couldn't help but think that he'd have been lucky to have a kid like any of them, and as long as they were his to look after, he would do what it took to keep them safe.

Mick and Jem were walking through the early morning light. They had stashed the Humvee in the woods two miles from the Theodore Roosevelt Memorial Bridge, the last standing bridge on the west side of DC.

They were presently carrying their rifles in case they had a foamer encounter. When they got close enough for Mick to see the island that the bridge traversed, they stashed their weapons in the trees alongside the road. Jem wanted to make it clear in case they came across any patrols that they were no threat.

Theodore Roosevelt Island had become the main outpost for the president's men. What had once been a scenic island was now a fortified base crawling with soldiers.

Mick and Jem hadn't put more than a foot onto the concrete of the bridge when a megaphone blared.

"Hands on your heads."

Jem immediately complied. Mick followed his lead, wondering if Jem was so calm because he'd expected this. Mick was anything but calm. His heart was racing as he looked ahead at the concrete barriers that had been placed across the bridge. Above the barriers were at least a dozen men, all aiming rifles at them.

"Slowly walk toward us. If you drop your hands, we will shoot."

Jem stepped forward and Mick followed. He hoped Jem had some sort of plan. Even though the walk was only about fifty yards, to Mick it seemed like he had crossed all of the Sahara.

When they reached the men, they were swiftly searched for weapons, then forced facedown onto the ground. The road bit into his face as his hands were cuffed behind him. This was the second time since the Primal Age began that he, a police officer, had found himself in handcuffs.

"Identify yourself," a soldier standing over them ordered.

"James Masters, formerly second lieutenant," Jem replied.

Mick didn't get a chance to introduce himself. Jem's response sent the entire force into a frenzy. Orders were barked as men rushed around. A hood was pulled over Mick's head as he was hoisted to his feet. He was shoved forward and thrown into what he figured was the backseat of a car. The last thing he heard before the door slammed was, "Take them to the Castle."

While the car carried him off, he wished he had listened to Kade and not left Houghton. Jem had offered him the chance to find new people who didn't know him, and that had been impossible to turn down. They had to expand, but he wished he'd taken the time to learn more about the guardsmen, and more importantly, to examine Jem's plan instead of just following him blindly. He'd owe Kade an apology if he ever got the chance to tell his former leader he was sorry.

A knock on the door sent Drew shooting straight off the couch, where he had fallen asleep. He looked through the open kitchen to the door, wishing he had X-ray vision and could see through it. He listened carefully for the breathing of his kids. All three of them were in a deep slumber. He lit up his watch to check the time: 4:23 a.m.

Drew had expected time to become unimportant after the end of the world, but within the president's province it had become even more defined. Everything revolved around shifts that happened exactly on time.

Opening a drawer in the kitchen, Drew lifted up a cutting board and felt around for the pistol James had given him. Had he not kept it hidden all this time, it would have been taken from him; civilians weren't allowed to have guns. Even the knife James had given Franklin would be confiscated if it was ever found.

Gun in hand, Drew approached the door. He tapped it twice and was answered in kind by five knocks, completing his security code.

"Who's there?" Drew whispered.

"We got two new people tonight," a female voice said from the other side.

Drew went back to the kitchen and opened a different drawer. This one held protein bars, gummy bears, and any other food he was able to either come across or skimp off his own rations. This was how he paid for information.

He cracked the door and slid a granola bar out.

"James Masters and Mick McCracken."

Drew felt his heart pound against his chest. He had been waiting months to hear that name. He slid a candy bar through the open door before he closed it.

"That's not all you should know."

Drew cracked the door open and slid out a pack of M&M's.

"They were arrested."

Drew put a hand over his face. He couldn't believe his luck. James had finally arrived but was unreachable. This was worse than if he hadn't shown up at all.

Drew slid a protein bar out and resigned himself to his new life.

"I can get you three minutes with him."

"What will it cost me?" Drew asked, wondering what he had that he could leverage.

"Five thousand calories."

Drew was close. With what he had already paid he had high three thousand, but he hadn't touched his daily ration yet. He could go hungry for a day. For the kids he could suffer anything.

Drew went back into the apartment and gathered up all the food he had to spare. He returned to the door, opened it, and pointed the gun at the soldier in the hallway.

She held her hands up. "You know I could have you arrested for having a firearm?"

"You know I could have you executed for providing a civilian with information," Drew replied as he dropped the food on the ground. "Why ruin our perfect relationship?"

She smiled back. "I agree. I'll escort you to the Castle and get you in. What I need you to do is give this food to the female prisoner. Fair trade?"

Drew wanted to know why, but if she had wanted him to know that she would have told him. He returned the gun to the drawer, put the food in a bag, and locked the door behind him.

He followed the soldier out of his apartment and through the war-torn Mall. The grass where people used to watch summer movies was now full of parked military vehicles. Drew wondered if he was actually going to get out of this labor camp, or if James was now trapped for good.

He looked at the woman next to him, who had been his informant for the past few months, but the person who connected them made it clear they were never to know each other's names. She was the closest thing he had to a friend. A friend he only talked to through a closed door and who only spoke when bribed. They didn't speak the entire time they walked.

Eventually, they ended up outside the Castle, a large stone building built in the 1800s that had served as the information hub for all the Smithsonian museums once upon a time.

"Go with whatever I say," she said as they knocked on the large wooden door.

The door opened, and a male soldier stood between Drew and the entrance.

"This is the guy I told you about. Lost his wife, just needs a release. Five minutes should do," she said.

"I'll give him three minutes. Don't want to spoil our commodity. Just skip the foreplay and try not to leave any bruises," the other soldier said. He fumbled with a key ring and pulled a key off. "This is the key to her cell."

Drew gave him a nod and walked past with the food still cradled in his arms. Once he was inside, they closed the door behind him. There was a row of cages that ran down the middle of the long building. There were four people in the cages.

He went down a short set of stairs and there was James, staring at him but not saying anything. Drew took the bag of food to a small Asian woman, who was cowering against the bars away from him. He understood what his three minutes were for.

"I'm just delivering these from a mutual friend," Drew said, passing the bag of food between the bars. She relaxed and took them without a word.

"James, I have three minutes," Drew said, moving over to his cage.

"One Willard Avenue. Houghton, New York. Say it back," James whispered.

"One Willard Avenue. Houghton, New York," Drew whispered back.

"We're being executed in seven days. If you choose to go there, let them know not to come for us. If you need a vehicle, ours is parked a mile north of the Theodore Roosevelt Memorial Bridge."

"There's gotta be a way I can get you out of here," Drew said.

"Your duty is to the kids. You need to leave tonight before anyone can suspect you are tied to us. I can't risk you leading them back to my friends. Understood?"

"I'll go straight to the kids. I know a guy who can get us out of the city. Then we'll head to Houghton," Drew said.

"Good." James let his head hang, like it had been a burden to keep up this long. "Tell the kids I said hello."

"I will."

The cool March evening clung to John's skin as he stalked through the dense woods surrounding Houghton College. He enjoyed seeing life coming back into the woods, which had been so desolate during the winter. Not that he had anything against pine trees, but seeing the bright leaves on the deciduous trees gave him hope that life would go on in the Primal Age.

He'd nocked an arrow into his compound bow as he scanned for movement. Everything about the task felt natural to him, unlike it had months ago when he had first joined Kade's group. Back then he was jittery and nervous; now, he at least had composure when he was armed and hunting. During their fight with a paramilitary group that called themselves the Tribe, John had killed two men. That in itself had caused much of his maturation.

After the fight, not only John had changed. Their group had spent much of the winter making defensive upgrades to their home. The campus bridges were now either destroyed or blocked off. A zip line had been drawn from their primary dorm, Lambian, to the Paine Science Center, where a team slaved away to correct the human reaction to the Feline Flu vaccine, which had turned a majority of the population into mindless beasts that foamed blood at the mouth.

The foamers had become far more terrifying in appearance since they'd first turned. They had become unkempt with long matted hair, their nails had grown into claws, and the males had sprouted full beards—the men in his group had cut their hair short, just to make sure they weren't mistaken for foamers. Despite all of this, Kade had decreed that no foamer was to be killed except in self-defense.

John's ears perked as he heard the clomp of footsteps on the soggy ground. Perhaps he had found what he had been hunting. A roar followed, and John spun while drawing his bow string, but the large foamer—who wore a tattered jacket that had an *A* on it—was already upon him. The creature bounded off of all fours and came in under the bow, tackling John to the wet earth. With the bow pinned between them, John used his elbow to keep the bearded face from getting close enough to sink its snapping jaws into his neck. There was a long scar that stretched across the side of the foamer's head from where a bullet had grazed him. The monster's jaws pressed closer to his neck, the smell of death emanating from his breath. Red foam bubbled from the corners of the creature's mouth. John recognized this foamer as the leader of the troop that lived in their area, the one they called Alpha.

The bow was proving to be John's greatest enemy at the moment, allowing the foamer to keep him pinned without leverage. John's free hand reached for an arrow in the quick quiver attached to the bow. His hope was the broad head of the arrow could be used as a weapon, if only he could free it.

A roar echoed from out of sight, and the foamer hesitated. When Alpha looked up, he was met full force by the shoulder of something far scarier than himself. The two opponents rolled across the ground like fighting wolves before their momentum separated them. The attacker reeled back on two feet and beat his chest as he roared again. Alpha stood on all fours like a cat waiting to strike, then, with a low grumble, relaxed and slinked off.

The attacker turned to John. He wore a blue-and-white ballistic mask that was painted to resemble a set of jagged teeth, like an angry jack-o'-lantern. Sticking up above his back was a katana. His right hand bore a set a blue rubber knuckles, and protruding from his hips were two Taurus Judge revolver pistols. This was not a man, but a living weapon. This was their leader. This was Kade.

Kade tipped the ballistic mask off his face, scanning John with his gray eyes. John could feel him probing for answers to questions he wasn't asking aloud as he offered a hand down to John and hoisted him to his feet. John couldn't believe how far Kade had taken his training. Since their battle with the Tribe, Kade had dedicated himself to becoming as deadly as possible.

"You know you shouldn't be out here alone, kid," Kade said as he picked up John's bow and handed it to him.

"You're easier to track now that the ground is wet," John replied.

Kade put a hand on John's back as they walked quietly through the underbrush. "And what are you tracking me for?"

"Xavier just got back from his grocery run and we wanted to get started on movie night, but I didn't want to let them start without you," John replied.

Kade rubbed John's fuzzy head. "Thanks for looking out, kid."

They trudged along in silence. Before the world had entered the Primal Age, John had been attending a prep school near the college campus he now called home. Family had only been a word to him until Kade took him in. Though Kade was his senior by a mere ten years, John saw him as a father figure. Kade had taken the time to teach John how to survive after the collapse of humanity, and had even forced him to continue studying. Kade claimed that the most valuable asset for the future would be knowledge. Living on a college campus that was renowned for its premed program left no lack of information to be gained.

"What do you do out here?" John asked.

"Do you know who Jane Goodall was?" Kade replied.

"The woman who lived with the gorillas? You're studying the foamers' behavior?"

"Exactly. Damian is up there in his mad scientist laboratory trying to figure out how to fix them; I spend time out here to understand them."

They crept out of the woods and onto the road that led back to campus. Every twenty yards, in alternating lanes, a car was parked with its tires deflated. This setup would force an approaching vehicle to swerve and prevent an attacker from gaining speed.

"If you ever want a hand with your research, I'd happily come along," John said.

The two of them stepped around a car, which blocked, broadside, the bridge that led to campus. On the other side of the bridge there was another car set up to complete their gate. These cars still had their tires inflated and were kept in neutral so they could be moved whenever a member of the cohort needed access.

"Stick to studying books for now. The foamers are becoming more accepting of me, but it still isn't safe to be in such close proximity to them." Kade pointed a finger at John. "Don't tell Tiny I said it wasn't safe."

If Kade was John's surrogate father, Tiny was his mother, and he was absolutely terrified of her. Few people in John's life ever intimidated him the way she did. She was, for the most part, a loving person who would do anything to help people—except when it came to protecting the cohort. If she was in her protective mode, it was a bad idea to end up on the receiving end of her wrath. For as scary as John often found her, he had never been so impressed by anyone. She had been a combat medic before being medically discharged due to a knee injury suffered in the line of duty. By far she was the most dangerous person in their cohort, Kade included. All of that aside, the thing that John found most compelling about her was how deeply she loved Kade. In all of John's life, he had never before witnessed a love like hers.

"I won't tell her. Unless she asks me. Then I'll have to tell her," John replied, his voice shaky at even the idea of disobeying Tiny.

Crossing to the north side of campus toward Lambian, they stepped carefully around the dozens of solar-powered walkway lights they had arranged across campus to give them an advantage at night.

Coming upon the dorm, John pulled the walkie from his belt. "Knock, knock."

As they closed the distance, a roll-out escape ladder clattered down from the middle third-floor window. Kade steadied the metal ladder while John climbed to their home.

Crawling through the window frame, John felt a pair of small but calloused hands grab him by the shoulders and help him through. Those tough hands belonged to Grace. She stood before him wearing a pair of overalls unhooked on the right side, with only a sports bra underneath. The overalls were streaked with dried grease, and her shoulder-length blonde hair was a few shades darker due to the lingering layer of dirt that perpetually stuck to her.

John had matured in many ways since he'd joined the cohort, but one of the areas in which he was still lacking—and which frustrated him immensely—was with girls. In the Old World, he would have had school dances and awkward first dates and any number of other ways to make an ass of himself. Here he didn't have that learning curve. Without that period of trial and error, he knew he only had one real shot with Grace. If he missed his shot, the window would close.

Kade climbed through the window and pulled the ladder in behind him, one rung at a time.

"Any bad news for me?" Kade asked, glancing over his shoulder at Grace.

"No, sir. Everything is tip-top," Grace replied.

Grace had been the youngest sibling in a family of contractors. At seventeen years old, she had been their jack of all trades. They'd relied on her for plumbing, electrical, and construction.

"Glad to hear it—and knock that *sir* shit off," Kade said.

"Yes, sir."

Kade smirked and shook his head. "You've got a spot of clean on you."

"You've got a spot of blood on you," Grace returned.

Kade noticed the dark red spot on his shirt. "Not a word of this to Tiny."

Brushing past Grace, Kade went into the hallway.

John's tongue lapped around his mouth like a tired dog, trying to formulate words, but none came and he stood there with a blank look on his face. He only hoped that, since the top of her head only reached his chest, she couldn't see how dumb his face felt.

"Excited for the movie?" Grace asked as they went into the hallway side by side.

"It'll be good to relax after being jumped by a foamer," John said, hoping to earn some pity points.

"Are you okay?" Grace searched him over for wounds.

John nodded. "Just my pride. I should be better than that."

"You are better than that, but we all slip up sometimes," she reassured him as they climbed the steps to the fifth floor, where their utility rooms were set up. In the six floors of the dorm, the first two were blocked off, the third floor was used for their entrances, they lived on the fourth floor, and the fifth was where they stored all of their supplies and had their designated rooms. They kept the sixth floor empty to be used as a protected vantage point.

"I just was lucky Kade was there to go Donkey Kong on the little bastard," John said.

They approached a door marked with three strips of duct tape that had been written on with a Sharpie:

The Theaterre
at the
End of the World

They pushed the door open and entered the room, which was set up with beds lining the perimeter, mattresses filling in the floor, and a high-def TV mounted to the wall. Grace had run a wire connecting it to the next room, where the solar batteries were stored.

In the far corner of the room, Ashton lay back between Xavier's legs, resting her head on his chest. Xavier was wearing what he always seemed to be wearing—a pair of blue jeans, a black T-shirt, and his trademark black cowboy hat. John considered X a renegade, but he still had an appreciation for him, much as he did for everyone in his new family. John didn't even mind the way X treated him with a cool distance since he treated just about everyone that way—with the exception of Ashton.

Ashton was a redheaded firecracker who took great pleasure in tormenting John. He figured that, since she was the little sister of Kade and Damian, she'd probably never had anyone to pass her frustrations down to, but that didn't make him any more accepting of the sibling-like abuse.

John deliberately cleared his throat. "You changed my sign again."

"Improved," Ashton responded, beaming a toothy smile.

"Well, it isn't. It's not. It's not better," John said, setting his bow against the wall and kicking off his shoes.

"Shush it and sit down," Ashton said, dismissing him with a wave. The freckles on her face matched the shade of her auburn hair, which made them stark against her pale skin.

John, figuring it was better not to start a verbal fight he didn't have the skill to win, went and took a seat beside Grace, who had already made herself comfortable on one of the beds.

The door opened, and Kade strolled in with Tiny behind him, who was producing a constant flow of reasons he'd been careless, which Kade didn't respond to as he crossed the room and took a seat between the two groups already on the beds.

Tiny's volley came to a close with, "You can't take these chances with your life for nothing. There's people depending on you."

"I didn't tell her," John quickly blurted, and even more quickly covered his mouth, wishing he could pull the words back.

Tiny's head snapped toward John, whipping her black hair across her face like a horse's tail. "Tell me what?"

Her brown eyes bore into John, and he wished he could find something to shield himself from the wrath he had just provoked.

"Tell me what?" she repeated.

John knew pain would be imminent if he didn't tell her something. He broke eye contact with Tiny long enough to gauge Kade, who gave him a single nod.

"Kade's been fighting foamers bare-handed to study them," John said.

"Snitch!" Ashton yelled.

"You've been doing *what*?" Tiny growled as she turned her piercing eyes back to Kade. Her usual milky face was flushed red.

Kade's hand rocketed forward, grabbing a handful of Tiny's long black hair, and pulled her face to his. She returned the kiss and dug her nails into his biceps. John had no idea if they were still fighting or making up.

In a whisper so low John could hardly hear, Kade said, "Trust me."

Their lookout's voice chimed through the walkie on Kade's belt. "*I think Jem and Mick are back. There's a Humvee at the bridge.*"

"Tiny," Kade said, and she left the room in a hurry. John couldn't grasp how the two of them communicated as efficiently as they did. John had seen this frequently and had expended a good deal of effort trying to decode it to see if it had to do with pitch or inflection. Perhaps it was simply their bond.

"Everyone, arm up and be ready. John, grab your bow and let's go," Kade ordered.

"What's the big deal if it's just our guys?" John asked.

"Protocol is we call in on approach. Jem and Mick don't break protocol," Grace said.

Feeling stupid for being corrected by his paramour, John grabbed his bow and followed Kade to the exit. They climbed down the ladder and mounted an ATV. They came to a halt on the opposite side of the bridge from the Humvee.

Across the bridge, the driver's door opened and a man climbed out. The man was taller than even John and was shaped like a muscle-bound triangle from his shoulders to his feet. Despite his outer toughness, John thought his eyes looked young. He didn't even have both feet on the ground before Tiny chimed over the walkie, "*In my sights.*"

"Hold until he proves a threat," Kade responded as he climbed off the back of the ATV. Kade slid his rubber knuckles into place, then attached one end of a handcuff to his wrist. He handed another set to John. "Remember how we greeted you?"

John remembered all too well; he had been handcuffed to a bed for an entire night with Kade's dirty sock forced in his mouth.

"Yes, sir," John replied.

"We're not taking chances. Stay behind me. Once he's subdued, we can question him."

John tucked the cuffs into his belt and retrieved his bow from the ATV. He nocked an arrow as they walked across the bridge. Sweat beaded on John's forehead. They hadn't had a stray since John, and that made him nervous for this man. He might not have the fortitude that John had to survive such an initiation.

"Is this Houghton?" the man asked as Kade approached.

"Sure is, friend. How can I help you?" Kade extended his hand. The man shook it. Fast as a mongoose, Kade locked the cuff on the man's wrist, wrenched his arm behind his back, and put him face-first on the ground.

A high-pitched wail came from the Humvee. Kade nodded for John to check it out.

"Do what you want to me, but they're just kids," the man howled.

John approached the vehicle like a timid squirrel. In the back he could see three kids huddled together; none appeared to have reached adolescence.

"Jem sent me. We're the ones he went back for," the man pleaded.

John motioned to the kids to come forward, and as they climbed onto the bridge he noticed one of the boys had a cat in his jacket.

"Who is Jem?" Kade said.

"James Eric Masters, and he was with a police officer named Mick," the man said.

"Let my coach go!" the kid with the cat yelled and charged forward, but John snagged him by the collar.

"Kids, stay back. It'll be okay." The coach cleared his throat. "James and Mick were detained. Jem asked me to come back here and tell you he's sorry, and not to come for them."

"I need more. He wouldn't send you without something undeniable," Kade said.

The kid pulled against John and said, "Jem loved my aunt. He saved us from the fire and led us back through the metro tunnels. He's my friend and promised me you're a good person."

Kade relaxed the tension on the man's arm. "What's your name?" he asked the kid.

"Franklin."

"He told me about you and your aunt. Welcome."

John felt jealousy rising from the pit of his stomach as they escorted the newcomers back to Lambian. Kade seemed to be welcoming these strays as if they were family, whereas John had been forced to assume the lowest rank and was constantly called *Stray*, which he found to be about the most offensive epithet one could be called by this group.

"John, would you mind taking the kids to my sister and having her set up a room for them? Then meet us in the quorum," Kade said.

John responded with a nod and led the kids back to the dorm, secretly hoping that someone else would start calling them strays.

Over the weeks since his introduction to the group, the name *Stray* had slowly dropped, but some members of the cohort still used it. Since Jem had given his seal of approval, these strays had been welcomed with a red carpet. They wouldn't have to endure a night of torment, nor weeks of shunning.

John stopped with the three kids at a door marked with a duct-tape capital *A* and knocked. Kade's sister Ashton, who was three years older than John at eighteen, opened the door.

"Kade wants you to get a room set up for them," John told her.

"Kade wants me to do what?" Ashton asked.

"Please," John said.

"Yeah, no thanks," Ashton replied, talking over the kids like they weren't standing between them.

"Your brother said so."

"And I'm saying no."

"I'll take your waste disposal shifts this week." Everyone hated that chore. Carrying five-gallon buckets of literal crap from the dorm to the creek wasn't fun for anyone. They had gloves, but that didn't stop the smell.

Ashton rolled her eyes and let out a huff. "Fine. But you'll still owe me another favor, Stray."

Stray. The word cut through him.

Ashton faked a grin and spoke to the children in a higher tone. John left her to wrangle the kids and jogged down the hallway to the meeting room. He swung the door open and flew into a seat, hoping he hadn't missed much of the briefing. The entire center line of the room was ordered with the standard-issue dorm room desks and chairs, set in a way that they had a fourteen-person table that resembled a make-shift boardroom. Sitting along the rows were the new guy, Tiny, Kade, X, and Grace. It was a weird feeling not having Jem or Mick present, since they were the usual culprits for calling a quorum.

"Are you sure we can't just leave them?" X asked.

"We can't leave them to be executed any more than I'd leave you to die," Kade replied.

"I can recall you leaving me once," X said. There was no malice in his voice; this was his way of joking.

"And I came back to find you as soon as we were settled," Kade replied.

"Kade did almost die coming to find you," Tiny said, smacking the back of Kade's head.

"He's almost died a lot, and he was looking for his little sister, not for me," X said.

"All the past. We need a plan to rescue Mick and Jem. Drew, you're sure there is no way to reason or trade with them?" Kade asked.

Drew shook his head. "The president is fricking crazy. I'm surprised Jem wasn't killed the moment they identified him."

"Why don't we just go get them back Bruce Willis–style?" X asked.

"We can't just fight through a thousand vaccinated National Guardsmen," Tiny said.

"Sneaking in will be hard enough. The place has been totally mobilized since James left," Drew said.

A long silence settled over the tables while everyone pondered the options. John didn't think there was anything they could do for those they had lost. Mick and Jem seemed as good as dead. The guardsmen sounded even worse than the Tribe. He couldn't even think of the Tribe without getting chills.

"We should get the Tribe to fight the guardsmen," John said to himself.

"Kid has a point. Maybe if we made the Tribe aware of the force in DC, they'd be more threatened by them than us," Tiny added.

X cleared his throat. "Not that I'm afraid of the crazy one-way ideas, but what do you expect to do—ride up to the Tribe waving a white flag and negotiate a truce, then convince them to help us get Mick and Jem back? Why not ask Satan to lend a hand while we're at it?"

CHAPTER II

THE DEVIL YOU KNOW

Blaire Cunningham had been a CIA agent with a list of credentials longer than the Statue of Liberty. Before that, she had been an orphan raised in the government system—until she was saved by being conscripted into the service of her country. Now she was the president's number one extractor of information, or inflictor of justice.

Growing up without a family, her only father had been the United States of America. Her brothers and sisters were those who had served beside her in the War on Terror. It still hurt to think that the terrorists were winning. That she had failed to see the threats.

The president had assured her there was nothing anyone could have done about it. That some of the terrorist agents claimed some of the attacks had been carried out by sleepers left over from as far back as the Cold War. It had been a long-term play with global cooperation against America, according to the president.

She took a special joy in drawing information out of those responsible. She could make it last for days—or weeks if she didn't have a busy schedule, but she usually did.

Standing over what was once an industrial kitchen sink, she washed all of her instruments in a bucket of water and sterilized them. She didn't want to give anyone the chance of taking the easy way out by contracting an infection of some kind. Lately, she had been working on two college kids who had helped raise a resistance to fight against the president and his men. She was hoping to learn that they had either been indoctrinated by one of the many terror groups that hated the United States, or that they were sympathizers who could give her information leading to finding more terror cells.

They may have wounded her father country badly, but America would never die so long as the president and his force stood. The fight would continue until the country was rebuilt and once again restored to its former glory.

She took in the smell of bleach—she had recently cleaned blood off her white uniform. The scent lingered around her like perfume, but she wasn't going to give up wearing white while she worked. It allowed her projects to fully appreciate the beauty in her art of torture.

Her dossier today informed her of one James Eric Masters, who had infiltrated the National Guard and then stolen a helicopter in order to rescue the number one most wanted terrorist in America, Damian Zerris. Damian had been the lead medical researcher on the Feline Flu vaccine, which the terrorist had used to cripple America's population. James had apparently returned to infiltrate their stronghold with the help of his friend, Mick McCracken.

Within their safe zone, Blaire had claimed an upscale steak house as her home and base of operation. The building was beautiful and had survived the battle for DC with minimal damage. From the balcony she had a breathtaking view of the Capitol Building, which constantly reminded her what she was fighting for. The former kitchen had metamorphosed excellently into her torture chamber. The space was large, filled with sturdy metal tables and plenty of places to hang things in place of pots and pans. Most conveniently, there were drains in the floor. She used a series of battery-powered LED lights to illuminate the room so she could see her work clearly.

Soon they would likely get back many of their old comforts. The president had put together a detail to head to the local water and power plants to see if they couldn't get things back in order. He had told her that once they had power and water they could stop looking for survivors because they would come like a moth to the flame.

She took great joy in each step of the rebuilding the United States and gladly offered herself to help in any way possible. Oftentimes this involved the great honor of sharing the president's bed.

The large kitchen doors swung open as two guardsmen walked a shackled man up to a metal table. She wrapped up the cloth sheath that held her instruments and went to meet her new project.

"My, my, James. It amazes me you were able to infiltrate the ranks of this great country's military for so long, since you were stupid enough to return after your escape," Blaire said.

The two guardsmen finished shackling the naked man to the table. Dismissing the troops with a wave of her hand, she was sad to see that her target had already been bruised. She much preferred a clean canvas.

James looked at her with blue eyes that reminded her of arctic waters.

"I was always a dutiful soldier," Jem said.

"I have evidence to suggest otherwise," she said, letting her knives clank along the table as she unrolled the sheath that held her instruments.

"I've already been sentenced to public execution. Do what you will," James said, resting his head back like he was getting ready to take a nap.

"I will give you one chance to tell me everything. Who are you working for? Where is your cell set up? Where is the terrorist Damian Zerris? You tell me these things and I promise your last few days on this Earth won't be painful."

Though she made the offer, she prayed that he wouldn't take it. She wanted to draw the information out of him. Let her hands do their beautiful work. Create a masterpiece, a piece of art the spilled blood of her countrymen deserved, and something so amazing that the president would be pleased with her.

"I've been through SERE school. Good luck," James said.

Blaire clapped her hands like an excited kid. "I'm glad you said that."

She always liked to start small to see what her quarry was capable of. The first things she pulled out were the sewing needles. Ten of them—one for each finger. Slide, slide, slide, blood, stop. With the first needle fully embedded under his pinky nail, she had to give this man credit—he hadn't flinched once. His strong jaw was set in defiance. Slowly, at a pace only the universe could truly appreciate, she started on his ring finger. A minute later, when she finished the insertion, he still hadn't let out so much as a gasp. She proceeded through the other eight fingers. Upon the insertion of the tenth pin, James's hands were flexed tight while small trickles of blood ran from a few of his nails. He hadn't made a sound. Excitement and worry danced inside of her as she recognized her victim's fortitude. No one had ever before re-mained silent through all ten nails. If she could break him, he would be her best work yet. She tried not to entertain the idea that he might not be broken. Blaire buried the worry and smiled to herself. She was in for a fun week.

Kade, Tiny, and X rode in one of the Tribe's Humvees and headed for their base, with a white flag sticking out of the top hatch. The plan wasn't perfect, but Kade figured since there had never been a follow-up attack, the Tribe wasn't necessarily a unified force. This meant they had a chance of discussing some sort of truce. The point was to con-vince them that they shared a common enemy now. A greater threat to both.

"There it is," Tiny said as the military base appeared on the hori-zon. She slowed the Humvee to a stop a few lengths from the gate, leaving enough room to make a break for it if they had to flee.

"Tiny," Kade said, and received a nod in return. Kade took a deep breath and opened the door. He stepped out of the vehicle and raised his hands above his head.

The gate was sided by watchtowers. Each tower held three men wearing drugstore breathing masks, all holding weapons trained on the Humvee.

"Identify yourself," the sentries called.

"Kade Zerris," he shouted back.

"Freeze," the man hollered, unable to contain the alarm in his voice. "Anyone else with you—exit the vehicle with your hands up."

"This was a stupid plan," X said as they opened their doors and climbed out.

Tiny smiled at him. "When does he ever have a smart plan?"

"Point taken," X said.

"Place your weapons on the ground," the sentry barked.

Kade had left his weapons in the Humvee, and as his friends set their guns on the ground, he was glad he had been training as hard as he had been. They couldn't take his hands from him.

The lead sentry chattered into his radio.

Kade met X's black eyes and said, "This plan is going great."

"Great?" X asked.

"They haven't shot us yet," Kade sincerely replied.

A feminine voice Kade recognized all too well came through the radio. "Hold fire. Contain them until the commander and I can get there."

"Yes, ma'am," the lead sentry said. He crossed the space between the two groups and stood an arm's reach from Kade.

The sentry slammed a punch into Kade's gut, but seeing the punch coming, Kade stepped into it. He took the hit to his flexed abs before the swing had the chance to reach maximum velocity. Though it hurt, Kade didn't flinch.

"I imagine you don't like me much, so I'll give you that one. Only that one," Kade said.

The sentry looked back at his line of compatriots and let out a laugh. "Only that one?"

Kade nodded and noticed X toss his cowboy hat to the side. He knew his friends would have his back if this turned into a brawl, but he hoped that these Tribesmen respected their leadership enough to keep this from turning into a gunfight. The sentry cocked to strike again. Kade slid into him and hooked his punch. Using the momentum, he spun the man's body, wrenching the arm behind his back. There was a loud snap, followed by a quieter one as Kade dislocated the sentry's shoulder, then broke his trigger finger.

A gunshot sounded that froze everyone in place, and a loud voice boomed over the group. "You were told to hold fire. I know we didn't spell it out, but I expected you apes to be smart enough to understand that means not engaging in a fight."

Kade realized then that during their battle the previous fall, they must have thinned the ranks of the Tribe's more able-bodied soldiers—otherwise they would have found themselves under attack by the overwhelming numbers. He knew the Tribe couldn't lead a full-on assault against DC, but they might have a few bodies that could help make Kade's mission possible. The fear that kept whispering in his mind was that opening communication with the Tribe was the biggest mistake he could have made. A truce would make them more vulnerable than they already were.

The man in command of the group sent the Tribesmen back to their posts, leaving himself alone with the three of them. The soldier was tall and broad, with deep eyes and short brown hair. Just the way he carried himself would have clearly indicated he was the leader. He walked over to where X's hat lay in the road and picked it up.

"The amazing Kade Zerris, who defeated the greatest soldier the Tribe had to offer, just casually shows up on my doorstep. What am I supposed to make of this?" the man said.

"Before we talk about anything else, I suggest giving my friend his hat back, or I can't be held responsible," Kade said.

The man crossed over to X and handed him his hat with a smile. "This would lead me to believe that you would be X the Fake Cowboy, and this would be the one they call Tiny, the—well, our source didn't give a positive descriptor for you."

"And you would be?" Kade asked.

"I used to be called Tall-Chief; now I go by Commander Henson," he replied.

A clacking sound rose from the pavement, and Kade's head hung lower with each click. The source rounded the fence, and a pair of heels attached to a long set of legs came into view. The legs extended under a short pencil skirt, which turned into a black blouse and was topped off by a familiar face in librarian glasses. They all belonged to the voice Kade had heard over the Tribesman's radio—the only person in the world he'd known before the Primal Age that he wasn't excited to see.

"Victoria. I am glad to see you well," Kade said, his eyes not leaving the ground.

She pulled her sandy-blonde hair into a ponytail. "Spare me the bullshit."

Victoria had once been Damian's fiancée, but he had left her when he went to work on the vaccine that later created the foamers. She had been part of Kade's original survival group but had left them to join the Tribe, believing they would provide her with better protection. She had been with the Tribesmen during the battle, but Kade had spared her life.

"It might not be good to see you, but I am glad you're alive," Kade replied.

"Ever the saint," Victoria said.

"As enjoyable as I find this banter, you are here for a reason and I have points to discuss with you. Mind telling what you came for?" Henson asked.

"A truce. DC is being run by the president, and he has over a thousand guardsmen, plus a few hundred civilians. Their soldiers are all vaccinated."

"That's a sizeable force, but it's unlikely they'd bring the fight to us. Why a truce?"

"Two of ours have been detained by the guardsmen and will be executed. We'll be killed on sight if we attempt to negotiate. We need people trained in infiltration," Kade said.

Henson turned his attention to Tiny. "I have one special forces soldier who has been itching for something more interesting than supply runs."

X let out a long fake laugh. "If he's so good, then why isn't he in the ground?"

Henson smiled in a way that reminded Kade of a casino dealer—authentically wanting the player to win, but knowing there wasn't a chance of that. "Unlike most of the Tribesmen, this man chose to remain a soldier. He isn't a pillager, like many of our force became under the old leadership." He paused, then added as an explanation, "Boy scout."

Kade held his hand up quieting his companion. "And what conditions do you have?"

Victoria handed Kade an envelope. As Kade opened the letter, he realized the Tribe had anticipated a point when Kade would come crawling for help. He immediately wanted to call off the truce, but Mick and Jem's lives depended on it. Not that he didn't believe in Tiny, X, or himself, but he couldn't throw away lives in the vague hope that they would be successful. He needed help, as much as he hated to admit it.

Henson put his hands on Victoria's shoulders. "Also, you have to take Victoria with you."

"That's not on the list," Victoria growled.

"It's nonnegotiable. Since you led that raid, the soldiers haven't wanted you around, and now with the Flu coming back, the civilians no longer welcome you. I can't lead the Tribe while always keeping an eye on your safety," Henson said.

Victoria cast her hand at her former cohort. "They'll likely lynch me on the way back."

"If I wanted you dead, you'd be dead," Kade said, looking over the list of demands. Victoria's rust-colored eyes had a fiery hatred that burned more ferociously than hell and all its minions combined, and that fury was fully directed at Kade.

"I want an assurance," Victoria demanded, crossing her arms.

Kade stared her down. "If death should befall your highness on an action that would be considered my—or one of mine's—fault, consider that a breaking of the truce. If you truly wanted to exterminate us you could. I have no reason to violate a treaty I came asking for."

Victoria smiled like a cat who'd just invited a mouse to lunch. He realized that she was playing him somehow, but he couldn't figure out her endgame. The demands he read over mostly covered setting up territory lines between the two groups to avoid conflicts, as well as trade negotiations between them. The only concession he had to make was returning half of the looted weapons and vehicles to the Tribe. Nowhere between the lines of the document could he see what play Victoria was trying to make.

Henson nodded. "Very good. If you find the rest of the demands acceptable, we can move forward."

John knew he couldn't complain to Grace. He already complained to her too much, and he'd already worn out her patience about being the stray. Kade would listen to him, but he didn't want to hurt Kade's feelings by expressing his unhappiness. Damian and Number Five were strangers to him.

He only had one option left. The door before him was marked with a capital *A*. Lifting his hand to knock, he hesitated, wondering if he really wanted to go down this path. But before he could make up his mind, the door opened.

Ashton shot him a glare—which almost made him want to die as much as when Tiny did—and pushed past him.

"What do you want, Stray?" she said as she started down the hallway.

John hurried to catch up. "I wondered if I could vent?"

"Do I look like Kade?" Ashton said, pushing open a door that was unmarked.

John shook his head and followed her inside.

"Then why are you still here?" she asked.

Ashton sat down on one of the three beds that lined the room.

John couldn't tell if she actually wanted him to leave or if she would listen. He knew whatever route he picked would be wrong. Swallowing hard, he made his choice.

"I just don't think it's fair that the new strays have it so easy. They're just magically accepted as part of the group," John said, sitting on the bed across the room from her.

Ashton ran a hand over her forehead and then gave John a sideways look. "That's what you want to vent about—that you were the only person who came into the group without an invitation and so we label you for it? News flash, Stray, everyone else was brought into the group by another member. You just turned up one day—"

"But—"

"Don't interrupt me. You know why my brother called you Stray for so long?"

"Because I was unwanted here?"

"No, you idiot. He had just lost one of his best friends to an ambush that he faulted himself for. On top of that, he had to consider the possibility that X and I were dead. Me, his sister, the only thing he ever cared for. You were named Stray so he could keep an emotional distance."

John's head was swarming with new information. "Kade doesn't call me Stray anymore."

"Use some logic, then."

"So he accepts me as one of the group now?"

"Ding, ding, ding, ten points to idiot-claw," Ashton said.

John ground his teeth. Plenty of other people still called him Stray, Ashton among them.

"You could lay off it," John said.

"Stray, I'll stop calling you Stray when you stop letting it bother you. Now, want to talk about problems? I'm not a babysitter. I've never taken care of another human being in my life, and I don't know the first thing about kids. I actually find kids gross. They smell, and poop, and puke," Ashton said, glaring at the door.

"I'm pretty sure these ones are potty trained," John said.

"I don't care. Jem or Drew better get back soon, or I'm going to kill the kids."

"By choice or accident?"

"Both."

The door opened and Franklin, Scott, and Meredith came in, each carrying a backpack. Franklin had the cat cradled in his arms.

"Hey, kids," Ashton said, her voice climbing to an unnatural pitch. "Hopefully you got some good stuff. This is going to be your room now. Feel free to set it up however you'd like."

Meredith bounded across the room to a free bed, where she plopped down and sorted through the contents of her pack. All were objects that John recognized from the room filled with random stuff from the former dorm rooms that had no survival purpose.

Neither Scott nor Franklin moved, but both stared at John. After a few uncomfortable moments, John decided he should attempt interaction.

"Nice sunglasses. Don't think you'll need them in here," John said to Scott.

Scott didn't say a word, only lifted his glasses to reveal his missing eye and scarred face. Ashton put a hand on her face and shook her head at John.

"Bristle doesn't like your big dog," Franklin said, setting the cat on the ground. This was the first time John got a good look at the black spotted cat. It was taller and leaner than a house cat should be and had a black mohawk running down its neck.

"It isn't my dog, and that isn't a cat," John said.

"She's *Acinonyx jubatus,* or as you would know it, cheetah. King cheetah, to be exact. Her name is Bristle," Franklin said proudly.

John shot a look at Ashton, who shrugged.

"Where did you find a king cheetah?" John asked.

"The zoo, where else? They aren't indigenous."

The little know-it-all was already getting on John's nerves, and even though he had a few more questions about the cheetah, he wanted nothing more than to be out of this room.

"Come on, Stray. Use that brain of yours," Ashton said, grinning at him.

Franklin turned toward Ashton as Bristle cautiously explored the room. "Miss Ashton, I am out of cat food for Bristle. I couldn't find any in the room you let us in."

Ashton looked to John for help, but he made sure to avoid her green eyes.

"I don't think we have any. We've never had a cheetah before. Whenever we run out of dog food, we just feed them people food until we can get some more," Ashton said, still maintaining that annoying high pitch.

Franklin shook his head. "I have to carefully regulate her food. She was separated from her mom too young, and if her diet becomes imbalanced at all, she could get sick and die."

John decided he would help Ashton by placating Franklin. "Don't worry. We can place an order with X and he'll go find it."

Ashton's eyes narrowed, and for a moment John was afraid she would cross the room and beat him up. Apparently X was a subject he should have avoided.

"X doesn't need any more grocery runs," Ashton said.

John didn't want to know where the conversation would go from here, and without a word bolted out the door.

Kade, Tiny, and X spent most the drive back arguing over whether or not they should have taken the deal at all, or at least certain parts of the deal. Most of the demands were simple technicalities to keep the two groups out of each other's way and divide the looting areas. Taking Victoria was by far the most taxing of the points. The next most difficult stemmed from a Feline Flu outbreak within the Tribe's camp. People were getting scared and were even willing to be vaccinated in an attempt to stop the spread, which only led to people turning into foamers.

Kade had been required to take on two Tribe civilians and Victoria. Kade's group would provide the Tribe a safe place to send the refugees.

When they returned, Kade sent word for John, Grace, and Ashton to meet him in his room. X and Tiny disappeared to prep their gear for the rescue mission.

Kade pushed open his dorm room door, which was marked with a duct-tape *K*. He hadn't seen the inside of it in a few days. Tiny preferred her room, so they tended to sleep there. If they weren't sleeping, he didn't have time to be in a room. He sat down on the sleeping bag–covered mattress and let out a long breath.

John came in, accompanied by Fenris and her pup. Fenris had once belonged to a farmer who had tried to feed Kade to his foamer grandson. The pup had been sired by Fenris and Argos, who had been Jem's dog before the Primal Age. He had been entrusted to Kade when Jem was called to DC by the National Guard. After saving Kade's life a number of times, Argos had fallen in the battle with the Tribe.

The pleasant surprise was that he had bred before Argos died. Now they had Rex. Rex was pitch-black with a single chocolate splotch on the center of his chest. Kade had been able to use the puppy as leverage to keep Jem there as long as he could, but Kade understood his friend had obligations.

On John's heels, Grace and Ashton entered the room.

"What did you call this all-important team meeting for?" Ashton asked as she petted Fenris.

Kade sat in silence for a few moments as he contemplated his next words.

"I know you guys are under no obligation to stay here, but I don't get the sense that any of you are planning to desert any time soon. I know nothing about these newcomers or how long they will stay. Two things I'd like to keep from them until we have a better idea. First is that Damian is responsible for the vaccine. Second is my Huntington's," Kade said.

"You have Huntington's disease?" John said in shock.

"How can you have been with us this long and not have known that, Stray?" Ashton toyed with the end of her braided hair.

Kade ignored his sister. "Yeah. Sorry. I think you met me just when, for the first time in my life, I wasn't thinking about it constantly."

"This isn't a joke? Like when you guys said my urine was better for me than water before a long run?" John asked.

"Not a joke, kid. One day I will die an unpleasant death. Until I am no longer able to lead this group, I don't plan to let it affect me in any way. With all the things that can kill me these days, I'd say it's pretty much a nonfactor," Kade said.

"Don't worry, we'll keep your secret," Grace said.

"Just be safe while I'm gone," Kade said.

Ashton shot him a glare, then went to the door. She paused. "Good luck." She stormed out, slamming the door.

"John, can you relay the situation to Damian so I can get packed?" Kade asked.

"Yes, sir," John said, and hurried out of the room with the dogs on his heels.

"You know she's pissed as shit at you," Grace said, sitting on his bed.

Kade walked over to his dresser and loaded his pack. He loved Ashton more than life itself and hated to knowingly cause her pain, but his odds of saving Mick and Jem increased drastically with X in the party.

"Ashton's been mad at me most of her life," Kade said.

He knew making her the caretaker of the children until Drew and Jem got back wouldn't sit well with her, but he trusted her to do a good job whether she liked it or not. It wasn't like he had many options. X and Tiny were out of the question. Damian was focused on his research. He didn't really know Damian's assistant, Number Five. Grace hadn't had a day of rest since they'd arrived in Houghton, and it didn't look like she'd have a break anytime soon. John was just a kid himself. Ashton was his only option.

"You're taking her boyfriend away and making her the town matron. I'd sleep with one eye open if I was you," Grace said.

"I already do. You ever going to give John a chance, or just lead the kid on?"

Grace gave him an uncertain smile. "He's great. He really is. I even find that nervous stutter of his cute. But if I'm with him because he's the only option, I'd rather just be alone. I don't need a boyfriend to feel complete."

Kade hadn't considered things from a stray perspective. His core cohort that started the journey with him had all known one another before the Primal Age. The relationships that had formed between him and Tiny, or Ashton and X, had been fully tested in the Old World and couldn't be considered settling. Kade sealed his pack.

"Maybe a better suitor will come along," Kade said, taking a seat beside her.

"Can't you find some completely hopeless movie star that can't take care of himself and get him to join?"

"I'll send a scout mission to Hollywood as soon as we return."

Grace reached over and put her hand on Kade's back. "I wanted to say thanks. I don't thank you enough for taking me in."

Kade got to his feet and sulked to the window. "This is why I don't tell people I'm dying. They get all sentimental."

Grace sprung up and followed him. "I just wish I'd known. That's the type of thing you tell family, and I'd call you family."

There had once been a time when Kade debated whether or not to execute Grace. With her standing beside him in grease-covered overalls, he couldn't imagine how that had ever been an option. Her trade skills had not only kept them alive, but also comfortable. He figured a little openness with one who gave so much for him couldn't hurt.

"The Primal Age has been the first time in my life I've felt alive since I was tested for Huntington's. Huntington's is one of the least likely things to kill me now. It just felt good to feel like a normal person again. It affects some things—like, I'll never have kids—but it's not an anchor around my neck anymore," Kade said.

"You just make a lot more sense now than you used to," Grace said.

Kade stared out the window. Huntington's coming up had been like someone stabbing a nearly healed wound.

"Don't expect me to write your eulogy," Grace said.

"It'll be a long time till I have to face that end."

"You said it is the least likely thing to kill you. I'd rather it be the most likely. I want you around as long as you can stay. You're the big brother I never had," Grace said, a quiver overtaking her voice.

Kade placed a hand on her shoulder. He couldn't express how much it meant to him that she thought of him that way, since she'd had three older brothers who were all dead now. One died at her hands to save Kade. "You've seen me shot, stabbed, burned, and beaten. If you haven't noticed, I am invincible."

"You're just really good at almost dying."

Kade rubbed the cigar burn on his neck. "Like I said, invincible."

From coast to coast, winter had taken its toll on the foamers. Most of the creatures that lived in a cold region and did not belong to a pack were unable to survive. The largest packs were situated in areas of high population density before the fall of society. Almost all of the cold-zone packs had survived by seeking shelter, either natural or man-made. However, when they were caught in snowstorms, the foamers would survive by pressing the entire pack into one single body.

Due to the abundance of vacant buildings, shelter wasn't the greatest hardship they'd had to endure. Most animals carry an evolutionary instinct to avoid the scent of humans. Though foamers weren't fully human, they still carried the same scent. Because of this, in the beginning, hunting had been a difficult procedure for even the strongest of packs, causing most to cannibalize their weaker mates to survive.

Winter eventually gave way to spring, and as time passed the foamers grew better equipped for the cold and the hunt. Some packs mastered communication among the ranks faster than others, and once the foamers could coordinate their hunting strategies, their survival rate increased drastically.

Alpha's pack had suffered its share of losses through the cold months, but overall his pack had swelled in numbers. There were now twenty-three foamers total in his pack. During Kade's research he would name the foamers, but amongst themselves they seemed to recognize each other by sight. A short stocky foamer that Kade called Beta had survived the winter as Alpha's number two, along with Pepper, who was named for the bird shot stuck in her cheek.

Because of the size of his pack, Alpha had come to not fear outside foamers, but he was wary of any foamer under his command. He had been challenged for leadership on more than one occasion but had never come close to losing his hold on the troop.

Alpha had taken to sleeping under the short deck of a vacant house. Pepper always joined him in the dark space that gave him an advantage over any would-be challenger. So far no foamer had succeeded in getting more than a few strides under the deck before Alpha awakened. At that point, it wasn't even fair. Alpha would have perfect night vision while his attacker was unable to see more than a few inches into the darkness.

Soundly asleep in his nest under the deck, Alpha was dreaming about something that didn't make any sense to him. He was sitting not on the ground, but on a raised device he had seen in some of the shelters they had slept in. His legs were bent at the knee over the device, while his back was flat against it. Over his legs was a flat top that had food on it, but it was strangely colored and wasn't bloody. Instead of digging in with his claws, he held two shiny things in his hands. In fact, he didn't even have claws and was hardly even hairy. Plus, he was covered in the colored things that he remembered from before winter, the things that had made it harder to relieve himself.

The strangest part was that he wasn't alone. There were two females, one large and one small. The small one had gray eyes and often spread her lips wide at Alpha, but she had no red foam around her mouth. Neither did the large one. Sounds came from their mouths, but there was none of the guttural emissions he understood. It was just noise.

Under the deck, without his knowledge, his hands worked an invisible fork and knife while he slept soundly, curled on his side. Pepper nudged his face. He awoke to a mass of red hair, and she nodded toward the one open end of the deck.

Alpha rose on all fours and stared at his attacker, who didn't realize the sleeping beast had awakened. Charging the opponent, Alpha came under his arms, pinning them in his grasp as he wrapped the creature up around the waist. Their momentum pushed them out from under the deck, but not before his opponent's head thudded loudly off the wood.

When they landed in the morning light, his opponent was stunned beneath him. Red foam gurgled out of Alpha's mouth as he sank his teeth into the foamer's exposed neck. He bit down hard, feeling his enemy's blood flow into his mouth. With his teeth deep inside the usurper's neck, Alpha thrashed his head from side to side, ripping apart the side of his opponent's throat. As the life drained from his foolish attacker, Alpha kept his lips suctioned securely to the wound. He swallowed a large mouthful of blood before separating to allow Pepper to drink her fill.

Alpha's eyes scanned the area for other threats, then reared back, beating his chest as he howled. With the exhilaration of the kill rushing through his body, he forgot everything that had to do with his dream.

Chapter III

The Rescue Party for the Rescue Mission

X's room had changed from just a simple dorm layout to a fully customized living area. A dartboard, perforated by throwing stars, had been attached to the wall. The dresser was filled with blue jeans, black socks, V-neck undershirts, and boxer briefs. His closet was packed with a wide variety of winter gear, and he had mounted a pull-up bar across the doorframe. What stood out as unusual was the mannequin he called Manny. Manny had once been in an upscale secondhand store, but the torso mounted on a metal stand was now home for his duster, cowboy hat, and weapons belt.

X was undressing Manny when Ashton came into the room. Her face was scrunched, meaning she was pissed, but since she wasn't already yelling, it wasn't at him—at least not when she came in. When he put his duster on, she went off.

"Oh, hell no. You aren't going after Jem and Mick. You don't even like them."

Crossing the room, X took her in his arms and kissed her. His eyes shot open as she bit down on his tongue.

"Et oh," X attempted.

She released his tongue and stood with her hands on his hips. "That shit might work for Tiny and Kade, but you can't shut me up by kissing me. There's no reason for you to go. I don't bitch when you disappear for a week on your *grocery* runs. I get it. Playing house isn't something you are engineered for, but I won't stand by while you risk your life in a situation that has already been handled, and that you aren't equipped for."

Not equipped for. Not equipped for. Did she forget when he fought off half a dozen foamers by himself to save her life? Or when he led all of Alpha's troop on a goose chase so she could escape? Or the time he got the draw on the Wilson brothers and ended the Mexican standoff? Or the time he broke into jail to free Mick?

Ashton moved closer and put her hand on his chest. "Look, I love you. I understand when you need to get away for a few days. But please, there's no reason for you to go along."

"This gives me a chance to earn back a white hat." X let his eyes wander over her freckled face, then he walked past her.

She kept after him, but he tuned her out as he made his way to the third-floor exit. The ladder was already hanging out the window. Without pausing, he descended the rungs. His shoes sank into the soft ground, and Ashton landed behind him. He went toward the road where Tiny and Kade waited.

Ashton grabbed two handfuls of his duster and reined him around to face her. "Fine. Don't listen to me. Don't stay for me. Go. But even if you earned that black hat at some point in your life, you've been nothing but a white hat in the Primal Age. And if you expect me to just be the good girlfriend watching the horizon for your return, you better think again."

She took him by the back of the neck and pulled him in for a long kiss, then shoved him away with such force he almost lost his footing before she stormed off toward Lambian. X felt like someone had tightened a noose around his heart and dropped the gallows door. She climbed the ladder while he suffocated in his panic. The reality that she might not wait paralyzed him. He didn't think there was anyone else in the group she would leave him for, but if he lost her, he had no reason to come back at all. She had long disappeared through the window when he made up his mind to go after her.

"X," Kade called.

X swung his attention toward the road and heard engines in the distance. One perk of the end of the world was that any human noises were easy to distinguish among the ambient sounds of nature.

He migrated back toward the other two while trying to convince himself that Ashton was her normal explosive self and wasn't being serious. She had been mad at him plenty since Kade had assigned her to X's car in the convoy when they'd first decided to come to Lambian. Yet a sliver of doubt was taking hold.

Kade and Tiny had donned their combat gear and were decked out in weapons and hiking packs. A Humvee came into view on the other side of the bridge. Though Kade's group had left the bridge unblocked, the vehicle still had to swerve through the obstacle course of cars.

X touched his palm to the handle of his pistol, grounding himself in the moment and blocking out his emotions. The Tribe's vehicle crossed the bridge and came to a stop in front of Lambian. X hadn't noticed at a distance, but the Humvee was in fact a Hummer, the civilian model. He wondered if they had captured enough of their military vehicles to put a dent in their arsenal, or if Henson just didn't want to risk another combat vehicle.

The passenger door opened, and all X could see was a pair of dress shoes. As the man they belonged to came around the door, X was surprised not only by his fancy attire but by his looks. The man was dressed in a vest, tie, and suit coat—Old World attire. Based on his gray hair, X put him in his midfifties. The affluence he exuded should have appeared weak in the Primal Age, but the man oozed power.

The back doors opened. X was still concerned this was a trap and kept his guard. However, he relaxed when a woman who looked like she had done her time in the Primal Age filed out. From the other side of the vehicle, Victoria emerged, looking anything but happy at the homecoming.

The driver's window descended, revealing a man in an army uniform wearing lizard-eye hologram sunglasses.

"Zack?" Tiny said, rushing to the door and bouncing with a giddiness X had never seen from her before.

"That can't be you, Doc," Zack replied, lowering his glasses down his nose.

"I can't believe you're here."

Kade cleared his throat. "I'll take the newcomers in and round up Drew, if you want to brief the Tribesmen on the situation."

Tiny waved a dismissive hand at Kade. "Got it."

Kade introduced himself to the people who'd come from the Tribe and led them toward the dorm. X stayed with the vehicle since he doubted Ashton wanted to see him. He watched Kade ascend the ladder and take one look toward the Hummer before he climbed through the window.

Mick paced in his cage, which was more like spinning in circles because he didn't even have enough room to lie down. There was a double row of cages that had twelve different cells, but only two others were occupied. He had been to DC a few times as a kid, but he had never been in the Smithsonian Castle before. The building had been the information hub for all the Smithsonian buildings, but due to its fortress-like nature, it was now a prison.

There was a tiny woman with short-cropped black hair framing her face doing pull-ups from the top bar of her cage. The other cage was occupied by a man who looked like a skeleton wrapped in skin with overgrown curly hair and a beard. The man appeared quite sickly, and Mick could smell the death emanating from the cage. Both the man and the woman wore plain one-piece jumpsuits that looked like they used to belong to custodial staff. Neither appeared interested in talking, and Mick didn't plan to start the conversation, so he paced. His best guess was that Jem had been gone four hours. He had no way of knowing for sure. It might have just been a half hour that felt like forever, but he doubted this was the case because of the pressure building in his bladder.

Once he started thinking about his bladder he couldn't stop, which only made the time drag on more. He looked for a bucket, or a guard he could ask to let him out.

The woman dropped from the bars and stretched her arms. Mick was tapping his foot and growing desperate for a solution.

"Excuse me," Mick said.

"I don't talk to cops. Did they think putting a different uniform on would get me to spill something?" the woman said, grabbing the bars they shared. He could feel her sizing him up as she swayed from side to side. Against her fragile features, her different-colored eyes stood out even in the low light. One was a bright green, while the other was a dark brown.

"I just wanted to know bathroom protocol," Mick said, squeezing his legs together.

"Get as far away from my cage as you can, and do your best to get it outside of your bars. They only clean our cells while we're with Cunningham."

Mick gave her a polite nod, then darted to the side of his cell, where he abutted no others and relieved his bladder. He turned back around to find the woman still staring at him.

"Who's Cunningham?" Mick asked, trying to break free of her trance-like stare.

She shook her head, sending her black hair swooshing side to side. "You aren't one of them, are you?"

"I'm not sure who *them* is," Mick replied.

"I'm Yuzuki, that guy is Anquan, and you'll know Cunningham," she said, and turned her back to Mick.

A set of doors opened at the top of the short set of stairs leading down to their cells. A soldier entered the room, dragging a barely conscious Jem by a jumpsuit that matched the other two prisoners' attire. His body bounced down the steps until the soldier reached the cages and tossed Jem into the one beside Mick. He sealed it with a keyed Master Lock, then left the room without a word.

Mick dropped beside Jem and tried to get some sort of response from him. What parts of Jem he could see had all been bloodied and damaged, and some wounds had even been stitched.

"He knows Cunningham," Yuzuki said flatly.

Kade climbed through the window after the other three. Fenris and Rex were the first to greet the newcomers with sniffs and licks. In the entrance room, John was waiting for them with Drew and Number Five. Number Five took her name from being the fifth test subject during the Feline Flu vaccination trials. She had been the only one from Damian's test group to survive. In an effort to not get close to her, Damian had continued to call her Number Five. The name stuck once Damian and Number Five joined up with the group.

Kade hadn't expected to see Number Five when he came through the window since she was rarely outside the science building, but she had a pack on her back as though she were planning to come along with them.

"Five?" Kade asked.

"I'd like to be more useful. I'm not really such a good lab assistant, and Damian has enough blood samples to last him a lifetime without me. I escaped DC with the rest of them, so I can help get them out," she replied.

"Lab assistant?" Victoria asked, looking at Kade.

Kade gave Victoria a nod, then said to Number Five, "Have you ever handled a weapon before?"

"Don't worry about me in that department," Number Five replied.

"All right. Drew, Five, head on down. I'll meet you in a few," Kade said.

Drew and Number Five climbed down the ladder. As Number Five's chestnut hair disappeared beneath the window frame, Kade realized just how little he knew about her.

"Sorry about that, folks. This is John. He's going to be showing you around and getting you guys situated. John, this is Emma, Wright, and an old friend of ours, Victoria. Take care of them until I get back," Kade said.

Kade tried to size up the newcomers. Wright had a power and

charisma to his presence that reminded Kade of his own father, who had been a businessman. The doctor carried himself like he was negotiating a business contract and gave no hint of the person behind the façade. Emma was the exact opposite. She was frail and had a nervous twitch about her, like a trapped animal. Even her voice sounded shaky.

"You guys can come with me. I'll show you to your rooms and give you the tour," John said, heading out. Wright and Emma followed him, but Victoria remained.

"Can we talk?" Victoria asked.

"How about after the—" Kade had a sense of déjà vu and changed his mind. "Sure."

She took off her librarian glasses and secured them in the top buttonhole of her shirt. "Thanks. I thought you should have a heads-up on what you've accepted."

Kade could not stop looking at her face. Images of her at Thanksgiving dinners and family gatherings clashed viciously with her in a ballistic mask, calling for his death. Now here she was, claiming to be forewarning him of some other danger.

"You mean, besides you?"

Victoria ignored his volley. "Emma is a British exchange student. She tried on several occasions to rally a group into Canada to see if she could find out some information. After the third time she was locked up because it cost the lives of four Tribesmen. At some point she's going to try to go."

"I don't see why she shouldn't be allowed to go," Kade said.

"The issue isn't if she goes—it's what she takes with her. Now, Dr. Wright, I don't like."

"I'm guessing he's not so bad then."

Victoria shook her head. "He's different. Goes on like the Old World is still a thing. I can't tell if he's detached or not, but he was dumb enough to try to get support to take over the Tribe. Besides, he's a shrink—I know how much you love those."

After he had been tested for Huntington's, Kade had been forced to see more shrinks than he knew existed. It had become his least favorite profession, and he had made two of them cry. Once that happened, Kade's father had decided to let him be.

"We're a lot farther from Canada than the Tribe, and I never asked to lead this group, so if Dr. Wright wants to challenge me for it he's welcome to," Kade said, then added, "Thanks for the heads-up."

Victoria smiled at him and pulled her glasses out of her shirt. "Damian is here?"

"He is."

"Does he know what I did?" she asked. Her eyes glossed over for just a moment, before her composure returned.

"He does."

Victoria put a hand on his chest. "By the way, I'm not happy to see you either, but I'm glad you're alive."

"Why did you tell me all that?" Kade asked.

"I'm a survivor. Right now, your being well-informed is my best chance at staying that way."

Victoria patted his chest and went into the hallway. Kade contemplated everything she had just dropped on him and decided he should swing by the science building on his way out to relay the information to Damian.

Sitting in the common room of the fourth floor of the dorm, John wondered if this would have been what freshman orientation would have felt like if he had ever made it to college. The room had two couches, a beanbag chair, and a table. He sat on a couch opposite Grace, with Fenris sleeping on the middle cushion. Rex was chewing on John's shoelace. Emma relaxed in the beanbag chair, while Ashton and the kids, cheetah included, filled in the other couch. Victoria sat across the table from Wright.

Damian stood before them, the spitting image of Kade. They were so close to identical that their only major difference was posture. Kade was more relaxed in front of a group, while Damian looked like he was always ready to defend himself from a verbal attack.

"My brother has asked that I keep things running smoothly until he gets back and make sure everyone knows the rule that no foamer is to be killed except in self-defense," Damian said.

John noticed his eyes traveled everywhere but to Victoria, who did nothing but stare at him.

"Those abominations would be better off dead," Wright said.

"He also said none of you are under any obligation to stay, but you are welcome as long as you would like. So long as the rules are followed," Damian said, as if he had never heard Wright. "We run a two-person guard watch all night long. We'll pair you newcomers up with one of us."

John tuned out the rest of what Damian said and found himself staring at Grace. He hoped at some point she would look toward him so he might be able to smile at her. But the longer he watched, the more she seemed like she would never turn her head his way. There had to be some way to show her how he felt, though he wasn't sure what else he could do to get her attention.

Damian wrapped up the meeting, and John let out a long sigh as he got to his feet. He had the last guard shift, and it would be a while until he had a chance to spend those hours with Grace. He'd have to head to bed now to get enough sleep to be alert for the night watch.

John was so lost in his own thoughts that he practically walked into Emma on his way down the corridor. With her small frame, it wasn't hard for him to believe he hadn't seen her. Everything about her was compact, with the exception of the one place John couldn't keep his eyes from wandering: her large breasts.

"Can you wake me up when it's our turn for guard duty?" Emma asked. She had sharp cheekbones, with large, knowing eyes, a button nose, and a strong chin. Her features reminded John of a mouse—a cute mouse.

"Yeah, sure," John said. He hadn't realized she was assigned to him.

"Thanks. I don't want to be late on my first day," she said, and disappeared into her room.

Alpha wandered among the trees, trying to find the scent of prey. If they were unsuccessful, he could always wander to the water and scoop out a fish. The water was close to the others, and he tried to avoid them whenever possible. They had things worse than claws. His head and shoulder showed the damage his body had suffered during his encounters with them. Many of his kind weren't as lucky.

He stopped to sniff the air, but couldn't pick up any scents—not even from the blue-faced other. Alpha hadn't caught his scent in a day, which was unusual. At least once a day the blue-faced other tended to be around his pack.

Alpha hadn't quite figured out what to make of the blue-faced one. The male seemed more like one of his than an other, but still wasn't quite like him. The interloper had harmed members of his pack, but only with his hands, the way Alpha's kind fought, not the others.

His nostrils flared as he caught the scent of two others. Silently, he moved his massive body through the darkness, trying to get them into his line of sight without giving himself away. He didn't want to face a boom stick, so stealth was key.

Their scent grew stronger and he heard voices. Moving into a clump of young pines, he concealed himself while he watched a tall and short other talk. He could hear the words clearly, though he no longer understood their meaning.

"You did very well sneaking out. Very brave," the tall one said.

"You said you'd hurt my friends if I didn't follow you. I won't let you hurt them," the short one said.

"Very well," the tall one said.

Alpha tried to see what happened next, but he couldn't get a good view through his hiding spot. He heard a zip, and then the two others were struggling, like two of his kind wrestling. Then there was gagging from the short one, and laughter from the tall one.

"I'm sorry, but my plan requires you to be dead," the tall one said.

Alpha's nose pricked up and his mouth started to water. The stench of blood was heavy in the air. It wouldn't be long before more of his pack arrived.

Alpha watched the tall one walk away, but he felt like the other was looking at him. Like the other knew he was there the whole time. Alpha was curious about the tall other, but he couldn't resist the smell of blood anymore and charged through the trees to where the small one lay on the ground with his throat slit.

Nudging the body once with his head, Alpha made sure the small one was dead, then fixed his mouth over the slash on the child's neck. After taking a long drink of the blood, Alpha bit down on the wound, tearing a section of the neck away. He was so lost in his feeding that he hardly noticed his pack joining in the feast.

Kade sat in the back of the cramped Hummer with X, Five, and Drew. Drew was a sizeable guy who was in terrific shape, having been a college athlete at the dawn of the Primal Age and then being forced into manual labor every single day since. Though he tried to hide it, Kade could tell his brain was torn at being away from the kids. Kade figured it was similar to how he felt every time he was away from Ashton.

Drew and Five were filling them in on everything they could remember about the stretch of land that used to be the National Mall, but now served as the base of operations for the president and his guardsmen. Kade had to hand it to the former leader of the country—he hadn't thought the doofus was capable of such tactical thinking. Despite using his power to create a police state, Kade wondered if the president would have shown half as much spine in the Old World if he would have actually won Kade's vote. From what Damian had said, the president was the main pressure behind the Feline Flu vaccine getting rushed into production, which made Kade wonder if he had been trying to orchestrate the Primal Age in the first place. Kade had to focus on the task at hand, though, which was saving his friends.

"Back before the end of the world, I took a class on propaganda during World War II to fill an elective block. The president makes the combined efforts of the Axis and Allies look like a child's lie to their parents," Drew said as he sketched the third copy of a DC map on a notepad. The kid was getting good at the maps, and Kade was hoping when they got back he could pair him with X on the grocery runs.

"In chaos, there is opportunity," Zack said. He had taken off the lizard-eye sunglasses and rolled up the sleeves on his army uniform. His dark forearms were covered in a peppering of brown scars.

"I'm a little pissed. The president convinces the entire population that the boogeyman is real, but my own friends didn't believe me when I held hard evidence that the world was ending," Kade replied.

"Even those that don't believe still agree with him just to stay protected. Everyone is scared, and what isn't to trust about the leader of the free world? He's made it sound like a worldwide community of terrorist sleeper cells in America coordinated one gigantic strike. Chemical weapons, dirty bombs—you name it, they did it," Drew said.

"I don't get why people would just follow that like sheep," X said.

"There is only one source of news right now, and that is the president. Look back to World War II, before there was a global media. Every country was able to spin the war to their own needs because no one else saw the other side of the story," Drew said.

"But you left. Don't other people leave? Don't they try to imagine what else is out there?" X asked.

Drew shook his head. "If you leave, you're automatically branded a terrorist. You must have been a sleeper cell that was gaining intel and now must report. It's why Jem was abducted on sight. The only people that ever leave the DC zone on orders are those closest to the president. The top of the food chain is still living like kings. For people that want power, this is a perfect opportunity," Drew said.

They were well into the night, with Zack at the wheel and Tiny riding shotgun, before their two scouts finished their report. Kade was about to let himself doze off when he saw Zack reach over and put his hand on Tiny's leg. Kade toyed with the cigar burn on his neck. Three seconds passed before Tiny removed his hand. Kade's eyes dashed back and forth between the two to see if anything else was about to take place, but neither stopped looking forward the entire time. Kade's heart ticked a little faster, and sweat broke out all over his body. Some voice in his head told him to yell at the Tribesman not to touch her, but he suppressed the desire.

Tiny looked over her shoulder at him and smiled her tight-lipped smile. Kade smiled back and felt his body slowly return to normal. He took a deep breath and tried to remind himself that people could make physical contact without any ulterior motives. In the Old World, Kade had never had a traditional relationship. He'd stayed away from Tiny because he knew he was dying and did not want to burden her, or anyone else. Now, in the Primal Age, he and Tiny shared a strange existence. There was no competition for her, and no one in their group ever got close enough to her to touch her. He would have to keep an eye on his jealousy to make sure he didn't overreact to a simple gesture between old friends.

They passed a highway exit sign that showed a slew of gas stations and food options off the next ramp.

"Mind if we swing off?" Drew asked.

"We don't need to refill the tank yet," Zack replied.

"I need to empty mine," Drew said.

X picked up an empty bottle that was rolling around on the floor and handed it to Drew.

Drew looked at the bottle, confused, then dropped it on the ground. "Not the liquid tank."

"I'll just pull over," Zack said.

Drew put a hand over his face that was clearly burning red even in the dim light of the car interior.

"I'm scared to shit out here. I haven't been living in the wild the past two months. I've still been dropping the browns with four walls around me. Can we please stop before I explode?"

Zack glanced at Kade for confirmation, who gave him a nod. Kade appreciated Zack's at least humoring him that he was still in charge. Zack flipped the headlights off and veered up the ramp in the moonlight. Full moons always amazed Kade. They gave no light of their own, but were able to reflect enough to light up the night.

Zack parked behind the first gas station off the exit. The back door to the station was hanging wide open.

"What's the call?" Zack asked.

"You and Tiny want to refill the tank. The rest of us will go in," Kade said as he and X took the time to equip their gear.

X led the way into the station with his .357 revolver out, and Kade followed him with both of his Judges drawn. It took a few moments for his eyes to adjust to the darkness, but the place appeared deserted, with most of the food racks having been plundered. Kade swung around the outer perimeter of the store, while X made a beeline for the bathrooms.

The door *whoosh-whooshed* as X ducked in and out, then called for Drew and Five.

While the others used the bathroom, Kade stared into the dairy cooler at the chocolate milk just sitting there. He knew the power had been out a long time, and the expiration dates had passed anyway, but it took all of his control not to chug down a half gallon. He spun around when he heard the sound of a plastic bag being filled. X was pillaging the tobacco racks.

"You don't smoke," Kade said.

"Your powers of observation have always astounded me, Watson," X replied, looking appraisingly at an e-cig.

"Should I ask?"

"Yes, you should."

Kade let out a huff as he made his way over to the counter. "What brilliant masterminding are you up to?"

"Imagine being two months without a fix. Then imagine you come across me, who has an abundance of smokes. Now imagine I can name my trade for a pack of cigarettes that were totally worthless to me. That is what I am doing."

"That is brilliant."

"Of course it is."

In front of Kade was a box of Snickers, Tiny's favorite candy bar. He snatched the box up like it was a Black Friday sale.

"I'm going to go see if the other two want to come in for anything." Kade headed for the door.

"Maybe she'll give you a thank you—" that was the last Kade heard before he was out the back door. The opportunities to do something thoughtful for Tiny were few and far between since he had to spend most of his day-to-day duties running Houghton. He was delighted to have one of those rare chances.

When he came in sight of the Humvee, Tiny and Zack were propped up on the windshield watching the stars. Kade felt the jealousy resurge with each step; they didn't notice him. The box of Snickers made a thud on the hood when he dropped them.

"Wanted to see if you guys needed to go in for anything," Kade said thickly, his voice sounding off in his own ear.

"Thanks, man, but I'm good," Zack said.

"I could go for a Snickers," Tiny said, hopping off the hood and heading for the station. Kade thought about telling her he'd brought her a box of them, but felt that the nice gesture had already been wasted.

"I can't believe I am actually getting to meet *the* Kade Zerris," Zack said, sliding to his feet.

"Look, I didn't want to fight the Tribe. I just wanted to be left alone. But I'm sorry if I killed any of your friends." Kade's body tensed for a fight.

Zack laughed, his bright white teeth reflecting almost as much light as the moon. "Not that. The world is a better place without people like Sarge. I'm talking about your girl. She told me all about you back when we were building sand castles in the Middle East. Looks like destiny wanted you two to end up together."

Kade had to admit, without the end of the world, he would never have been able to put his Huntington's behind him so he could move on with his life and have a normal relationship. If he could go back in time and do one thing, he would have told his brother not to make the vaccine. But if he could have done two things, he would have told his younger self to get out of his own way. "I'm lucky."

"That you are, brother. She is the best of the best." Zack smiled, and Kade could tell he was looking at a memory. Inside, he was burning to ask Zack if he had been with Tiny in the Old World, but he wasn't sure he wanted to know. He couldn't get mad at her for it. It wasn't like he had been loyally awaiting the end of the world, saving himself for her.

He used a deep breath to push the thought from his mind. "Want me to take a turn at the wheel?"

"I'd love to snag a quick nap before we get there. In case I'm asleep, we'll probably want to refill about an hour out, so after the job we have enough gas to put distance between us and the weekend warriors," Zack replied.

No food. No water. No sleep.

Mick was spread facedown on the metal prep table. The smell of bleach lingered in the air; even though he couldn't see Cunningham, he knew she was somewhere nearby. He was about to begin his third session with her. His chest had been cut up pretty well, but she had been going easy on Mick compared to what she had done to Jem. The only good thing about the sessions was that he got escorted by a soldier across the Mall to the restaurant Cunningham used as her headquarters. That brief time outside felt like heaven—a few moments away from the misery of a cage and the smell of his own defecation. He had considered making a break for it during the walks, but he noticed more than one rooftop sniper watching his progress. Even if there weren't snipers, he doubted he had the strength to make a run for it. Just staying on his feet took all of his concentration.

With what little he had learned about Cunningham, he knew there was a reason she was showing favorites. He'd like to have said he'd rather be the hero and take the brunt, but he doubted he'd be able to hang on to any information if he'd had to endure what Jem was going through.

A hand wrenched his head back, and standing in front of Mick was the woman in white. Cunningham held a metal tin with an oven mitt. When she brought the tin close to his face he could feel the heat. She rattled the tin, and Mick wasn't looking forward to finding out what was inside.

"Before you terrorists struck, I used to love the game Yahtzee. Now I've made my own version. I'm going to ask you a question. If you give me an answer, I won't roll these on your back. If not, I'll enjoy my game."

"I'm not a terrorist. I'm a police officer," Mick said.

Cunningham slammed his head onto the metal table and rolled the contents of the tin onto his back. He wasn't sure what they were other than there was five of them and they felt like fire on contact. A second later, they stopped hurting, so he could only imagine how hot they were to sear his nerves that fast. They weight was removed from his back, and he heard them being plunked back into the can.

"You only speak when I ask a question. Where is the terrorist Damian Zerris?"

"He's not a terrorist," Mick said between pants.

He clenched his teeth as the hot masses rolled along his back. She plucked them up again.

"At least you didn't deny knowing him. Let me try that question again."

On Cunningham's table, time held no sway. She controlled the passage of time. On a number of occasions she had to reheat the tin, and in those moments of peace he could feel the blisters sprouting on his back. By the end of the session, he could smell his own skin cooking. When she deemed his time was up, Mick still hadn't given up any information.

When they finally returned him to his cell, there was no way for him to sit comfortably, so he knelt and lay forward over his own knees. No matter which one of them came back from a session, no one spoke. Neither asked what had happened or if any information was given up. They all sat together in silence.

Mick was in pain, craved food, needed water. He needed nourishment if he was going to get through the days until his execution. The best idea he could come up with was sleeping, but the moment he closed his eyes there was a rap on the bars of his cell.

"No sleep. They'll make the torture worse. Wait," Yuzuki said.

It took every ounce of strength Mick had to nod that he'd heard her.

CHAPTER IV

THE DEMOCRATIC EMPIRE OF WEST VIRGINIA

John stood at the northwest corner of the roof, watching the sky lighten on the horizon. He hadn't spoken much to Emma through the course of their shift. On a number of occasions he had wanted to, but he wasn't sure what to say. He didn't want her to think he was into her, and he didn't want Grace to think he was interested in someone else. Plus, he was really terrible at talking to beautiful girls. If he opened his mouth, he would only make an ass of himself. Perhaps by remaining silent he would come off as quiet and mysterious.

"Is guard duty always this dull?" Emma asked, coming up beside him.

"Yeah, for the most part," John replied, stumbling over his own tongue.

"Do you people ever leave this dormitory?"

"Sometimes. Occasionally. We're usually working on something. But we explore from time to time. X does a lot. You probably didn't meet X," John said.

"Ever make it to Canada?"

In all of John's life, he had hardly seen anywhere but Houghton. Every once in a while the older classmates would make a Canada run so they could drink or gamble, but he was still a ways from eighteen, so that had never been an option for him.

"Are you Canadian?" John asked.

She raised her eyebrows, and it reminded him of a butterfly's wings getting ready to fly. "Seriously?"

John wanted to kick himself. Or at least literally put his foot in his mouth so he could stop saying stupid things.

"Sorry, I know you're English."

"British."

"Sorry, I know you're British. I say stupid things around pretty women." John couldn't believe those words had actually come out of his mouth. Like he had on many occasions in his life, he wished his words had a leash so he could pull them back.

She smiled a toothy smile at him and put her hand on his forearm. "Don't worry. It's endearing."

By the time he finished sighing, his lungs felt like a deflated pair of balloons. "How'd you end up here? Long swim?"

"I was a freshman at MIT—"

The door flung open, causing John to jump. He immediately scolded himself for being so easy to startle. Ashton rushed through the opening. Her face was ghostly white, and she looked around more rapidly than a chipmunk with ADHD.

"Did Scott come up here?"

John pointed at his eye, trying to remember which one was Scott, but thought Emma would be upset with him if he said *cyclops* out loud. Ashton nodded rapidly.

"Haven't seen him," John said.

"I've checked all the rooms. I can't find him anywhere," Ashton said, pushing her hair out of her face.

John went over to the edge of the roof and peered down. He could see the escape ladder swaying from the third-floor window.

Ashton came over. When she saw the ladder she shoved him, almost knocking him off his feet. "How didn't you notice the ladder going down?"

"That wasn't my . . ." John stopped himself, hoping he wasn't too far gone to avoid throwing Emma under the bus. That had been her zone to watch. They always divided the roof in half for guard duty.

Ashton had heard enough and stormed past John to Emma. John

stayed close enough to stop Ashton from physically attacking Emma, but worried what would happen to him if he had to do that.

"You haven't even been here a full day, and you've already screwed up." Ashton pointed a finger in her face.

To John's surprise, Emma didn't seem bothered by the outburst or accusation. He might actually get lucky and not have to break up a girl fight.

"I believe the child was your responsibility. And you would do better to stop yelling at me and try to find him," Emma said.

"Can you track him down, Stray?" Ashton said, then added, "Please."

"Mind coming along to watch my back?" John replied.

"I'll finish watch—you can take the new stray. I want to be here when the other kids wake up," Ashton said.

New stray. John was no longer alone on Stray Island.

"Don't worry, we'll find him," John said.

X awakened to a full bladder and was glad to see they were already stopped. The sign outside the Hummer read *Welcome to Maryland.* They had just halted in the middle of the road, since there was no reason to pull over.

"Drew, top off the tank from the reserve can," Kade said.

X climbed out of the Hummer at the same time as Kade, both of them heading for the tree line.

"I'll cover you, you cover me?" X asked.

"I'm going first," Kade said, pulling down his pants the moment they crossed into the trees.

The seconds that passed during Kade's turn felt like minutes as X's bladder wanted to explode. He danced back and forth, trying his best to keep his pistol up while watching Kade's back. Finally, his turn came. He holstered his pistol and undid his fly. The most glorious moan escaped his lips as he finally found relief.

"Kade!" Tiny hollered from back on the road.

X zipped up and had turned to run when Kade grabbed his wrist.

"They're in trouble, but there hasn't been a gunshot. Let's see if we can get the drop on the situation. I'll go wide to the left, you go to the right," Kade said.

X nodded and pulled out his revolver. He went through the trees at a quick jog before he swung back to the road. There was nothing to use for cover once he left the trees, so he stayed low to the ground, letting the grade of the road conceal him. He was around twenty yards north of where the Hummer was parked.

There were two men and a boy who looked like they'd walked out of a Mad Max movie. The man in the center had an arm around Drew's neck and a revolver to his head. The man to the left had a hunting rifle, and the boy had a shotgun that looked like it would knock him on his butt if he fired it.

Zack was on the near side of the Hummer with his hands up and his rifle hanging across his front. Five was still in the back of the Hummer, and Tiny was on the far side with her rifle propped across the hood.

X lined up his sights on the man holding Drew hostage, but he didn't feel confident attempting the shot at this range with a pistol. The boy's eyes settled on X.

"Pa, another one," the boy said.

The man with the hunting rifle glanced toward X. "Why don't you set that pistol down and come join us."

Drew's eyes were panicked. He looked afraid to breathe, and sweat was pouring from his forehead. X wanted to take the shot, but he'd as likely hit Drew as his assailant. Letting out a defeated sigh, he set the revolver down and walked toward the others, trying to devise a plan B.

"Now if you could just tell the nice lady to put her rifle down, we could talk like adults," the man with the rifle said.

"You apparently haven't met her yet, or you wouldn't call her nice, or a lady," X said.

"Regardless, we are representatives of the Democratic Empire of West Virginia. If you hand over your supplies, we will leave you with your lives," the rifleman said.

Kade charged in and, with a powerful swing, took the head cleanly off the rifleman's shoulders. His body stood for a moment before collapsing to the ground.

X charged at the hostage-holder while drawing his knife. The man pulled the trigger, blowing the side out of Drew's head, then turned the pistol toward X, but it was too late. X threw his body into the man, crashing to the asphalt. The boy aimed his shotgun toward X, but Tiny's bullet cut through his throat.

The man struggled under X, but X pinned him under his knees and pressed the tip of his knife to the man's chest.

"He's dead. Leaving behind three kids. Three kids that he took in as his own. I want you to go to hell, knowing, fearing, that someday I will follow you there. And when I get there, this will be pleasant in comparison."

X plunged the knife into the man's chest, then twisted the blade as he pushed it as deep as he could. The man's blood ran all over the ground, and within moments he stopped twitching. Pulling the blade clear, X cleaned it on the man and crawled over to Drew's body.

He knew there was no point, but he checked Drew's throat for a pulse. As he expected, he found none. Drew was gone. Needlessly and senselessly. X closed Drew's eyes and turned his attention to Tiny, who was crying for the first time he had ever seen.

"He was just a boy," Tiny said, wiping the silent tears from her eyes.

Zack had his rifle drawn to his shoulder, scanning for other dangers. "He was a threat. Nothing more."

Kade holstered his sword and walked toward Tiny.

"Jesus Christ, people. Have you ever considered the practicality of your costumes?" Zack said, his glaring eyes cutting like lasers between Kade and X.

"What?" was all X could muster.

"The urban cowboy and the city-slicker samurai. If either of you had a rifle, that situation would have resolved without Drew getting his head blown off. His death is on you two."

"Zack, you're out of line," Tiny snapped.

"No. I've been playing nice, blowing smoke up Kade's ass because you told me he was in charge. But he's going to get us all killed if he's leading this mission. You know as well as I do the best thing we could do would be to leave them and finish the mission ourselves," Zack said.

They were an hour away from DC. X couldn't imagine being left out now, but at the same time wouldn't be terribly upset if he was. As much as he had wanted to get away from Houghton for a bit, he was anxious to get back and smooth things over with Ashton.

"Tiny?" Kade said.

"He's not wrong about our best chance of success," Tiny said, wiping her eyes.

Kade looked like he had swallowed hot coals. His face contorted in pain and he kept opening his mouth to say something, but nothing came out, until finally, he said, "Let's bury Drew and see if we can't find their supplies. Then I will defer to Tiny. I trust you to do what's best."

Alpha stalked two others through the woods. Neither was the interloper he had become accustomed to, and they both carried things that were worse than claws. The others were on their way toward the place where his pack had found easy meat. Alpha had scattered them when he caught the scent of the others, but he wanted to remain close enough to observe these others whom he didn't recognize.

John wiped his forehead as he followed Scott's footprints—or at least the footprints he thought were Scott's. The area where the ladder reached the ground had been so traveled it was more mud than grass, so he guessed at which footprints were Scott's based on size.

John guessed Scott had no idea where he was trying to go, and it appeared he was going in circles. This baffled John, since even at night it wasn't difficult to find the campus.

From time to time John was reminded that Emma was searching with him when she would step on a twig or brush past a branch. She seemed scared out of her mind. She was sweating like they were on the surface of the sun, and her grip was so tight on the rifle he was sure she would snap it in half.

He tried to keep his thoughts off of her and on his task, but when she stopped and backed herself up against a tree, he didn't have any choice but to wait as she hyperventilated. She slid to the ground as her breathing became faster, and John went to join her. He sat beside her, not sure how to help her calm down. Her chest rose and fell in jerky motions. He attempted not to notice the effect it had on her breasts. John put his arm around her and took deep, slow breaths. She fought her breathing to match his, and breath by breath she was able to regain some control. Her long straw-colored hair was another reminder that she wasn't used to living in the current state of things. The women of their cohort either had short hair, or never left the door with their hair not tightly under control.

Finally, Emma found her composure, but now her face was turning a deep shade of red. "I'm sorry. I'm not sure where that came from. Please don't let that taint your impression of me."

John thought back to his first day with the group. He had been so scared he had frozen when walking. He had topped off his amazingly brave performance by shooting Kade when they'd been swarmed by foamers.

"Don't worry. You're off to a better start than my first day," John said, getting to his feet and offering her a hand.

"I'm just nervous. I've never even held a gun before," she said as John hoisted her to her feet.

John remembered when Kade was on the ground with two bullet holes in him because John hadn't spoken up about having never fired a gun. John instinctively covered his leg where he had shot Kade and recognized the same could happen to him.

John set his bow on the ground and took Emma's rifle from her.

He demonstrated to her as he spoke. "If we get in trouble, I want you to push the safety so you see the red dot, then aim at forty-five degrees and fire."

"How will I hit anything if I'm aiming in the air?" Emma asked, taking her rifle back.

"Exactly."

John resumed his pursuit of Scott's footprints and made a mental note to tell Kade that Emma needed some weapons lessons. He wondered if any of the other newcomers would also need training.

His thoughts came to a halt when he saw something lying in the mud ahead. Emma came to a stop beside him, but neither of them spoke as they looked at what they couldn't deny was a body on the ground.

"Stay here and holler if anything moves," John said.

As he approached the body, the number of footprints increased to dozens, as well as handprints to match. Scanning the area around him, John made sure there were no foamers lurking before he knelt beside the body. Had it not been for the scarred eye socket, he would have had trouble saying for certain that it was Scott. The body looked like someone had taken a meat tenderizer to it and then ate that meat. His arms and legs had been cleaned to the bone, and his chest and head had lost all structural consistency. John hurried back to Emma.

"Is he dead?" she asked.

"Let's go find Ashton," John said grimly, walking past her and making sure she couldn't see his eyes. He wanted to tell himself that this wasn't his fault—that Ashton should have been watching him, and Emma had been in charge of that sector. But he knew that even if he wasn't at fault, he could have prevented Scott's death.

Kade drove in silence. X was beside him, but neither of them had the stomach for talking. After they buried Drew, they found their attackers' camp. They had a gigantic pickup truck that was attached to a horse trailer with two horses inside. Kade didn't know much about horses, but since they were progressing to a farming society they decided it was a good idea to bring them along. The truck bed was loaded with enough gas for them to make the trip back without having to stop. X and Kade were more than happy to volunteer to drive the truck. Tiny hadn't dismissed Kade and X yet, but he had a hunch she would cut them the moment the real mission began.

Kade had spent so much time training to be a weapon he hadn't thought much about using a weapon. His entire thought process had been so intrinsic that he was now questioning everything he had done over the last two months. He had kept not just himself internally focused, but all of Houghton as well. They hadn't explored beyond X's forays. He didn't have any idea what the world was like outside of his own small section of it. If he had been more willing to explore, he might not have been in this predicament in the first place.

Drew was dead. That was the only thing for sure at the moment. And he was dead because Kade didn't carry a weapon that could kill someone who stood more than a yard away. Zack was right. If he'd had a rifle, he would have been able to drop all three attackers before they even knew he was there. Hell, he had been able to run all the way up to them before they knew he was there. He had cost Drew his life.

"Just so I know, what's the plan? Should we put up a fight when they tell us we aren't going?" X asked. His voice was dull and lacked its usual energy.

"We let them make the call," Kade said.

X slammed the back of his head against the headrest. "I guess I should have listened to Ashton."

"Sorry for asking you along. I've just been used to us being able to handle things," Kade said.

"Not your fault. But I feel like I was asleep and someone just threw a bucket of ice water on me," X said.

"Ever think we aren't good enough for them?" Kade asked.

"Always. Without all other options dead or foaming, how would either of us deserve them?" X said.

Kade laughed. "Apparently Ashton has wanted you since she was in diapers."

"Really?"

"I thought I was the only one that didn't know that," Kade said.

Despite X being seven years older than his sister, Kade didn't mind the pairing. He couldn't say for sure if he would have felt the same way in the Old World. X was his oldest friend, and if Ashton was going to date anyone, he'd rather it be someone he could stand.

"Any idea how I can get out of the dog house on this one?"

"I stuck her with babysitting duty. I'm sure if you take the kids off her hands when we get back, she would forgive you for just about anything," Kade said.

"But when we get back, Drew . . ."

There was a long silence between the two of them.

"Jem will take the kids over," X finally finished.

That was the moment it dawned on Kade that Jem might not make it back—and to make things worse, that meant Tiny might not either. The thought of losing her made him feel like someone was wringing his intestines.

The walkie sitting on the center console rang. Tiny's voice said, *"Final stop."*

Kade followed the Hummer off the road and parked in the trees. Through the foliage sunrise burned the sky pink.

They climbed out of the truck.

"Grab your stuff. We're going to set up camp on the other side of the road," Tiny said.

Kade and X followed their orders without a word and let Tiny lead them over the road and into the trees. Each step Kade took felt leaden. In his own mind, he had been courageous, rushing into the battle to create an opening for Tiny to save Drew. He hadn't thought that if he'd had a rifle, he would have been able to save Drew without anyone's assistance.

His sword was over his shoulder, his Judges were on his hips, his knuckles were on his fist, but he felt entirely unprepared. He didn't know who he thought he was, trying to play commando. He had skills that made him a half-decent leader back in Houghton, but there had been nothing in his life to make him think he was qualified for this rescue mission.

The people who had surprised them weren't even military—they were just a ragtag group from some place called the Democratic Republic of West Virginia. A bunch of nobodies had got the drop on him. They were so desperate for people, they'd sent a boy.

A boy that Tiny had cried over. He had seen Tiny cry a handful of times in her life, but never during the Primal Age. Something didn't seem right with her on this trip. He was trying not to be offended by the fact that she hadn't noticed the box of Snickers he brought her, especially after she'd gone off to get herself a Snickers. And Snickers were better than roses to that woman.

Everything she had done since Zack arrived was out of character.

Zack—the man he knew nothing about, but who the love of his life trusted like he was sent from on high. Kade watched Zack as he did a quick sweep of the area.

Since the dawn of the Primal Age, Kade had been puzzled by how Tiny could move in such a mechanical yet fluid way. Her body was always moving as one cohesive unit.

Watching Zack move, he understood that it was their training. Months spent conditioning each fiber of muscle to function as one. They made Kade feel childish about his own abilities.

He had been feeling so sure of his capabilities, but all of his knowledge was limited to what he had taught himself. Not that there wasn't a mountain of knowledge he had consumed over the years, but never truly believing the end of the world would happen, he'd only studied subjects that he enjoyed.

Even Grace, the dark horse of their group, had proven to be more valuable with everything she knew about construction. Kade stood amongst the trees feeling like a child lost in the woods.

Zack finished his sweep, and the five of them regrouped.

"Looks like we're clear here. No signs of anything that is or was human," Zack said, putting his back against a tree and sliding to the ground.

"Take some rest. I'll brief the other two," Tiny said.

Zack nodded and propped his gun on his knees. He closed his eyes, and a second later his head drooped to his chest and he fell asleep.

Number Five took a seat by Zack. Her eyes met Kade's for just a moment before they flicked away. That brief connection was all he needed to see the emotion—the same emotion he had seen for most his life when people would make eye contact with him. She was sorry for him. He felt like screaming, crying, and hitting something all at once. Her brown eyes that usually held such warmth for him had turned cold.

"We're going to rest through daylight. Zack and I will infiltrate DC tonight. We're about forty-five minutes from the Mall. Five is going to be waiting for us to come out. You guys will start the trek back to make sure we have a clear path when we get out of there."

X took his hat off and ran a hand over his buzzed hair, letting out a long sigh. "I'll give you two some space."

As X stepped away, the air became weighted with silence. Kade clenched his hand into a fist, channeling his frustration into his balled hand. She wouldn't leave him behind. She knew what he could do. Kade cast a sideways glance at the sleeping soldier.

"I can't believe you would let him bench me," Kade growled.

"It was my choice," Tiny said.

Kade curled his hand around a low branch. Zack and Tiny had served together, which meant she had a level of trust with Zack that she didn't with Kade, but it didn't make Kade enjoy being cut out. "I understand you have history with him, but I thought you'd have more faith in me."

Tiny glanced at Zack, and her face softened. "It's not like real history. We just slept together a few times."

There was a loud snap as Kade broke the branch. He stared at the stick in his hand, like he was confused how it got there, as the torrent of emotion that swirled through him settled on rage, clenching the branch with such force he felt every ridge of bark imprint on his hand. The teeth in his mouth felt like they were going to crack under the pressure.

Tiny's eyes went wide. "You didn't mean history like that, did you?"

Kade shook his head.

Tiny dropped her gaze. "Sorry, Kade, but we both have pasts. I can't help mine is here now. But you're my present."

"Since your old fuck buddy is back, you're just going to send me away. Seems like I don't really matter to your present." A lump rose in Kade's throat.

"Kade, this has nothing to do with him. I'm trying to keep you safe. Our best chance of success is if just Zack and I sneak in and out." She pulled her ponytail over her shoulder and picked at the split ends. "If this were a fight, I'd want you right beside me. If we were trying to steal something other than people, I'd want X. But Zack and I are the only two actually trained for this."

"You've been so different since he arrived." The branch splintered in Kade's grasp.

He felt like an angry child throwing a tantrum. Even as the words spewed out of his mouth, he knew they sounded immature. He had never felt emotions like this before in his life.

Her eyes locked on his, and for a moment they showed their usual warmth, before they took on a steely resolve.

"Things have been different since he got here."

"I never thought that if I let you in, you would walk away," Kade said, turning his back.

He cast aside the branch and picked a direction to go. She started after him, but caught herself against a tree and retched. Buckling in half, she spewed up their last meal. Even though Kade wanted to be angry with her, seeing her so vulnerable made most of his rage dissipate. He went to check on her, but she held up a hand.

"You don't get to say what you said, then act like you care. Screw off," Tiny said before another spell hit her.

A hand rested on Kade's shoulder. Zack stood beside him, wiping the sleep from his eyes.

"Let me take this bullet," Zack said.

Kade's first instinct was to punch Zack in the mouth, but he kept a tight leash on that desire and let it pass. The thought of punching Zack sounded appealing, but the person he wanted to hit was himself. He was the one acting like a child. Jealousy was a monster he was not used to fighting.

He shrugged off Zack's hand and walked away.

CHAPTER V

WOUNDS

Mick was exhausted, but the only thing he could do was stand— which was painful, but less painful than sitting. Anytime he bent or swiveled, his back throbbed from the countless burns. During his last session, Cunningham had basically used his quads as pin cushions.

He was proud of himself for not giving up any information. The idea crossed his mind to give her fake answers and earn himself a brief respite, but he needed to be able to communicate that plan with Jem, who was currently in one of his sessions. Since their arrival, Yuzuki and Anquan hadn't been taken, but Mick figured they would resume their usual sessions once he was executed.

His cloud of pain was broken by Yuzuki doing sit-ups in her cell. She was short enough that she could actually lie back in her cage.

"Yuzuki," he whispered. "Shouldn't you save your energy?"

She stopped mid-sit-up, holding the position. "I can't let myself get weak, or I have no chance."

"When do we get fed?" Mick asked. He figured if she was training that hard, there had to be calories coming in.

She shook her head and looked away. "About once a week. Just enough to keep us from dying."

"How are you so strong when he's so frail?" Mick asked, nodding toward Anquan.

She went back to doing sit-ups. Mick waited for her answer. She didn't seem like she was going to give one. He thought about asking again, but he didn't have the energy.

Letting his head fall against the bar, he closed his eyes. He wondered if he could sleep against the bars like that, and a moment later, as he drifted to sleep, Yuzuki's small hand tapped his cheek. "No sleep."

Mick's eyes followed hers, and he saw there was a soldier at the top of the stairs with a sack in his hands.

"Certain soldiers like to take advantage of a commodity I have. No one wants a skeleton, so they keep me healthy. Please, no sleep. They're more gentle when there are witnesses," Yuzuki pleaded.

Mick nodded, forcing his eyes open. What he watched Yuzuki go through was the hardest thing he'd had to endure yet. The police officer in him wanted to do something, to strike out, or yell at the man, but he restrained himself, feeling anything he might do would only make things worse for Yuzuki.

When it was over and the man left, she covered herself in her jumpsuit and opened the sack of food. She gave a protein bar to Anquan and held one through the bars to Mick.

His eyes darted from the bar to Yuzuki. Everything she just suffered replayed in his mind. Unlike him, she didn't have a death date. After what she'd gone through, he couldn't imagine taking that food from her.

"No, thank you."

She shook the bar at him. Tears ran from her green eye, and yet she didn't say a word.

Mick backed as far away as he could. "I'm dead in a couple days. You need your strength."

She stuffed the protein bar in her mouth and turned her back to Mick.

"This is a tricky one. Mostly the same as the last one, but a few differences," Ashton said to Meredith and Franklin.

Ashton was in the driver's seat of a car they had found in a townhouse complex off campus. Meredith and Franklin were sharing the

passenger seat and learning how to drive. Bristle crawled across the
two kids and onto Ashton's lap.

"Franklin, I told you to leave her in the dorm," Ashton said.

"I can't leave her," Franklin replied.

Ashton clenched her jaw, then put on a smile. "Then control her, or
I'll toss her out the window."

Franklin quickly wrangled the cheetah onto his lap and kept the
purring creature there, encircling her in his arms.

Ashton was moving the car for their most recent defensive project, which they called the south wall. Most of the campus sat in a
water-formed wishbone, which gave them a good defensive perimeter.
However, anyone approaching from the south had a wide area from
which to easily access the campus. One of the main roads crossed both
the river and the stream running east and west. What they had been
doing was finding cars and driving them into a solid line of vehicles in
a lane. Once the car was part of the wall, they would remove the tires
and syphon whatever gas was left.

Many of the cars had been brought to the area by X while he was
out on his grocery runs, and on the maps he kept he had marked areas
where there were full parking lots. Ashton's goal for the morning was
to keep Meredith and Franklin occupied while maybe teaching them
to drive enough to be able to put a car into place in the wall. She cared
far less about their driving skills and more about keeping them from
asking where Scott had gone.

"This is a manual car. You have to use this stick and the clutch to
change gears as you drive, but you guys won't need to be able to do
more than first gear for now," Ashton said.

She walked them through how to get the car into gear, and after a
few demonstrations let each of the kids have a crack at it. Seeing as it
had taken her most of a day to teach John to drive stick, she doubted
these twelve-year-olds would pick it up on their first try.

Holding people back from driving because a law said so had always been a stupid idea to her, even before the Primal Age. If someone

had a desire and ability to do something, she didn't see any reason to stop them. Now it was necessary for these kids to learn as many skills as they could to increase their chances of survival, and one skill that made a huge difference was the ability to drive whatever car you ended up in.

Meredith had tried to drive first, and after a half hour of stutters and stalls, Ashton gave Franklin a crack at the task. She hadn't decided yet how she felt about Franklin. The kid reminded her of Damian, and she still wasn't sure how she felt about her own brother. They both were naturally smarter than the average human by leaps and bounds, and they both expressed their intelligence at every possible occasion, but neither understood how it could feel demeaning to others.

As Franklin put the car in first gear and drove the car at a rolling pace on his first try, she tried to look at the positive side of his intelligence.

Victoria stood in the doorway of Damian's lab. She saw he had put a cot on the floor, which didn't surprise her. He had always been married to his work. It had been almost two years since he'd broken off their engagement, and she had not seen him since.

His back was to her while he worked, so she decided to watch him for a while longer. Too much had happened in these two years. He had left her to go work on the Feline Flu vaccine, leaving her with wedding invitations sent, venues booked, and no groom.

She could have suffered all the humiliation and pity in the world if she hadn't had to lose him in the process. It was strange to see him with his hair so disheveled. Damian had always been meticulous about his appearance. He'd barely been legal when she'd met him. Naive in so many ways, but so incredibly brilliant. Her little man-boy. A smile crossed her face as she remembered how nervous he'd been the first time she had invited him out with the rest of their team. He had clearly traded his social development for his pursuit of knowledge, but he was cute. At first he was cute like a monkey in the zoo, but over time his childlike heart won her over.

Most people in their field were in such competition with each other that they would step on anyone to advance themselves. Damian had been totally different. If his team failed, he'd personally feel responsible. He'd always step down to allow someone else to step up. It was about the only trait he shared with Kade.

It hadn't just been Damian who'd changed. She had gone through hell and back since the vaccine had been released. If she'd known what she knew now back when she'd deserted Kade and his band of misfits, she would make the same choice again. However, the Tribe hadn't turned out to be what she thought it would be. Her mind became her weapon, and her body became her tool. She'd been forced to use her body as a means of survival—she, who had always been so proud of her brain.

First she used Sarge for protection, but after She-Chief ordered Victoria's return to Houghton with a war party, she knew that was going to be a short-lived affair. She did everything she could to sabotage the mission, but to Kade and the crew it would never look like that. They would think she was just saying this now to try to get back into their good graces. The problem with being a survivor was anyone who knew your game always figured you were playing an angle, even if you were being honest.

After Sarge and his soldiers met their end, she knew she would have to climb the hierarchical ladder fast or she would end up raped, or murdered. Henson had become her best chance, and she clung to him like a life preserver in open water. Once the Feline Flu resurfaced, she used the mass deaths as a time to solidify her place.

One morning, two of the three chiefs hadn't awakened.

They had died of natural causes.

She'd had absolutely nothing to do with it.

She had been with Henson all night long.

Henson was such a sound sleeper, it amazed her.

With Henson as the ranking leader, she had been able to effect some change in the Tribe, and between the two of them they brought a modicum of civilization to the people. She was never safe, though. Losing close to thirty soldiers meant there wasn't a single person in the entire camp that hadn't suffered a loss because of the mission from which only she returned.

She never strayed from Henson in the camp's public areas and spent most of the time he was occupied locked in his quarters, learning what she could from the limited supply of books in the camp. That was when she hatched her plot to leave the Tribe, but the only place she knew she could go was back to Kade. She played the part and got her way.

Now here was the man who was supposed to have been her husband. Too much had changed for them to ever find their way back to each other.

"Kade said you would be stopping by," Damian said without turning around.

She hadn't been aware that he knew she was there, or that Kade would have predicted she would come here first. "Did he?"

"Care to lend me a hand?" Damian lifted himself from his work and faced her. His hair was a greasy mess, and the splotchy beard made him look like a homeless person. He'd lost the boyish energy he used to exude. His face had aged nearly a decade since she'd seen him last. "I screwed up."

"You were only at your best when you had me on your team," Victoria said, flashing a smile.

He gave a few slow nods and turned back to his work. "That I was."

Victoria went to his side, and he slid her a folder as thick as her wrist. She'd have her work cut out for her, but if there was anything she could do to pretend that her time with the Tribe had never happened, she would pursue that option.

She opened the cover and began to read his neat, handwritten notes on the Feline Flu and the vaccine he'd helped to create, which had turned 60 percent of those that had received it into foamers.

X's hat was tilted down over his face so it looked like he was sleeping. At the moment he felt like this was his best chance to avoid getting caught in the crossfire between Tiny and Kade.

They were in the first serious fight he had witnessed between them, and they seemed to be arguing over Zack rather than the fact that she had told Kade he would be useless in a stealth penetration of DC. Zack didn't like Kade because he wasn't a traditional soldier. And Zack knew Kade would try to find some reason for them to go along. X couldn't admit it out loud, but he was glad that they were being left behind. Ashton was livid with him already, and the sooner he could get back to make things right, the better. He didn't want to leave Jem and Mick to die, but if Tiny really thought X would just be in the way, he would stay clear of the operation. It would be impossible to fix things with Ashton if he was dead.

A gentle foot nudged his quad.

"I hate to interrupt your fake sleep, but I need to use the ladies' room."

X tilted his hat back. Number Five stood beside him with a military rifle slung across her chest.

"Wouldn't Tiny be the better pick?"

"I don't want to get in the middle of that triangle," Number Five said.

His bladder was full enough, so he jumped on the opportunity. He pulled out his revolver, and he and Number Five went deeper into the trees.

When she stopped, they could hardly see the others.

"You face that way, I'll face this way," Number Five said as she undid her pants.

X turned away and kept his pistol at the ready.

Zack's words echoed back to him now. When they'd lost Drew,

Kade and X had been doing the same thing he was doing now.

X loved his .357. It was comfortable. Familiar. He knew its strengths, its limitations. While he stood there, he came to terms with how little he actually could do with a six-shooter. His range was small. He only had six shots.

Though Kade wanted everyone in Houghton to train with rifles, X had always skipped those sessions. He was who he was, and he didn't want to be turned into a soldier. He was a thief—a damn good thief. Now he wished he had picked up a rifle.

More importantly, he wished he had listened to Ashton and not come in the first place. He could be safely bickering with his gingersnap.

"I'm good," Number Five said.

X holstered his pistol and drained his bladder.

"Kick some leaves over it," Number Five said when X finished.

He kicked around the foliage until he covered up his wet spot. Even the woman without a name seemed more suited for this life than he.

"I think this might have been our longest conversation to date," X said.

"I spent my time in the lab, and you spent your time away," Number Five replied.

X usually made it a rule not to even look at Number Five if he could help it because he knew if Ashton saw the way he'd look at her, she'd probably gouge his eyes out. Number Five looked like she'd walked out of a centerfold and into their lives.

"I'm in no rush to go back to the forest of awkward silence," X said.

"Are they always like that?"

"Kade and Tiny have always been volatile. There's a lot of repression and aggression in their history. This is ugly, though, because Kade never learned to deal with jealousy as a kid because of . . ." X cut himself off before revealing Kade's Achilles heel.

"His disease. Remember, I spend all my time with his brother."

"What is going on there?" X asked gingerly.

Number Five shook her head. "I don't know. I never thought I would care about someone like him. He's so focused on his data and experiments, I don't think he sees the world around him."

"I can't believe he doesn't notice you." X held his arm out like he was presenting her to a crowd.

She let out a laugh. "The exact opposite. I'm a walking experiment."

"Number Five."

"That's all I am to him. I stay close to him because I don't know where else to go."

"No other home for you?" X asked.

"I was probably the second most excited person for the end of the world, behind Kade. I used to live in Portugal, but then this young strapping Navy seaman convinced me he loved me. I crossed my family and moved to the States to be with him, but—"

The air was cut by a high-pitched scream. The sound came from back near the road. X and Number Five broke into a run. X's legs ruffled the leaves as he barreled through the trees. He reached the road and sprinted across it, heading toward the screams.

He crested the far side and stopped in his tracks. The horse trailer was surrounded by five foamers that may have once been a biker gang. They were still wearing most of their riding leather, which seemed fairly intact. Three were large bruisers, one was a sizeable woman, and the last was an emaciated old man. Like all foamers they had come across recently, these were matted with filth, and their fingernails had grown into long claws.

The foamers were taking turns attacking the trailer, each provo-cation causing terrified whinnies from the horses within. X drew his pistol. Before he could aim, Kade flew past, knocking his hand down.

"Don't shoot," Kade called as he hurled himself down the bank. He already had his knuckles and mask on.

X stood dumbfounded as Kade landed on the skinny man, who fell to the ground with a terrible sound of cracking bones. Kade reared back and beat his chest with a loud roar, drawing the focus of the remaining four. They charged at him from all sides.

Kade landed a dazing blow on the first one, then rolled over the creature's back, booting the foamer to the ground from behind. Jumping back, he dodged the swipe of the next attacker.

"Should we do something?" Number Five asked, arriving beside X.

"He said don't shoot," X replied.

Kade grabbed the next swipe and pulled himself toward the foamer, landing his knuckled fist squarely into the monster's face. One of the large bruisers tackled Kade to the ground.

X holstered his pistol and drew his knife, ready to charge into the fray.

Kade reared his head back and slammed the mask into the bruiser's face. The creature closed its claws around Kade's shoulders.

X rushed into the fight, but before he could reach Kade the other bruiser swept him off his feet. The two bodies flew through the air before they crashed down with X on the bottom. The ground drove the air from X's lungs, but his knife had lodged itself in the creature's chest. The foamer pulled out the blade and lumbered away into the trees, leaving a red trail behind.

X pushed himself up to his feet, trying to regain his breath. Just as he was feeling ready to rejoin the battle, a foamer launched through the air toward him. His blade came in front of his body on instinct, but he never needed it. Kade crashed into the creature in midair. The two tumbled to the ground and Kade landed on top, but the foamer had his knuckled hand locked up in its grip. Kade pinned the foamer's free hand with his. The foamer pushed Kade higher off its body, but Kade bucked all his weight up into the air. The creature's arms folded under the quick change of weight, and Kade torpedoed mask-first into the foamer.

The foamer's nose cracked under the mask, and the monster lurched forward with a cry of pain and bit down on Kade's trapezius muscle. Kade never let out a sound as he repeatedly drove his knee into the creature's ribs until it let go.

Kade rolled his knuckled hand free from the foamer's grasp, but not before slicing his wrist on the creature's claws. He pulled back and landed his knuckled fist on the creature's throat, causing it to let out a hollow croak. The foamer was still alive, but the only focus it had now was getting enough air.

The first foamer charged at Kade again as Kade tried to put himself away from the second one. X dropped a shoulder into the creature, knocking it against a tree. The foamer let out a howl of pain but was quickly silenced by X's knife. The body dropped to the ground, and X surveyed the scene. The first foamer Kade had landed on was still writhing like a deer that had been struck by a car. Kade's final opponent was dragging itself away, still fighting to breathe. The last fully functional foamer showed nothing but its rear as it ran away.

Kade walked to the broken foamer and drew his katana.

"Sorry," he said as he arched the blade through the air and decapitated the creature.

He wiped off the blade, put the sword away, then tipped his blue mask back onto his forehead. "Thanks for the help."

"Couldn't leave you hanging," X said.

Kade stood amidst the wreckage, his sleeves torn and bloodied, looking like the angel of death.

A slow clap resounded through the trees from the road.

"That was badass," Zack called down.

Kade and X made returned to the road, where Number Five, Tiny, and Zack were watching.

"That was like watching King Kong versus Godzilla," Zack added.

"Someone should check on the horses, and we'll have to move the vehicles," Tiny said, pushing past Kade.

"I wish YouTube still existed. That would have gone viral," Zack said. Kade just stared back at him. X laughed at the concept of something going viral. In this world, that had such a different connotation.

"I'll grab a kit and get you cleaned up," Number Five said.

X thought Kade looked more alive the closer he was to death.

John stepped down on the spade, penetrating the ground. He loaded the head and tossed the dirt clear of the hole—the hole that would be a grave.

Since John had joined the group, the only loss they had suffered was Argos the dog. His only interaction with Argos had been his first night, when the dog had been left to guard him. The dog's death had affected him as a member of Kade's cohort, but he hadn't felt it on a personal level.

Scott had spent even less time with the group, but John felt responsible for his loss. Even if it wasn't John's sector to watch, he had been on guard duty with a brand-new person when Scott sneaked out. He should have been double-checking Emma's territory. If he had paid more attention, he could have prevented the kid from dying.

Scott's death was John's fault. No matter how many other people had messed up, John had been the final line of defense, and he had failed.

He passed the shovel to Wright, then climbed from the grave. Damian had given the approval to have a ceremony, the first they had ever had for a death, but neither he or Victoria were present.

Emma stood on one side, with Grace across on the other side of the grave. At the head, Ashton had her arms around Meredith and Franklin. Her head hung so low John could only see the part in her hair. Franklin held Bristle tight to his chest.

Wright helped John hoist the sheet-wrapped body of Scott and lower the lifeless form into the grave. The kid looked like a mummy, the sheet was so tightly wrapped, and John felt a chill run down his spine as he considered if Scott would rise to haunt them. The kid would have every reason in the world to torment them. John could practically picture it: the Ghost of Lambian Hall. Scott, with his one good eye, wandering the halls, howling at those who'd failed him. Maybe Scott would get his other eye back when he died. But maybe not, since it wasn't buried with him. Maybe John could find an eye to put in the grave.

Wright clapped his shoulder and went to the foot of the grave. John knew he wanted to be as far from Ashton as possible. She hadn't lashed out at him yet, but he knew it was coming. Wright was going to be leading the ceremony, so he didn't want to be on his side. That left Grace or Emma.

Grace stood tight and upright with her hands behind her back. He couldn't see any signs of distress in her, but Emma looked like a wreck. Her mascara had made black circles under her eyes, and she hid most of her face behind a white cloth.

Though John wanted to be close to Grace, the extra bit of awkwardness she made him feel wasn't something he wanted to deal with at a funeral, so he decided to go stand beside Emma.

Wright ran a hand through his shining gray hair before he straightened his black suit coat and vest. Of everyone present, he was the only one dressed properly for a traditional funeral.

"Today we say goodbye to a young soul. A soul that should not have had to leave our world so soon. The soul of a loving and trusting boy who continued to make the best of bad situations," Wright said.

Emma turned away from the grave, throwing her arms around John and burying her head into his shoulder as she sobbed. John lifted his hands, unsure of where to place them, and after trying a few different spots wrapped them around her waist. He bowed his head and continued to listen to Wright.

"Scott was a fine example of what a person should be. At least now he can transcend into a perfect world. A world without pain. A world where he can be safe. May he rest in peace."

Classically conditioned, John muttered an *amen*. When he looked up from the prayer, he found Grace glaring at him in a way he only ever saw Tiny bore into someone. Her baby-blue eyes were wide and bulging like they were going to pop out of her skull.

Wright grabbed a handful of dirt from the pile and sprinkled it over the grave. Grace broke her stare and followed Wright's lead. Ashton and the kids were next, followed by John and Emma.

The procession continued back to the dorm, leaving John with Wright. John retrieved his spade and cast shovels of dirt over the body. The dirt scattered over the white cloth, slowly burying from sight John's mistake.

"You don't have to wait with me," John said as he kept shoveling.

Wright squatted down, careful not to get any dirt on his nice clothes. "You seem to be having some issues at the moment."

John hefted another shovel full of dirt into the grave. "My problems don't seem to be that big of a deal right now."

"Scott was the type of boy who wouldn't have wanted you to avoid counsel on pretense," Wright said.

John looked down at what little of the cloth still shone through and silently asked Scott for his permission to be selfish. "Grace. I've been head over heels in love with her since I met her. I've even written her poems, but she wants nothing to do with me. Today, when I stood beside Emma, she looked like she wanted to murder me."

Wright chuckled. "I would never want to trade places with you. You have now learned the number one secret to getting a woman's attention: stop giving her all of yours."

"I don't want to be an ass." John cared too much about Grace to try to play games for her heart. Mostly he couldn't imagine there was a game at which he could beat her. She beat him at everything they'd ever played, even checkers. If he tried to win her, he knew he would lose.

"I'm not telling you to do anything you wouldn't do already, but I'm sure there's some way you could spend time with Emma normally," Wright said.

John hauled another load of dirt into the grave. Wright did have a point there. She did need to learn how to shoot. There were plenty of things he could teach Emma, things that Kade would probably put him in charge of if he were here anyhow.

"I'll let you think on that, but do you mind if I ask a question?" Wright said.

"Sure," John said, wishing that if Wright was going to continue standing there, he would at least find a way to lend a hand.

"These creatures you guys call foamers—why aren't we hunting them? If there is a pack that close to where we live, why don't we just eradicate them?"

"Kade says we are only supposed to kill them in self-defense. He wants to learn more about them," John replied.

Wright stood and ran a hand along the right side of his head, smoothing out his hair. "That makes no sense. As a leader, he should be removing the threat. There isn't a reason to learn from them when we could exterminate them. They've just killed a boy. I would call any action we take against them as preemptive."

"Kade's orders are Kade's orders. He's kept us alive this long."

"You're throwing dirt on evidence to the contrary," Wright said.

John stopped midthrow. The dirt cascaded off the sides of the spade, trickling like sand in an hourglass. The foamers had killed Scott. They could kill again.

Wright waved the conversation away and walked toward the dorm. "I also find it peculiar that Damian, our interim leader, wasn't present for the boy's funeral. I'll need to have a word with that man."

Tossing the remaining dirt into the hole, John couldn't stop his mind from wondering if things would have been different had they eliminated the foamer pack. Scott would still be alive. Maybe Kade *didn't* know best.

Before the collapse of the United States, the country was constantly trading out leaders to keep progress moving forward. Though he wasn't of voting age and had never cast a ballot, John decided democracy might not be a bad thing in Houghton.

Alpha stood over the body of the one like him that had been dumb enough to challenge his leadership. Rearing back, Alpha smashed both fists down on the foamer's face to make sure he wouldn't get up again.

Normally he would take a victory feeding from his challenger, but this one had landed a solid set of gashes against his shoulder, and Alpha wanted to get it clean. He walked painfully on all fours toward the creek. He hoped the others wouldn't be out so that he could wash the wound in peace.

Descending the bank to the creek, he noticed that Pepper was on his flank. It was nice to know there was at least one of his kind that watched his back. With Pepper standing guard, he waded out into the shallow creek and let the water run over his wounds. He winced against the sting of the cold water. Despite the pain, the water felt cool as it washed away not just the blood, but also the matting of dirt on his skin. Climbing out of the water, Alpha dropped his shoulder into the mud, caking the wet dirt over his wounds.

With his natural bandage applied, he ascended the bank and nuzzled Pepper. She returned the affection, and the two returned to the cover of the woods.

Mick's head lolled around, giving him a peripheral of Cunningham's chamber. He had given up on holding his head up because each time he mustered the effort, he practically concussed himself when his neck gave out.

Today he was in for something new. His arms and legs were strapped to a chair. This was the first time he would be upright for whatever followed. Cunningham stood in front of him with a hand on her chin, like an artist appraising her canvas.

Mick would have rather been lying down. Many of the blisters on his back had ruptured and were oozing. Just the pressure on the wounds was enough to make him want to pass out, but Cunningham wouldn't allow it. He had spent so much time with her he hardly even noticed the bleach smell.

His chest was a patchwork of bruises and cuts. As bad as his wounds looked, he was hardly damaged compared to Jem. Cunningham seemed to have a special kind of hatred for Jem.

She put a hand on Mick's forehead and lifted his head so he had to look at her. Her white uniform was spotless, which meant he was in for a long day. Cunningham squeezed his jaw open and put a small square film onto his tongue. It reminded Mick of a breath strip, but he didn't think she cared much about his breath.

The beats of his heart grew faster, while his body felt warm and fuzzy, almost blissful. His mouth dried up; he would have done just about anything for a drink of water.

Cunningham ran a small penlight in front of his eyes and then let his head drop. Mick felt a growing pit of dread forming in his gut. His breath caught short and his heart raced. He was doomed.

Cunningham let out a cackling laugh.

A witch must be in the room, Mick thought. Long shadows stretched across the spotless kitchen.

Cunningham lifted Mick's head by the hair. Her eyes flicked between his. Mick wished he could curl up like an armadillo and hide.

"You'd better buckle up—this is going to be a long trip," Cunningham said, showing him the sharp edge of her razor knife.

Kade knelt shirtless while Number Five tended to his wounds. His rubber knuckles hung from the breakaway chain around his neck. Tiny had always been the one to patch him up, and Number Five's touch was unfamiliar. He didn't say anything as Five did her best to put him back together. He was lost in his own mind, which was a dangerous place to be.

Had he just avoided the Tribe entirely, Zack wouldn't be here. Tiny wouldn't be acting so weird. He wouldn't have to deal with being jealous, and everything would have stayed normal. Tiny was often mad at him, but this was different. She wasn't just mad. She was mad, tapered in disappointment, and dunked in disgust.

The only idea he had to make things right was to give up fighting with her about going into DC, but even that wouldn't be enough. There was no get-out-of-jail-free card on this one.

He flinched as Number Five pinched together the thumb-claw gash on his wrist.

"I'll patch this one up, but Tiny will need to stitch it when she gets back," Number Five said.

Kade just gave her a nod. Tiny and X were moving the two vehicles to another location. Tiny had said they were going to take a while to make sure it was a safe place since they wouldn't be close enough to the horses to guard them. No one said it, but everyone knew she was just looking to get away from Kade.

Number Five closed up the med bag. "You're as good as I can do, Humpty."

"Thanks," Kade said, staring at the trees in front of him.

She walked away with the bag, and Kade didn't bother moving even enough to put his shirt back on. He sat still as a monk in meditation while he tried to figure out how to make things right with the woman he loved.

A hand clapped him on the good shoulder as Zack took a seat beside him.

"That was pretty sick," Zack said.

Kade didn't acknowledge him.

Zack held his hand out for Kade to shake. "I feel like we got off on the wrong foot."

Kade didn't even look at the hand.

"I listened to her talk about you for months. I already understand her version of you. I'll never understand why she loves you, but I understand you. I'm Zack. I'm regarded as an asshole because I'll tell you exactly what is on my mind, and when it comes time to make decisions I do what is right without considering feelings."

"I'm not looking to be friends," Kade said, glaring at his hand.

"Neither am I. I just want you to understand, I respect you for what you are. But you don't use a screwdriver to do a hammer's job, regardless of how nice the screwdriver is. I get that you don't like the idea of her going into danger without you, but I'll be with her. I've watched her back before, and I love her as much as you do."

Kade turned toward Zack, wanting to throttle his throat.

"Relax, Congo. All her love belongs to you. But I'll give my life before I let harm come to her. So, man to man, I'll keep her safe. Just do your best to make things right before you leave, so I don't have to worry about her thinking when she should be acting," Zack said.

Kade sat for a full thirty seconds, letting his brain process Zack's words. It wasn't his ideal situation. Sending Tiny off alone with a man who just told Kade about his feelings for her didn't seem like a wise option. But it did mean she would be protected. And the only way Kade could make things right is if she came out of the mission alive.

Kade took Zack's hand and gave it solid pump. He'd do better to make an ally than an enemy.

"For what it's worth, I've always been sorry she loved me," Kade said.

"Trust me, she never told me anything that would make me believe you deserved her. But it doesn't change that you're the only person she has ever loved. And if she hadn't, she wouldn't be alive today. I like to believe everything happens for a reason," Zack said.

A few months ago, when Kade first met Grace's family on the road, her oldest brother, who later tried to kill Kade, asked him if he was a man of fate or coincidence. It had stuck with Kade ever since. Every flip that had landed tails for Kade had turned out to have a heads along with it. He still believed the world was ruled by coincidence, but fate was starting to get a stronger piece of the pie.

"Take care of her, please," Kade said.

"We both know she doesn't need taking care of, but I'll keep my eye on her. Just promise me you'll never take her for granted. She deserves someone better than either of us," Zack said.

He couldn't agree with Zack more. "Deal," Kade said.

X and Tiny's footsteps could be heard coming through the trees.

"I'm going to go nod off," Zack said, getting up.

"Thanks for the talk," Kade said.

Kade was surprised he actually felt better. Zack did profess his love for Tiny, but at least Kade knew where they stood now. Zack was a self-proclaimed asshole, but he wasn't a snake in the grass. Kade felt better knowing he'd have her back.

"I hear you need stitching," Tiny said as she approached Kade, who hadn't moved from where he was kneeling.

Kade held up his bandaged wrist, which had already bled through.

"What am I going to do with you?" Tiny said with a tight-lipped smile.

Kade smiled back as she undid the bandage.

"You're going to have to grin through this," Tiny said as she prepped her gear.

"I've survived worse," Kade replied.

Tiny gave a nod. "I wish you would stop trying to set a new record."

"I'm not trying."

"You could have shot every foamer there and taken no risk."

"I thought about it, but we aren't that far from DC. I didn't think it would be wise to attract attention."

The needle slid through Kade's flesh, and he did his best not to move. She surveyed him to see how he was handling the pain.

Kade gave her a smirk. "I can't tell you how grateful I am for the Primal Age," Kade said.

"Funny thing to be happy about."

"As much as I wish I could have let myself be yours in the Old World, it wasn't going to happen. I needed this to get out of my own way." He paused. "I'm sorry I fought you about staying behind."

Her fingers made another pass at the wound, sealing it a little more.

"Then I'm glad for the end of the world too."

"And I am sorry I got mad about Zack. I can't get mad at you for having a past when it's my fault you have one in the first place."

"Kade, stop," Tiny said, and paused her stitch. "I don't want to hear it. You're making this sound like I'm not coming back."

"I don't want to take a chance—"

"Jesus, Kade, I'm mad at you. You're mad at me. This is what happens in relationships. Tomorrow, when I haul our stupid friends' asses out of jail, we can fight it out and have makeup sex. Today, I want to focus on the task at hand," Tiny replied.

With this being Kade's first relationship, he was still adjusting to what was normal. He didn't like the idea that she might not make it back, but he hated the idea that she would go in there while they were fighting.

Drew had educated them well on the ins and outs of the president and his men. He had a thousand soldiers to patrol a few square miles. Even though there were resistance efforts, the president didn't stretch himself out beyond the boundaries of his territory. He was calm and calculating, a complete one-eighty from the man who hadn't gotten Kade's vote.

Drew had made maps of DC for each of them. The kid had shown such promise. The amount of initiative he had used during his time with the president's men had shown what a logical person he had been. The best he could do for Drew now was to get Jem out to take over care of the kids, and he couldn't even do that. The best thing he could do was stay out of the way.

"Can I at least hear the plan?" Kade asked.

Tiny ran a salve over his stitches. The immediate cooling effect felt wonderful.

"Heading in from the west. We'll do a quick recon, then run a diversion. We will run up the Potomac River. When the soldiers come out, we'll go in," Tiny said.

"Shouldn't you guys take more time to survey the situation?"

"We're not going to be stupid about it, but we only have a couple nights left. If we need more recon, we will wait. If we can take it, it'll be tonight," Tiny replied.

"Once you're in?"

"Just slip through the darkness to the Smithsonian Castle. Break in, break out. Then drop into the metro tunnels and haul ass to Number Five."

"Seems simple enough."

"The fewer moving parts, the less things can break. By the way, I am so pissed at you for researching foamers like you have been."

Kade let out a single laugh.

"They deserve the fair shake," Kade said.

"It was really hot. But I'm still pissed."

Kade looked into Tiny's eyes. They had retaken the same fireside warmth he was used to. It was good to know she was only pissed on principle.

"How can I make it up to you?"

"Well, I've got in this bad habit of falling asleep with some asshole who never listens to me, and now I have trouble sleeping by myself. I need to get some rest before sunset. Think you could help me out?" Tiny asked.

Kade pulled her into a kiss.

To John, the room looked like an action hero's wet dream. Weapons were stacked, leaning, and hanging everywhere. The dressers were filled with small arms and ammo. The closets were loaded with rifles. They had everything from military-grade to children's pellet guns. John remembered the first time he had been in this room and felt completely overwhelmed by the arsenal. Later that day, he had accidently shot Kade.

Emma stood against the wall just inside the door, as if she were trying to stay as far away from the weapons as possible. She hadn't spoken since they came into the room. John didn't think he would ever had met someone as afraid of the room as he had been, but she looked like she would have been more comfortable in a pit of cobras.

Pulling open the bottom drawer of one of the dressers, John found the air rifle. It fired BBs and was powered by manually compressing air. It was the simplest gun he could teach someone to use, but the weapon wouldn't kill anything much larger than a rabbit.

He grabbed the gun and got to his feet as Grace appeared in the doorway.

"Can you give me a hand with some repairs on the furnace?" Grace asked.

Emma had a look like she was postponing her execution.

"Sure, but not right now. I promised Emma I'd teach her how to shoot. Once I—as soon as I teach her the basics, I'll come find you," John said.

Grace noticed Emma standing there. "Never mind. I'll ask Dr. Wright. Fenris needs to go out if you guys are going down."

Grace disappeared as fast as she had arrived. John didn't mean to cause a brash reaction from Grace, nor was he proud that he seemed to be learning how to play the game, but it was a nice feeling to have the power paradigm shift a little.

John loaded his pockets with containers of BBs, then retrieved his bow. He had Emma climb down the ladder before he went through a process he hated, but not as much as Fenris did. Rex and the cheetah were small enough that they could be hauled down in someone's pack. Fenris wasn't as lucky. She was strapped into a hiking harness pack and hooked to one of their many pulleys. John then had to force her out the window, where he lowered her a few feet at a time, all the way to the ground.

It was tiring, time-consuming, and terrifying. By the time John got Fenris to the ground, he understood why Grace had him take the dog along.

Once John had climbed down he led them to the south wall, where they were building the solid line of cars. There were a few cars that had been left along the wall but not put into place. John had hoped to be able to multitask.

Fenris took off like a black streak, bounding all over the campus but never staying out a sight for long. John couldn't blame her—she was confined much more lately with Jem and Kade gone, and it must have been nice to have a respite from being a mother.

When they reached the wall, which was almost three-quarters the width of the campus, John pulled a small can of orange spray-paint from his pocket and made a pie plate–sized circle on the door of a black Honda. He showed Emma how to load and pump the rifle first. She seemed more nervous to hold the gun than John felt talking to Grace.

"It isn't going to bite you," John said as he turned her body to take the stock to her shoulder.

"I just don't like it," Emma said.

"Just relax. You'll get more comfortable over time," John said.

Emma broke into booming laughter. "I think my first boyfriend told me the same thing."

"He showed you how to fire a gun?"

Emma glanced over her shoulder, and John got the impression she was searching him for something. "You aren't kidding?"

"No?"

An ear-to-ear grin took over Emma's face. "You could say he showed me how to fire a gun."

"Why don't you show me what he taught you?"

"You poor boy," Emma said, and pressed her back into John's front. The hand she had on the barrel of the rifle she dropped to her side. John wondered if this was some sort of English form of firing a rifle, but then he felt her hand climbing up his leg.

Panic spiked in John's brain as he pushed her so hard away from him, she almost fell on her face, then dropped the rifle.

"Bloody hell, John. You could have just said no," Emma said, snatching the rifle from the ground.

"I'm stupid. I mean, sorry. I've never done anything like that," John said.

"Never?" She raised an eyebrow.

John shook his head. Never. Not even a kiss. But he didn't want to say that out loud.

"Why don't we just forget about that for now, and you teach me how to use this stupid thing?" Emma said, approaching him.

John stood behind her, giving a few inches of space, and showed her how to place her hands and how to aim down the sights. She gently pulled the trigger as he instructed, but as the rifle fired, Emma jumped back into John. The BB hit nowhere close to the orange circle.

John put his hands on her shoulders and stood a little farther behind her so he could see along the barrel.

"Just focus on the target. Let everything else fade away," John said.

She pulled the trigger, and John had to catch her in his arms as she jumped at the sound of the air rifle. His arms were tight around her waist, and he could feel her heartbeat rapidly resonating through her body.

He steadied her again, trying not to think about how she felt in his arms, and had her take another shot. She was still way off target, but it was a start. Disappointment coursed through him when she didn't jump back into his arms.

After a half hour, she had the process down and was putting more in the orange than she wasn't. He left her to keep practicing while he pushed a car into the wall. While pushing the car from the trunk, he came up with an idea and added an orange circle to the driver's door.

He explained to Emma how to lead a target and instructed her on how to hit the target as it moved past. Then John pushed the car as fast as he could. His feet bent against the pavement as he locked his shoulders and charged forward. Building speed, he cleared the wall to where Emma was waiting.

The rifle fired, and a deafening echo sounded from his nose. The sting penetrated through his entire body as he covered the bridge of his nose and felt warm blood running into his hands. The car rolled to a stop, and Emma was by his side.

"Bullocks, I'm sorry. I led the wrong way," Emma said, putting a hand on John's shoulder.

John held his nose with both hands. "That would be following."

"That makes sense," Emma said.

"I think we are good for today," John replied, grateful it hadn't been a larger-caliber rifle.

CHAPTER VI

HIT THE FAN

M ick rocked back and forth in his cell, covering his eyes. His eyes were lying to him. He wouldn't let them lie to him. He'd hide them. No monsters could lurk in shadows if he couldn't see them. He'd hide.

Anquan sat with his back to everyone, slowly breathing and wasting no energy. Yuzuki kept a standing vigil at the corner of the four cells.

Jem squatted and scratched at his forearm. His face and body were completely covered in bruises and gashes. There was no inch of his body that could be traveled without finding some form of damage. His nails dug into a gash on his forearm.

"Something is in there. Something's in there. Need to get it out," Jem said as the wound opened.

Mick took his hands away from his eyes. He watched Jem dig into his own arm. The thought crossed his mind that there might be something in his arm too. He ran his nail over his skin and began to dig.

"Stop it," Yuzuki shouted while reaching through the cages and grabbing both their wrists. Mick didn't want to anger a witch so he ended his dig, but Jem did not.

Yuzuki pulled Jem face-first into the cage bars. He stopped cutting at his arm and looked around the room with a puzzled expression, like it was the first time he had ever seen it.

As the drugs claimed Mick's mind, he hoped for his and Jem's sake they would be executed soon. There was no telling how much longer he could go without revealing any information.

Kade never fell asleep as he lay next to Tiny. Between the pain in his body and the thoughts on his mind, he could hardly even close his eyes. He knew he had to let her run the mission but was worried about not being by her side. She was the strongest person he had ever met, and if he had to put his faith in anyone it would be her. He was glad to have spent most of the day laying with her as they waited for the cover of night to approach.

Zack approached them, already suited up for war in his ACU loaded with a sidearm and holding his rifle across his chest. Kade hugged himself against Tiny, then rolled away from her body.

"Can—"

Kade held his finger up to his lips, shushing Zack. Using his feet like rakes, Kade moved the leaf debris around until he struck a stick that was a few feet long. He loved Tiny, but waking her up was a dangerous task.

He poked her in the kidney with the stick.

As if he had pushed a self-destruct button, she thrashed over, snagged the stick in her left hand, and broke it with her right. She glared at him as she took deep breaths.

"Wakey, wakey," Kade said.

Tiny took a few more controlled breaths.

Zack clapped Kade on the shoulder. "Thanks for not letting me put my hand in the bear trap."

"Assholes," Tiny said through gritted teeth.

"Game time," Zack said to Tiny.

"Just give me a minute to get dressed for the ball," Tiny replied.

A half hour later, the five of them stood with the vehicles. Tiny and Zack reviewed the plan for everyone, but it was simple for Kade and X. All they had to do was get in the truck and drive home.

The short briefing ended, and X went to feed the horses. Number

Five climbed into the back of the Hummer, waiting for the other two.

Zack gave Kade a nod. "Remember your promise."

"You too," Kade replied.

Zack climbed into the passenger seat, leaving Tiny alone with Kade.

"What was that about?" she asked.

"Guy stuff. Be careful, okay?"

"I'll see you the day after tomorrow." Tiny hugged him tightly and kissed him before he could initiate. When their lips separated, she averted her eyes. With a final pat on his chest, she left for her ride.

Kade watched until he could no longer see the Hummer in the distance. He wished she would have looked back just once, but like she said, he'd see her in two days.

"Ready to ride?" X called from the driver's side of the truck.

He wasn't. He would rather have stood there watching and hoping that his walkie would chime, saying they needed him. That wasn't going to happen, and he might not like it, but he had to accept it. Sunset was upon them, and soon the other half of the group would be running the rescue mission.

Kade turned and marched back to the truck. He climbed in and tossed his stuff in the back with the rest of the supplies, which included the weapons they'd gathered from their earlier attackers.

"My mom used to always say *hay is for horses* whenever I said *hey* instead of *hello*. I didn't see anything else in the trailer to feed them. So, horses do eat hay?" X asked.

"Does a bear shit in the woods?" Kade responded.

"Speaking of shit. Holy gigantic crap—the floor is covered."

Kade didn't know much about horses. Animals had never been his thing. Most people expected to outlive their pets; it wasn't a luxury Kade had as a kid. However, he doubted that they would enjoy a long drive standing in their own fecal matter.

"I wouldn't want to stand in my shit for that long. Give me a minute," Kade said, climbing out of the truck and going to the trailer.

He unlatched the back of the trailer and stared at the back ends of two large horses. Kade was amazed by the size of the creatures. One horse, which was pure brown, turned his head far enough for Kade to see one of its gigantic eyes. The animal looked miserable.

Kade spotted a snow shovel hanging from the side of the trailer and retrieved it. He did his best to scoop up the majority of their feces, but he also made sure to keep his distance from the animals since he didn't want to spook them. With the thickness of their hooves, he figured it would hurt a little more than his rubber knuckles.

He hung the shovel up and walked around to the driver's side, where X was smoking a cigar. X took a few puffs, then rolled the cigar around his fingers. "I never saw the appeal of these, but never knock it until you try it."

Kade pointed to the cigar burn on his throat that had been given to him during his fight with the Tribe a few months back. "They remind me of Sarge."

"You mean the time you kicked ass and saved the day? Horrible memory," X said.

"Think we can walk the horses?" Kade asked.

X's brow creased. "Like a dog?"

"They just seem really unhappy."

"Don't think that has anything to do with us killing their owners?"

Kade rubbed his neck. "That could be part of it, but they aren't meant to be in a cage."

"They could run off."

"It's not like we know what to do with them once we get them back."

"Why not try?" X said, giving in and getting out of the truck.

The process didn't go smoothly. They found it was far more complicated than just attaching a leash to a collar. At one point the brown horse ran away from them, and after a half hour of trying to catch it, the animal came back to the trailer on its own. The other horse, which was black and white, seemed much more content to just stand around than to walk with them, and neither X nor Kade wanted to try that hard to force the huge animal to move.

The George Washington Parkway had been a scenic drive, so it had remained relatively undamaged when the guardsmen waged their war on the surrounding area. It provided an easy enough drive, with plenty of cover to allow Number Five, Zack, and Tiny to feel safe. Despite Number Five telling them that the bridge would be heavily guarded, they didn't have much of an option other than to drive the entire way around to the other side of the city. They would get close enough to recon the entrance, then decide the best diversion to run.

Zack was confident he and Tiny could manage a way in. They disembarked about a half mile away from the bridge and proceeded silently through the night. The forest was entirely different from the desert they had stalked together, yet it felt almost normal to have Tiny with him.

It broke his heart to know he would have to wait years if he wanted another shot with Tiny. From the day he had met her, he knew about her feelings for Kade, who had been just a name to him. Back then she didn't think there was ever a chance she would end up with him, which gave Zack the window he needed to make a move on the most awesome woman he had ever met.

What he thought was the start of a strong emotional connection had been for her the equivalent of taking out the trash. They slept together on and off during their tour, but it was always on her terms. He kept hoping that their relationship might develop into something, but it never did. Now that she had her knight in shining armor, he knew his time would most likely never come. The only thing he had going for him was that Kade wouldn't live a full lifetime, so there was a small, tiny, minuscule sliver of hope that he might have another chance.

They came to the edge of the woods near the Theodore Roosevelt Bridge. Toward the near side of the bridge was a barrier fully staffed with soldiers underneath generator-powered floodlights. The island beyond the bridge was clamoring with noise even in the night.

"Any ideas?" Zack asked, trying to think of a way past the guards that didn't involve swimming.

"There's no way we can get close without being seen," Tiny said, keeping her rifle tucked into her shoulder.

"That is a ton of light. They're making themselves night-blind," Zack replied.

Tiny looked at him with wide eyes. "If that was us, what would we have?"

Before he could answer with *night vision snipers*, two shots rang out in the night. Zack's arm burned as a bullet grazed him. He dropped to the ground as the second shot slammed into Tiny's chest. She smashed back into the tree behind her, then toppled forward. Her head sounded like a watermelon as it cracked off of the edge of the pavement.

Zack scurried forward and scooped her up. He threw her over his shoulder and took off into the woods as more shots rang out. Jostling her about without knowing her injuries was a concern, but he had to get enough distance between them before he could do anything to help her. Keeping her steady, he pulled the walkie from his belt and called Number Five for a pickup. He sprinted, trying to cover as much ground as he could by the time she reached him.

With the headlights coming toward him, Zack moved into the road to get Number Five's attention. She swung the vehicle around so it was ready to leave. Zack threw open the back door and gently laid Tiny across the backseat. Her head was bleeding from the impact with the road, but she hadn't been shot. The bullet was imbedded in her sidearm.

"Go. Try to catch Kade. I'll make sure you aren't followed," Zack said, slamming the door and heading back the way he came.

The better part of an hour went by before X and Kade finally got both horses situated in the trailer and were ready to drive again. By now Kade figured the mission was underway since nighttime was upon them.

X took a puff from the stub of his cigar, the cherry lighting up in the night. "Remind me to save some of these for myself."

Kade reached into one of the packs sitting in the back and pulled out two protein bars. He tossed one to X and saved one for himself.

"I miss real food," X said as he tore into the bar.

"We'll be farming before you know it," Kade replied.

"I'm not saying I want to work for food. I miss being able to walk into a grocery store, put a real fine steak down my shirt, go home, and toss it on the grill," X replied.

"You don't call that work?"

"Hey, man, that was fun."

"Hay is for horses."

X punched Kade in the shoulder.

"Shall we get moving? Your pissed-off sister is waiting for me when we get back," X said.

Kade gave him a nod. This was how it had to be.

X stepped down on the gas pedal as the walkie on the dash blared static mixed with what Kade thought was a frantic voice. He couldn't make out any words. Then, just like that, silence. Kade and X shared a confused look.

"*Kade*," Number Five's voice chimed through the walkie. "*Kade, are you in range?*"

His body reacted faster than his brain as he snagged the walkie. "What happened?"

"*Come*"—crackle—"*meet*"—crackle—"*motion*."

"On our way."

The book on agriculture couldn't be much more boring. John had nodded off three times in the cozy beanbag chair. He usually did his studying in the library, but with fewer bodies around these days, he was trying to act more like Kade would and stay in the dorm whenever possible. There were more distractions in the common room than before, but overall the book doomed itself.

Kade wanted them to move into an agricultural society as soon as possible. The issue was that none of them had any background in farming. John was trying to be a useful member of the cohort by spending most of his study hours on that project.

His mind kept recalling how he'd felt when Emma's hand had been on him, which wasn't helping his cause any. He was more confused now than he had been when he'd just had Grace on his plate. Grace was still the person he wanted to be with, but there was a voice in the back of his head telling him it was never going to happen. Emma might not have been Grace, but she wasn't no one either.

"You alive?" Wright said, waving a hand in front of John's eyes. He hadn't even seen the man arrive in front of him.

"Sorry. Just a lot on my mind. I usually talk to Kade when I have problems," John said.

Wright waved him along. "Step into my office."

John debated for a moment, but knowing he wasn't going to make any more progress on the cycle of beans, he gave up his seat and followed Wright into his room. The amount of work Wright had put into his room in such a short time impressed John. The bed was neatly made, with Wright's PhD hanging on the wall. A desk had been arranged with two cushioned chairs across from it. There were two photos on the desk. One was of two children, a boy and a girl, in sports gear. The other was a much younger but still powerful-looking Wright with a woman in a wedding dress.

"Did any of your family make it?" John asked as he took a seat opposite the desk.

Wright shook his head. "When I got home from work, my wife was the only one left alive. The kids had been torn to pieces. She had turned into a foamer. I don't know if the kids were or weren't before she killed them. I wish I understood how the vaccine does this to people."

"You could ask Damian," John said, and immediately bit his tongue. He wasn't supposed to tell the newcomers about Damian's role in the Feline Flu vaccine.

Wright's eyebrows rose. "What can he tell me?"

"I'm not sure. Don't know what he knows. But he's been doing some research on the foamers," John said.

Wright gave him a half smile. "Thanks, but I am more interested in the vaccine. So, tell me what happened."

"While I was teaching Emma to shoot, she sorta, kinda, touched me, in a way—"

"In a physical way. How did you feel about that?" Wright straightened his vest as he sat tall.

"I was scared."

"This is a new experience for you?"

"Yeah. And I was worried that Grace would find out."

"John, are you and Grace in a relationship?"

"No."

"Are you attracted to Emma?"

"Yes."

"Perhaps you should change your target. In months Grace hasn't done anything to show interest in you, but within days Emma has. You can't put Grace on a pedestal." Wright tapped a pen on a notepad.

John leaned in his chair, staring at the ceiling. "But she's so amazing, and tough, and beautiful."

"I'm sure you'll find just as many things to love about Emma if you look closely."

"I think I already blew that chance."

"You might need to create the window this time."

"How do I do that?"

"Just be yourself."

John crossed his arms. "I've been myself for months, and that hasn't worked with Grace."

"Make eye contact when you are talking. Watch her lips when

she is talking. Make small physical contact whenever possible. The window will open in no time."

John pondered the words. He wasn't sure if he wanted to give up on Grace, but Emma did seem interested. He cared so much for Grace. She had been the recipient of all his energies since he met her. The hope that she would come around to him in time had been keeping him waiting, but maybe she never would. Maybe he would spend forever waiting for her.

Emma wouldn't make him wait forever. She seemed interested in him now, and it wasn't like she was undesirable. If anything, he was just as physically attracted to her as he was to Grace. He'd be lucky to have either, but he could only have one.

"Something you said after the funeral has been sticking with me. I was wondering why Kade is trying to learn about the foamers," Wright said.

"His brother is trying to figure out how to fix them, and it's Kade's way of helping," John said.

"What exactly is Damian fixing?"

John's daydreams of which woman to choose came to a halt. Kade had asked John not to reveal his brother's part in the vaccine, but John didn't know how to answer the question without giving away too much. He tried to think of a way to tell a version of the truth without breaking Kade's trust.

"Damian was a medical researcher. He's trying to reverse the effects of the vaccine," John said.

"How do they know it was the vaccine that caused the foamers in the first place?" Wright asked.

John froze. He'd never even considered that this wouldn't be a survivor-wide concept. His group was partial to that knowledge because of Damian.

"It's the common theme among the survivors here," John said.

Wright shook his head and leaned back in his chair, straightening out his vest. "Don't you find that strange?"

"That most of us aren't vaccinated?" John asked.

"No. That two brothers and a sister, as well as their closest friends, all survived this together. In the Tribe, no one had family left." He turned a photo on his desk so John could see a woman and two children. "None of my family survived."

"I guess they were just really lucky."

"Or they knew something the rest of us didn't. Either way, it doesn't seem fair."

John sat rigid, like his chair was made of nails and if he budged an inch he would be skewered.

Wright turned the picture back around and gazed at it. "I guess nothing's really fair about this life anymore. Look at poor little Scott. I hate to say this, but do you think he's part of their research? It's been bugging me how a child could escape this dorm without notice. It almost seems like someone had to have helped him."

John thought back to that night he had been on guard duty. He might not have ever been looking out the side that Scott left from, but he had never heard the ladder. Most of the time they just heaved it out, and it sounded like a bag of wrenches on the way to the ground. To have kept it so quiet Scott would have had to lower it rung by rung, which would have taken a ton of strength and patience. More than a child would possess.

"And all I know of Kade is that he turned down the Tribe's help to maintain control of his little empire, which cost many Tribesmen their lives. Even one of his own left him over that choice. I just can't help but wonder what kind of leader he is," Wright said.

John had never given much thought to the fact that Kade could have prevented the fight with the Tribe by joining forces with them, something he now chose to do willingly when it was convenient to him. He didn't like the direction his brain was turning, but he couldn't help but think of how adamant Kade had sounded when he said he planned to lead this group until he was unable to because of a disease he knew he had that would kill him. Logically, he should want to find safety and a leader for the group, not parade as its champion.

But Kade was his surrogate father. He couldn't believe that all of this, all of their survivals, was just something he was using to stroke his ego.

The one thing John was sure of, though, was that the newcomers didn't make him feel like the stray.

"All I can say is he took me in and has kept me alive this long. You'll have to excuse me—it's time for my shift," John replied, wishing he could push the new thoughts from his mind.

Chapter VII

Humble Pie

Ashton ran from door to door, flinging them open. Meredith was close on her heels. Somehow she had lost Franklin. She had put the two children down for bed and had gone to do some studying, but just like in the Old World she was asleep before she knew it.

She threw open the door to Kade's room, but no one was in there. She kept moving down the hall, hunting for her missing kid.

The cheetah, Bristle, mewing at the door was what had awakened her. Meredith had still been sleeping, but Franklin's bed had been empty. After losing Scott, she couldn't let something like that happen again.

The first place she had checked was the main exit to the dorm, but the ladder was still rolled up. She couldn't find the kid anywhere, and her panic was about to go to full-blown terror. Being in charge of the kids was something she had not wanted in the first place. If she'd had anyone to pass the task to, she would have done it the moment Scott died. She was in charge of only three human beings, and it had taken her less than twenty-four hours to let one of them die. She was a horrible matron.

Ashton reached Wright's room and threw the door open. He was the first person she found home.

"Franklin's disappeared."

"Calm down and say that again," Wright said.

"I can't find Franklin. Have you seen him?" Ashton said, getting control of herself.

Wright crossed his arms over his chest. "I haven't seen him, but if you'd like I can keep Meredith with me while you search. I'm good with kids."

She wasn't sure if it was her panic that made her feel like his last few words had been an attack on her, or if he was trying to be helpful. Either way, she could cover more ground without Meredith in tow.

Wright welcomed her warmly, and Ashton found herself glaring at the psychiatrist for immediately being better than she was with the kids. She put the bitterness out of her brain and resumed her hunt.

After searching the rooms, she headed straight for the roof—not that she expected any of their incompetent guards to actually have seen something, but maybe she would get lucky.

When she burst out onto the roof, John hurried to put distance between him and Emma. Ashton wanted to tell him she expected the stray to suck at his job, but she didn't have time to insult him with the current state of things.

"Have either of you seen Franklin?" Ashton asked.

"No, but there is a light on in the science center," Emma said.

Emma was right. There was a light on in Damian's lab in the neighboring building.

"Can you guys walkie over?"

John called over to him, and in the minute it took for Damian to respond, Ashton swore she could hear her own heartbeat.

"*He's here*," Damian said over the walkie.

Ashton snagged the walkie out of John's hand. "Do not let him out of your sight. I will be right over."

Everything flew past as she rushed to the science center. She threw the door to the lab open, and immediately remembered being trapped in this very room a few months ago by a pack of foamers. X had come to her rescue. Thinking of X put her in a worse mood than she had already been in, which her brother must have picked up on, because he put himself between her and Franklin.

"I'm sorry, sis. I assumed you knew he was here," Damian said.

Victoria looked up from her notes for a moment to take in Ashton, but went right back to work.

"Franklin, come here," Ashton hissed.

Franklin stepped from behind Damian and strode toward her. "Don't be mad at them. I thought I'd be back before you were awake."

"You cannot wander off without telling me. I am responsible for you," Ashton scolded.

"I didn't mean to make you mad," Franklin said.

"I'm not mad. I am concerned."

"Can I stay? Your brother is teaching me how to use all the equipment," Franklin said.

Ashton took a deep breath. "If one of these two promises to escort you back when you are done."

"I'll make sure he gets back in one piece," Damian said.

"Don't keep him out too late. He's just a kid," Ashton said.

"Sure thing, Mom," Damian replied.

Ashton pointed an angry finger at her brother. She'd love nothing more than a chance to let out all her pent-up frustration.

Franklin tugged at her sleeve. "Miss Ashton, Bristle needs different food. She doesn't have a healthy diet," Franklin said.

"I'll check some things out and see if I can't make a trip tomorrow," Ashton replied.

Franklin threw his arms around her. "Thank you. She doesn't have a mom to take care of her."

Ashton looked down at the kid like he was made of gold, then slowly closed her arms around him. "We'll get her taken care of."

He separated from her and Ashton left to go check X's maps. Maybe she could do something good for these kids after all.

"Flash them!" Kade yelled as he pointed at the oncoming vehicle. Both of the vehicles were driving by the light of the full moon. The half hour it took to reach Number Five felt like an eternity.

X toggled the high beams and slowed the truck.

Before it came to a stop, Kade had already jumped clear off the truck and was running for the Hummer. Number Five slammed on the breaks, practically sliding into Kade.

He flung open the passenger door to find Tiny sprawled across the backseat. Kade climbed in and hit the dome light.

Her eyes were open but completely dazed. The left side of her scalp was bleeding all over. Kade placed a hand on the seat as he moved in closer to examine her, but at the pressure change on the cushion she let out a roar of pain.

There it was. Halfway down her combat harness, just below her breasts where her sidearm hung, the pistol was dented from a bullet.

"It went to hell fast," Number Five said.

Kade drew Tiny's Ka-Bar knife from the other side of her harness.

"Where's Zack?" Kade asked.

With a quick swipe he cut her harness free and let the busted gun fall away from the impact zone.

"Zack got her to me. Then he told me to go, that he'd cover the escape. I'm not sure what happened to him."

Kade lifted Tiny's shirt at the waist and sliced it all the way to her shoulder. He peeled the shirt back. Tiny's rib cage was already purple from breast to hip. Kade pulled a flashlight off of her torn harness and shined it in her eyes. Her pupils didn't respond at all.

"What's the plan?" X asked.

Kade examined every remaining inch of Tiny, looking for more wounds.

"Not to tell you what to do, but it might be time to cut our losses. Mick and Jem knew the risk they were taking. We've already lost Drew. She needs attention," X added.

Seeing Tiny like this made him want to kill all the president's men, every last one of them. But he couldn't leave Jem or Mick to die either. Every ounce of his being wanted to walk across their last bridge and tear every man stationed there limb from limb.

Then it hit Kade—no one would leave themselves only one exit.

"What did we do when we knocked out the bridges?" Kade asked.

X shared a confused look with Number Five. "We created a controlled way in while protecting our ways out."

"And when we boarded up the first two floors of the dorm?"

"We stopped people from getting in, but made ways to get out."

This wasn't a military base. It was no different than Houghton—a survivor colony. The president may have created ways to prevent people from getting in, but he still had to have ways to use those very same things himself. Kade had been so stuck on his fight with Tiny that he hadn't even considered the task at hand.

"Shit. He's got an idea," X said.

Kade turned away from his wounded love and faced X. "I've trusted you to look after the things I love the most in this world. I need you to take Tiny home. Five, I need you to go along and"—he choked on the next words—"keep her alive."

"Kade . . ." X said.

"I'll also need the Hummer, a cigar, your handcuff key, and your word you'll get Tiny to Houghton safely."

"It was one thing when we both had to leave. You can't expect me to sit back and let you run your own suicide mission," X said.

Kade pointed to the burn on his neck. "It worked last time. Now, your word."

X titled his belt and pulled the handcuff key out of its hiding spot. "You're a son of a bitch."

"My mother was a very nice lady."

X gave Kade a quick hug with a single pat on the back. "Don't die."

"I'm invincible, didn't you know?"

"Just don't go knocking on the front door."

Mick was in a state of half-sleep when the door to the Castle burst open. He looked over to Jem's cell to see if he was being brought back from a session, but Jem and the others were in their cells.

Instinctively, Mick moved to the back of his cage, wondering if they were coming for him. Two soldiers came into the room hauling a large, dark man between them. The man was dressed like a soldier, but showed some signs of being roughed up pretty badly. The man had a bright smile, which was slowly tinting red from his bloody lips. The two soldiers threw the man into the cage next to Mick and locked him in.

With that, the two soldiers left the Castle.

"Which of you is Mick and Jem?" the man asked.

Both Mick and Jem looked at the man, but neither took ownership of their identities.

"I'm Zack. I'm from the Tribe, working with your friend Kade on a way to rescue you two," the man said.

Mick wasn't sure what Cunningham was trying to pull when she added a new prisoner to their group. The Tribe and Kade were two pieces of information that could only have been learned from Mick or Jem, but whoever was trying to lure them into giving information had their facts wrong. The Tribe and Kade were enemies—they wouldn't be working together.

Mick and Jem both looked at each other at the same moment, realizing that one of them had given up information. Cunningham might not have been able to put the puzzle together properly, but she at least had some of the pieces.

Mick did not blame Jem. They were both heavily drugged. They had had no sleep, food, or water since they'd arrived. Mick, who had sustained less physical torture, was hallucinating more than he was coherent anymore.

The Castle doors opened again as a soldier approached the cells. The soldier opened Mick's cell and hauled him out. Any escape plans were now gone. His only goal was to make it to his execution without giving up his friends.

For a few minutes he was able to feel the night air on his skin. Compared to how painful walking was, the fresh air felt like heaven.

He wondered if he would be able to walk back, or if they would have to haul him in the wheelbarrow again.

It wasn't long until they reached Cunningham's HQ and the soldier put him on the table and stripped his jumpsuit, but for the first time he wasn't shackled. The smell of bleach reached him before he saw her.

"I am truly sorry for your treatment. Our new captive shed light on your predicament for us. He said that James was responsible for everything and that he forced you to come along by threatening those you cared about. I'm going to patch you up, and we'll keep you here only as long as it will take you to heal. We'll need to keep you in the cells until James is executed. After that we will properly house you until you're well enough to travel home," Cunningham said as she wiped his back with alcohol.

Mick didn't know what to say, so he just lay there. He tried to think the situation through, but it felt like the Grand Canyon stretched between his thoughts. Cunningham went about cleaning up his wounds and stitching the worst gashes.

"Oh dear," Cunningham said, pausing at Mick's lower back. "I'll need to lance a few of these blisters, then I'll patch you right back up. Don't worry, though—I'll give you a sedative."

The next thing Mick remembered was waking up in his cell. He pulled his jumpsuit away from his body and looked down at the bandaged wounds. For the first time in days his brain didn't feel totally fried, only slightly derailed. He didn't know if he had dreamed, hallucinated, or actually experienced what he remembered. The best thing, he figured, until he could think clearly, was to keep it to himself.

John hoped his life would get easier when the others returned. He was on his second leg of guard duty for the night. Ashton had asked John to cover her leg since she was doing research into nearby stores.

The worst part was his second leg of guard duty put him opposite

Grace. Before Emma he wasn't sure how to act around Grace, and now he had no idea what he was supposed to do.

"Some strange weather," John said, for lack of anything else.

Grace glanced around at the surrounding campus, then back at John.

There was nothing strange about the weather. It was a spring night. No precipitation. No weather fluctuations. Just a cool clear night.

"You been getting enough sleep lately?" Grace asked.

"Not really," John said.

Grace came over and took a seat beside John, facing the opposite direction. She was wearing yoga pants and a grease-covered sweatshirt large enough for her to swim in. There was nothing flashy about her, but her simplicity was one of things he found most attractive. Emma was beautiful and nice, but she wasn't Grace.

"Worrying about Kade?" Grace asked.

John hadn't been worried about Kade, but the moment she put the idea into his brain it was the only thing he could think about. The end of the world made no promises about tomorrows—that was something Kade always preached. However, knowing that Kade had an expiration date was daunting. It was like knowing he had Superman on his side, but it wouldn't be long before he left to find his home planet—which had been destroyed, so it wasn't like he could find it anyway. But he was leaving, and that feeling of invincibility he gave John would leave with it.

"Dr. Wright doesn't think he's the best of leaders," John said.

"The quack can think what he wants," Grace said.

John's eye caught movement down by the creek that ran near the dorm. He tapped Grace's shoulder and pointed to where he watched a foamer slurp water from the creek.

Bringing the rifle to his shoulder, John put his sights on the creature. The mangy male looked like a shipwreck victim, all bushy-haired, clothed in only scraps that hardly clung to him. This might be the monster that had killed Scott.

"It's just a foamer," Grace said.

Kade had asked John to keep the foamers alive, but Wright made a good point when he said it was preemptive self-defense. This foamer might have the potential to kill one of them at a later point.

His finger rested on the trigger.

"Relax. You know Kade's orders. We don't harm foamers," Grace said.

The palms of his hands grew slick as he debated if he should pull the trigger.

The foamer was a monster, a soulless creature that was nothing more than an animal. If that had been a wolf drinking from the creek and it had just killed Scott, he would take the shot. He wondered if Kade's orders would change once he knew Scott was dead.

John's hands shook and he cast the rifle aside with a frustrated release of guttural syllables.

"I'm so tired of not knowing what to do," John said, storming across the roof to the opposite side, where he could see to the south wall of cars. The place he had attempted to teach Emma how to shoot.

The scab on his nose from where the BB had sliced him still throbbed. The night breeze, the kind that holds whispers in its gusts, brushed passed him as he stared at the ground from the sixth floor.

"WWJD," Grace said, placing a hand between his shoulders. Her touch grounded his feet and banished the whispers in the wind.

"What would Jesus do?" John asked.

Grace laughed. "What would John do? You've got great first instincts, but you think your way out of them."

She had a point. But he didn't know if she was right. He rarely ever followed through with his first thought.

"I think I need a vacation," John said, without thinking.

"That's a great idea. I haven't been to the beach in forever. Give it a couple months until the ocean warms up and we can make a beach trip," Grace said.

John smiled at her. "I haven't been to the beach in ten years. All I remember is digging up sand crabs."

She patted his cheek, and John remembered the time she had planted a kiss there. "You poor thing. My brothers"—she took a long pause—"we used to go every summer until the last few, when business picked up."

"It's a date then," John said, feeling his cheeks flush.

"It's a date," Grace added.

John looked into her eyes. John would kiss her. He leaned in, closing the distance. She closed her eyes as he neared. They were so close he could feel her breath. He would finally get the kiss he had spent months anticipating.

The roof door slammed open, and Ashton emerged with a map in her hands. John lurched away from Grace, feeling like his mom had walked in while he was on the wrong website.

"Stray, you can catch some sleep. I found what I was looking for," Ashton said.

The first time ever Ashton did something kind toward him had to be at this exact moment. John's eyes still hadn't left Grace's lips, which still seemed to be waiting for him to close the distance. But he couldn't have his first kiss with Ashton watching, and he couldn't exactly tell Ashton to go away.

"Good night, Grace," John said, heading for the door.

"Remember what I said," she called after him.

Before John could make his way into the stairwell, Ashton put an arm out to stop him.

"Stray—I mean, John. I was wondering if . . ." She stopped and swallowed hard. ". . . you would be willing to help . . ." She looked away. ". . . me. I've got a grocery run to do, and I'd rather not go alone. Plus, you owe me one more favor."

John knew he wasn't her first choice, but he was her only choice at the moment. Damian and Victoria weren't going to leave the lab. She wasn't the type to trust newcomers, and though it had never been laid down as a rule, Grace was kept out of most dangerous situations.

"Sure," John said, descending into the stairwell, each step taking him farther away from where he wanted to be.

It might as well have been the front door he was going to knock on. Kade took a deep breath. Though it was spring, the night air still held a bit of a chill. Judging by how light the eastern sky was, it wouldn't be long until morning, and he wanted to be gone before the Mall woke up. Standing in Lady Bird Johnson Park, he peered out across the bombed-out Arlington Memorial Bridge to the remains of the National Mall. From this distance it looked like a protective bubble had been dropped around the Mall, with everything outside of its perimeter turned to rubble.

He felt naked without his usual assortment of weaponry, or even his normal clothes. The plan guaranteed he would get searched, so he'd left his mask and katana with X and Number Five. Instead of his usual weaponry, he had the shotgun and pistol from the Democratic Empire of West Virginians.

Standing in the mild spring night, Kade had the enemy pistol around his waist and the shotgun in his hand. It was a nice break-action shotgun, which meant it opened in half to put in a single shotgun shell. Kade had no intention of shooting it, but it would have been suspect if he showed up unarmed.

He had kept most of his clothes, but he was wearing one of the leather jackets from the foamer he'd decapitated. Hanging out of the corner of his mouth was one of X's cigars. He did his best to keep puffing on it, but he kept getting lost in thought as he retraced the image of the map Drew had made. The one grounding feature of his look was the knuckles hanging under his shirt from the breakaway chain around his neck.

The final piece of his new wardrobe was the foamer that X had killed. The wound to its neck was duct-taped shut, and he had zippered its jacket all the way up to conceal the silver lining. He had also dressed its hands in a pair of gloves to conceal the talons that would have been a dead giveaway.

Standing at the jagged edge of the bridge, he looked down at the moving water and thought he saw something dragging along the surface.

"Stay where you are!"

Kade held up his cigar hand to show he was no threat. Across the empty space that used to be a bridge, two soldiers pointed weapons at him. Only two. He had a chance. To be put in charge of guarding a bridge that no one could walk across gave Kade the confidence that neither of these were the best of soldiers. If the president was the man pulling the strings, the best soldiers would be guarding the high-probability entry points—and the president himself.

"On the ground!"

Kade dropped to one knee and then the other, setting the body down beside him before lying facedown on the macadam. He put his hands close together. His cigar cherry glowed red as it picked up the wind.

One of the soldiers went to a metal winch that was mounted on their side of the bridge and rotated the arm of the machine. The *click, click, click* of a crank sounded over the river below. Kade watched two cables rise up out of the water. The cables were bound by planks, creating a footbridge that was connected to the two halves of the bombed-out bridge. The planks didn't look safe, covered as they were by enough algae to choke a catfish. However, there were places on the planks where it was clear that feet had traveled.

The way Kade had lain down, he had unintentionally left himself staring into the face of the dead foamer. Its eyes looked like they were ready to pop, and its mouth seemed forced open at an awkward angle.

The soldier crossing the plank bridge took forever. Kade understood the caution but was in a rush himself and growing impatient. Finally, the soldier's boots neared his prone form. The first thing he did was kick the shotgun out of Kade's grasp.

"What are you doing here?" the soldier asked with a loud yawn.

"See the dead guy?"

"Yes?"

"His name is Henry. We met up a few weeks back. He said he was Secret Service working for the president. I figured he had just lost his mind. Not like the president is still giving orders. Something about being sent to scout Camp David for the president's relocation. Like I said, horseshit," Kade said, keeping his head down.

"If you don't believe him, why are you here?" the soldier asked.

Kade took a gulp of air. He had been rehearsing this story for the last half hour. His only hope was to sell it.

"I'm a man of my word. Yesterday we got hit by a pack of . . ." Kade paused remembering what Drew had called foamers. ". . . rabids. He saved my life at the cost of his own. The last request he made was to bring his body back to his wife, and to tell the president what he learned. Like I said, I don't believe the delusional stuff about the president, but I'd like to get Henry back to his wife."

The soldier stooped over and rummaged through the foamer's pockets. Kade had already done the same thing earlier. The license belonged to Henry Rabbenstein, who lived in the District of Columbia. All good lies needed a kernel of truth.

Replacing the wallet, the soldier nudged Kade with his foot. "Leave the shotgun on the ground and get on your feet."

Kade did as he was told, and for the first time he got a look at the man. He was over forty but less than sixty. Kade couldn't peg him any closer than that because he still had a full head of hair, but it was mostly silver-gray. The man appeared to be in shape with the exception of a bit of a belly.

The soldier came around and patted Kade down. Kade was quick to cooperate and show him the pistol. The soldier was just as quick to relieve him of the sidearm.

"Take Henry and cross."

Kade put the body over his shoulders in the fireman carry, the cigar still in his mouth, and then took his first careful step onto the planks. They were slick but sturdy. Without his hands free, he felt like a top that even a small gust could send crashing into the river below.

One foot after the other, he crossed at his leisure, gaining as much information as he could. The second soldier, a much more portly man, held his rifle to the side while he leaned against the crack mechanism that adjusted the bridge. The man was huffing and puffing and didn't seem to be focused on anything other than not passing out. Kade wanted to shoot a quick look behind him to see if the silver fox was as encumbered as he had hoped the multiple weapons would make him, but he couldn't see around Henry.

When his feet hit the concrete of the original bridge, Kade took a deep breath to steady his nerves, but a breath was all the time he could afford. Ducking his head, he heaved Henry off his shoulders at the portly soldier. The soldier attempted to brace himself against the flying foamer but only managed to end up on the ground under the corpse.

In half a second, Kade reached the winch and hit the release on the bridge. The cables zoomed out of the spool. There was a brief, almost cartoonish, moment when Kade met the eyes of the silver fox, who seemed suspended in midair as the supports fell out from under his feet. There was a first splash as the bridge sank into the water, followed by the plop of the man dropping into the river.

Kade scooped up the fallen rifle and aimed it at the soldier who was trying to squirm out from under the foamer. The solider stopped squirming, but a smile stretched across his face.

"You pull that trigger, and you'll be dead before you can blink," the soldier said.

Kade smiled in return. "I've been dead a long time. You have two choices. First, you can take off your clothes, jump off the bridge, and take your chances with the water. Second, I can shoot you in the head, remove the clothes from your dead body, and take my chances."

"*Hel—*"

Kade leapt the distance to the soldier, landing the heel of his foot into the man's face. Dropping the rifle, Kade fell beside the man and covered his mouth while drawing his rubber knuckles from under his shirt.

The soldier bit down on Kade's hand. Kade gritted his teeth and smashed his fist into the man's head. During his repetitive assault, he felt guilt welling up inside him. While his knuckles shattered the man's face, it dawned on him that this was the first time he had ever killed someone as the aggressor. He continued landing punch after punch into the man's face until he went limp.

After rolling Henry off the man, Kade stripped the soldier of his uniform, then pushed him over the edge of the bridge. Before Kade did anything else, he listened to hear if anyone was coming.

Feeling safe, he opened up Henry's jacket. Underneath, the foamer's pale flesh was covered by three strips of silver duct tape. Kade removed the tape and reached inside the body, pulling a blood-covered dry bag from the gutted belly. Opening the bag, he pulled out all the supplies he had hidden inside. He was reunited with his Judges, his roll of duct tape, map, handcuff key, and lighter.

Dressed as a soldier, Kade pulled out Drew's map and checked his location. The Smithsonian Castle was a little farther down the Mall. He said thanks to Henry, then pushed his body into the river. With the Judges hiding under his shirt and the soldier's rifle in his hands, Kade continued on his mission.

It took everything in his power to keep himself from running down Independence Avenue, but he figured he looked less suspicious walking. The Mall grounds had been turned into a motor pool for all the vehicles and weapons at the president's disposal. Kade figured there were enough tanks to take over a small country. He'd put together some story about being on patrol in case someone happened to stop him, but he didn't run into another soldier until he reached the Smithsonian Castle.

The building lived up to its name and truly looked like an English castle that had been dropped in the center of the capital. The Castle was made of red stone and was three stories high—four at the rook-like buttresses posted at the corners and center. The formerly beautiful windows had been shot out, and the garden that had once surrounded the building was nothing more than a mud pit, but against the back-drop of the war-torn city it looked regal. Kade contemplated sneaking in through a broken window but assumed this would draw attention. So far, the front door plan had been working for him.

As Kade hurried up the short steps that led to the entrance, the sky was turning a light pink. He pulled on the door, but it wouldn't budge, so he tried knocking. A moment later the door inched open.

"Did they screw the schedule up again?" the soldier on the other side asked.

"I guess so," Kade said.

"If you don't mind, I'll take the rest of the night off. Got a civvy I wouldn't mind meeting up with," the soldier said.

"Sure thing," Kade replied.

"Great, man," the soldier said, opening the door and walking past Kade.

Kade caught the door and waited for the man to descend the stairs. He stepped inside and let out a huge sigh. For someone who never felt like luck was in his favor, he couldn't believe how easy it had been to get this far. Perhaps it was his proverbial lucky day.

Inside, the building had high, decorative ceilings. The structure was long but narrow. Kade cautiously made his way down a small set of steps and surveyed both directions as far as he could see. It looked to him like the entire interior had been retrofitted as a prison, with small cells running two wide down the center of the room. The entire place smelled like a toilet.

There were five prisoners, each held behind separate fencing. Be-cause of Mick's bright red hair, he was the first one Kade recognized. Jem and Zack were housed beside him.

Kade couldn't believe how lucky he was to have made it this far. Jem and Mick looked beat to hell. They were covered in bruises and dried blood and seemed to have lost a good bit of weight. Standing at the cages, he could see their pupils were gigantic, making their eyes look alien. He could only guess that with pupils the size of black holes, they were in a delusional state.

"Everyone else seeing this, or am I hallucinating again?" Mick asked, catching sight of Kade.

"That you, chief?" Jem asked. His icy eyes had lost their shine.

"One and only," Kade replied.

Jem beat a drumroll in childlike excitement on the bars of his cage. "Mick's gay."

"Not a surprise," Kade said.

Mick bounced his forehead off the bars of his cell. "Why does everyone keep saying that?"

"Can we discuss this once we get out of here?" Kade closed the distance to the prisoners.

Zack came to the edge of his cage. "How is she?"

"Alive and on her way home," Kade said.

Zack's head lifted like a weight had been removed. "Great."

"What's up with those two?" Kade approached Zack's cell.

"They haven't had the nicest of stays. The president has been trying to get your location out of them. How'd you get in here?"

Only able to see the bruised and cut faces of Jem and Mick, he could only imagine how badly damaged the rest of their bodies were. Kade surveyed the locks on the cages. They required keys.

"I just walked right in. Getting out is where I am going to need the help."

Behind Kade, someone roughly cleared his throat.

Alpha slept soundly with Pepper curled up with him. While Alpha slept, he again went to a different place. He saw himself with his hair cut short and rust-colored instead of long and filth-ridden. He didn't have a beard, and he wore skin covers like the others did.

He lay on a soft floor holding a tiny other in his arms. The other had a head much larger than its body, and it was wrapped so tightly he couldn't see its arms or legs. He knew the tiny creature was a girl, and she was propped up on his chest, and her large gray eyes stayed locked on him like he was the only thing in the world.

His eyes shot open and his cheeks were wet. There was a pain in his chest for which he could not find a source. He didn't know where he was going when he closed his eyes, but something called him toward it like he had to return. Shutting his eyes tight, he waited to return to the other place.

CHAPTER VIII

FOREST THROUGH THE TREES

Ashton had fallen asleep on her back with an arm and leg hanging off of her dorm bed—the exact position in which she had landed after her guard shift.

Her room had posters across the walls of Olympic soccer players. The bed was two singles pushed together, and she had a light-blue queen-sized bedspread that X had brought back from one of his grocery runs. The only memento from her former life she displayed was her soccer cleats, which sat atop her dresser like a trophy, a reminder of the future she once had as a top-tier soccer player who was offered scholarships from almost every Division I institute in the country. That was before she had torn her Achilles. In hindsight, though, if she hadn't taken a semester off to recuperate from her injury, she would now be dead or a foamer.

Franklin quietly pushed her door open, holding Bristle over his shoulder like a baby about to be burped. The cheetah had become too large to cradle in his arms.

"Miss Ashton," he said, shaking her hanging arm. The only answer she gave was a zombie-like groan.

He set Bristle on her chest. The animal spun around in a few circles and then kneaded the spot where she wanted to lie down.

Ashton's eyes shot open, and she was greeted with the purring of Bristle. Her head snapped to the side. She tried to hide the hellfire from her eyes, but at that moment she wanted nothing more than to tear the child's throat out for waking her before she was ready. Every time she had the second guard shift, she needed a little more sleep to get the day started. Now the little pip-squeak had brought her out of her slumber too soon.

She did her best to suppress the desire to murder the child. "*What?*"

"Meredith isn't waking up," Franklin said.

Ashton tossed an arm over her eyes to block out the morning light. She must have forgotten to close her blinds before she went to bed. The sun hadn't fully risen yet, and she was in no rush to get up either.

"Did you ever think she might just not want to wake up yet?" Ashton said.

"Today is her birthday," Franklin said.

Ashton let out a long whine. "I like to sleep in on my birthday."

"Miss Ashton, I can't wake her up. She's hardly breathing. I don't know what to do," Franklin said, with tears welling up behind his Coke-bottle glasses.

"Fine," she snapped. "Take your cat, and I will be over in a moment."

"She's a king cheetah," Franklin responded as he left the room.

Ashton let out a growl and kicked off her sheets. She pulled on a pair of shorts and tossed on a sweatshirt. She stumbled, barefoot, down to the kids' room.

Inside, Franklin knelt beside Meredith's bed. Ashton went right up to her and gave her a shake.

"Hey," she said loudly.

Meredith's body responded like a rag doll, showing no sign of waking. The lack of response sobered Ashton out of her sleep grog, and she dropped beside the bed. She placed two fingers on the artery in Meredith's neck and felt a slow pulse.

"Franklin, go get the walkie out of my room," Ashton said.

The boy took off with all the coordination of a fish. Ashton checked Meredith's breathing and tried again to wake her, but had no luck. Franklin tripped on his way back into the room and fell onto the bed. Still, Meredith gave no response.

Ashton held the walkie to her mouth. "Damian, I need you in the kids' room now."

"*On my way, sis,*" Damian responded.

A few moments later, Damian rushed through the door, huffing and puffing like he was going to collapse.

"I've got to quit smoking," Damian said, raising his arms to assist his breathing.

"She won't wake up," Franklin said.

Damian took one look at Meredith, and Ashton knew what she had feared was true: Meredith was in the coma leading up to the ending of death, foamer, or immunity. Damian didn't say anything and continued his volley of tests on Meredith.

By the time he finished, everyone else had filed into the room. Damian didn't seem too thrilled to have the zoo of people and animals watching him work, but he continued on, ignoring comments and sniffs.

"She's been vaccinated," Damian said.

"How?" Ashton said.

Wright leaned against the doorframe. "I heard you've been doing research on the vaccine."

Damian never turned around, but Victoria stepped into Wright, planting a finger against his sternum. "If you're going to make it with this group, you better learn how to speak straight, shrink."

"If someone was shot, we would look to the person with the smoking gun. Damian is the only one of us that has vaccines," Wright said.

Victoria let out a cackle. "What reason would we have to vaccinate anyone? We've been doing research on how to fix the problem."

"You have vaccinated subjects, and you have access to foamers, but you don't have anyone in the process of transition. Maybe you needed a new subject. Aren't we all expendable to you science types?" Wright said.

Damian's head remained stooped as he knelt beside the bed. Ashton knew he had no way to defend himself. The entire Primal Age had been his doing. Indeed, the entire population had been nothing but test subjects to him.

Then a thought that scared her came into her mind. What if Wright was correct? She didn't believe him and wouldn't believe the accusation, but she felt a tingle of fear dance along her spine.

"I'd like to call a trial to prove that he has been experimenting on Meredith, and maybe even Scott," Wright said.

"Where do you think you are right now? We don't do trials," Victoria said.

"Then I would like to call the first. I will prosecute, Damian can defend, and the rest of you will be the jury," Wright said.

Franklin broke into sobs. "Why would you teach me how to do research if my friends were the subjects?"

Wright came into the room and wrapped a protective arm around the boy.

"If she wakes up, she will be able to tell us what happened," Victoria said.

"And if she doesn't?" Wright said.

"You can have your trial," Damian said with such force all other chatter stopped.

Ashton didn't like the idea one bit. Even on the shred of doubt she had that her brother was capable of such an act, he was still her brother. As much as she was against a trial, Damian seemed adamant about it, which meant he had to believe he would be proven innocent.

"I will stay with the child to make sure Scott's fate doesn't come to her as well," Wright proclaimed.

"Like hell. I'll watch her," Victoria retorted.

"You could be just as guilty," Wright said.

"For the time being, I am still in charge," Damian said, getting to his feet. "Dr. Wright and Victoria, you will both stay with Meredith. Everyone else out." He ushered the two dogs, cheetah, and remaining people into the hallway. "Go. You all have work to get to."

Ashton sent Franklin and Bristle to her room, but waited with her brother until everyone else left.

"I hate to ask, but did you do it?" Ashton asked.

Damian's eyes were miles away. "Was it the vaccine that I invented that did this to her? Yes. Did I personally do it? No. Does that make me any less guilty?"

Her brother walked away before she could say anything. Even though she believed Damian was innocent, his feeling of guilt was something she had no control over. She did still have the ability to affect the kids. One was dead, one was in a coma, and the last one was probably nearing a breakdown. What energy she had she needed to put into taking care of Franklin.

Kade's grip tightened on his rifle. He didn't know how many people were behind him. They hadn't shot yet, so he wasn't entirely sure what the situation entailed.

"Identify yourself," a soldier hollered.

"Henry Rabbenstein," Kade said.

"Put your rifle down."

"Wait, what if he is one of the civilians they just promoted?" a different soldier said.

Trying to avoid the click, Kade flipped his safety off. He hadn't gotten this close to be stopped now.

"Four, seven, and nine," Zack murmured.

"He can still put his rifle down," the first soldier said to his comrade.

Kade spun and found his targets exactly where Zack had called them. He tapped the trigger as he faded across the line. His first shot winged the man on his nine, the second dropped seven, and he completely missed the man on his four.

The man he missed took off running. Kade hurried after him, while putting another bullet in the first man. The last standing soldier bounded through the door with a large bag in his arms, making it clear to Kade why he hadn't been shot.

"Kade," Zack called. "Get us out of here."

He took one last look in the direction the man had fled before he searched the other two bodies for keys. His fear was by letting the soldier escape he'd have to face a greater force. Either way, escaping would be a challenge. Finding a ring of keys, he returned to the cages and let Zack out first. Zack went to gather weapons from the downed soldiers while Kade opened the rest of the cages.

Kade stood before the two people that didn't belong to his cohort. "Neither of you have to come with us. You're welcome to stay, but decide quick."

The man looked like he had come from a concentration camp, but the woman looked remarkably fit. He figured she hadn't been in captivity long. They both aligned themselves with Kade.

"Come up with a plan to get us out of here yet?" Kade asked Zack.

"I had hoped your pilot buddy would be able to fly us out, but I'd take any drunk over him right now."

"Just walk out through the metro tunnels," Jem said.

Zack and Kade shared a look.

"It's not a bad plan. They cleared most of the resistance out, so if we can get past their line we should be good," the female prisoner said.

"Who are you?" Kade asked.

She held her filthy hand out to him. "Yuzuki, and this is Anquan. I led the American University resistance force."

Kade shook her hand.

"They're in here!" came echoing from outside the room.

Zack handed the spare rifle to Anquan and the pistol to Yuzuki. Yuzuki swapped her pistol for the rifle.

Kade took Jem under the shoulder while Yuzuki did the same with Anquan, and Zack took Mick. As delicately as he wanted to handle the wounded, if they didn't cover a lot of ground fast, they'd all be dead. Their injuries would heal, but he couldn't bring someone back from death. They led the group across the Castle to the second entrance, where Kade cautiously pushed open the door to the back gardens.

* * *

John walked down the hallway winged by Emma and Grace. They had just left Meredith's room. No one spoke until they were one set of doors away from Damian.

"I can't believe he would prey on the children like that. I'd like to have seen him try that on me," Emma said.

Grace looked past John to Emma. "He didn't do it."

"The simplest explanation is usually the right one. He's a scientist who does research on people. He needed subjects, so he found them," Emma said.

"He's a Zerris. He wouldn't do that. John, you agree, right?" Grace said.

John held his silence for as long as the girls would let him. He continued to walk, feeling them both staring at him as if he was going to preach the eleventh commandment.

"It isn't that hard to believe. Look at what he's already done," John said, then realized he let information out that he promised Kade he wouldn't.

They had just entered the common area, and John saw his agriculture textbook still sitting open where he'd left it.

"I have to run to the library," John said, and jogged to his book and then away from the girls as fast as he could go. Grace would be mad at him for not siding with her, but even angrier that he'd disobeyed Kade. Emma would want more information. Neither situation could end well for him.

John was in such a rush that he didn't even arm up before climbing out of the dorms. He felt naked when he hit the ground, but he sure as hell wasn't going to go back and face both the girls. Foamers tended to stay across the water from campus these days, so he was less afraid of an attack than he was of the two women.

John crossed the street, then the quad, to get to the library. The footpaths carved by college students cutting corners had mostly grown back in. In his hurry he hardly had time to appreciate the beauty of the sunrise. He entered through the front doors and sped past the checkout desk to the first couch he could throw himself onto.

The couch was as comfortable as a medieval torture device, but it was somewhere to hide. He dropped the book to the ground. Maybe in a minute he would get up and go look for a more interesting book, but for now he just wanted to feel sorry for himself.

The swoosh of the doors brought him out of his self-pity, and he snatched up the book as he jumped to his feet. It was the first weapon he could think to grab. If he couldn't hit them with it, he could at least read them to sleep.

Emma came around the corner, and John dropped the book. She stopped where she was with her hands tucked into the pockets of her peacoat. The thick black coat was tied tightly around her waist. A sly smile came across her face as she stood watching John; he had the distinct feeling he understood what a mouse felt like when staring down a cat.

Her brow furrowed as she took a step toward him. "I thought I could help you study."

John stepped back, his heels hitting the edge of the couch. "You know about agrigora—I mean agro—farming. You know about farming?"

"I did a little gardening," she said, the heels of her knee-high boots clicking on the floor as she continued toward him. "Like, where do you plant seeds?"

John's brain raced for an answer. 1492. Buzz Aldrin. Lance Armstrong. Water runs downhill. Negative nine point eight meters per second squared. Every piece of information he had ever crammed into his brain came flooding back in.

Finally he spit out, "Dirt?"

"Brilliant," she cooed as she loosened the belt to her coat and let it drop from her shoulders. She stayed her course toward John as he took in her white button-down and black jeans. "What do plants need to grow?"

Thank god for biology class. "Water."

Emma undid all the buttons on her shirt but the last one, leaving the shirt hanging open like a sail. John tried to back away from the bra-clad breasts approaching him, but ended up falling onto the couch.

Her legs squeezed tight on either side of him as she straddled his lap and put her hands on his shoulders. "What else?"

John wanted to look her in the eyes, but he couldn't pull his gaze from the crests of her breasts. This was the closest he had been to boobs since Tiny buried his head in her chest when she was shooting over him. He had never seen naked, real-life boobs.

"What else?" Her voice sounded like honey. She pressed her thin lips to his forehead and gave him a long kiss. She could take as long as she wanted. The closer she moved to him, the nearer her breasts came to his face. In an attempt to suppress his desire to touch them, John went to put his hands in his pockets, but ended up placing them squarely on her quads. She didn't do anything to relocate his hands, so he figured it was best to let his accident pass as intention.

"Sunlight," John got out through ragged breaths.

She undid the last button of her shirt. "Such a bright pupil."

She took his hands and guided them to her shoulders. She let them sit for a moment, but when John didn't do anything, she helped to guide the shirt over her shoulders so it was nestled around her wrists.

John closed his eyes, letting his hands wander along her arms, feeling the warmth of her smooth skin. A rattled breath escaped his lips.

"How do plants make food?" Emma whispered into his ear.

Crap. John couldn't remember. Something about chloro-something-or-other. His eyes shot open in panic.

Emma sat back, her arms hanging at her sides, still linked at the wrist by her shirt. The faint indents of her abs led his eyes to her white bra and continued up to the defined lines of her neck. As if she knew he was studying the portrait, she turned her head to the side to accent her neck. He had followed the lines all the way out to her sharp chin before he remembered he was supposed to be giving an answer.

He couldn't even remember the question. Afraid to ask in case she would penalize him, he kept thinking. Something about plant food.

"Photosynthesis!" Thank the dear Lord and sweet baby Jesus for Mr. Maney, his middle school science teacher.

"Top marks," Emma replied. Her hands disappeared behind her back, and then her bra fell forward off her shoulders. John's eyes went wide as he saw his first pair. His hands moved like the Itsy-Bitsy Spider up her ribs. Every inch he climbed, his eyes would dart from her eyes to her breasts. This seemed too good to be true, and he expected her to stop him at any moment.

Just before his hands reached their objective, they shot back like he had been electrocuted.

"Grace," was all he could say.

"I'm Emma," she said, putting her elbows on his shoulders and leaning over, hanging what John wanted just in front of his face.

"I know. But Grace," John said, forcing his eyes to look into hers.

Her arms tightened around his head, tucking his face between her breasts. John fought to keep his focus, but the warmth of her breasts had him struggling to remember his own name.

"John, John, John, you are so sweet, but don't mistake my intentions. I am not trying to steal your emotional desires from Grace. All I'm doing is enjoying the moment. You've helped me; I'm helping you."

She leaned back, resting her forehead against his. Her breath was sickly sweet on his face as she ran a hand under his shirt. Her delicate fingers worked their way up to his sternum. She rested her hand just over his heart, and he could already tell she was feeling the rapid beats.

"I'm not asking for your hand in marriage. I'm asking for nothing more than friendship. If you say no, I'll put my clothes back on and walk away. This never happened," Emma said.

No is what John knew he should have said. Even if Grace wouldn't have him, his heart was still hers. But—

Emma placed a long lingering kiss on John's lips. John's first kiss. In the movies people always closed their eyes, but he was so stunned he couldn't stop watching her face. The kiss could only have been a few seconds, but he felt like time had stopped.

She pulled away, locking eyes with him.

"I'm sorry. I should have waited for your answer," she said.

No more is what John should have said, but he wrapped his arms around her hips and laid her under him on the couch. Her fingernails scratched against the back of his neck as she pulled his lips to hers.

Her tongue explored his mouth, and he met it with his own. She pulled away and coyly smiled at him. She tore his shirt clear off his head and pressed his bare chest against hers. Any defense John planned to mount was destroyed as he pressed his lips into the nape of her neck.

They burst through the exit of the Castle, and Kade hurried with Jem to the end of the building using the jut of the rook tower as cover. The soft light of morning reflected on the former grounds of the Castle gardens, which was now one big mud puddle. Kade released Jem to peek around the corner of the building to make sure it was safe. When he went to motion the others to follow, Jem was already standing out in the open. Realizing he couldn't leave him unattended, Kade ran back, grabbed Jem, and hauled him to the corner. Once he caught his breath, he motioned for the others to follow him.

They had just turned off of Independence Avenue, and when an old-fashioned air raid siren blared through the early morning, he was fully convinced all of his good luck had been used up. Once they rounded the corner, they would have no cover all the way to the Smithsonian metro stop, which was straight down the road from them. The only option they had was to run for it.

Anquan and Yuzuki took off at a dead sprint as Zack and Kade each dragged Jem and Mick along with them. When they reached the stairwell, the first two had already made it down both sets and were out of sight. Bullets zinged through the air. It looked like someone had kicked a hornet's nest as uniforms appeared everywhere.

Zack and Kade had made it halfway down the stairs with the two injured men when they heard gunfire coming from below.

"Stay," Zack said to Mick and Jem, then motioned for Kade to follow him.

They crept up the stairs on their hands and knees.

"They've got us bottled. Just cover me for like five seconds, then get the hell out of here," Zack said. Bullets whizzed overhead like bees cutting through the air.

"I'll wait for you to get back," Kade said.

"Not this time, Sundance. I'm going to put a lid on you guys. Those two won't get out of here without your help," Zack said.

"You can take them out of here. I'll stay," Kade said.

"She'd hate me forever if I let you do that. I'd rather be dead," Zack replied.

"She'll hate me too."

Zack clapped him on the shoulder. "She'll have to get over it. You're going to be a father."

The entire war zone faded away from Kade's mind, and he was trapped in a silent panic.

"Make sure she knows I told you before she did," he said with a crooked smile. "Now cover me."

Zack sprang to his feet and ran toward the Washington Monument. Kade popped up and opened fire on the closing assortment of soldiers, drawing their fire away from Zack.

Zack sprinted through the war zone, past the bullet-torn Washington Monument, and to a row of tanks. He climbed on top of the nearest one and dropped down through the hatch. Bullets pinged off the tank. Seated inside the vehicle, he bled from a number of bullet wounds. The metal beast roared to life as it headed for the open subway steps.

Kade ducked beneath the lip of the stairs like less of a man. If roles were reversed, he wondered if he would have been able to be as self-less. Tiny was what he wanted most, but the idea of giving up his life so she could have what she wanted seemed out of his reach.

The spray of bullets that had been cutting the air above his head ceased. He peeked over the top of the staircase to see a tank rolling toward him. His first thought was to dive down the stairs and get away from there as fast as they could, but then he noticed the president's men were all focused on the machine.

Kade retreated a few steps down while the tank rumbled overhead, sealing the entrance off from their attackers. A chorus of heavy fire and explosions followed as the concrete stairs shook from the barrage.

A scream echoed up the stairway, and Kade spun in a panic, thinking Mick or Jem had moved themselves into the line of fire. They were both still wandering around safely on the platform below. Kade slung his empty rifle over his shoulder and rushed down the steps.

Grabbing Mick and Jem, he dragged them along and forced them against the wall at the bottom. Ahead of him, Yuzuki tucked herself in behind a bend in the wall, while Anquan was sprawled in the center of the corridor leading to the turnstiles. Kade couldn't tell if Anquan was dead or just wounded, but he wasn't moving.

Ten yards down the cement corridor were two bays of turnstiles joined by a ticket booth. Behind the turnstiles were four soldiers. With hardly any natural light getting around the tank, it was almost impossible to see anything that the soldiers weren't illuminating with their flashlights.

"Stay," Kade said to Jem and Mick, then rushed across the corridor to join Yuzuki.

Kade leaned forward so his face was over Yuzuki's shoulder and whispered, "Rifle's empty."

"Me too," she replied.

"Anquan?" Kade asked, eyeing the pistol in the center of the corridor just out of the man's grip.

"Dead."

Kade set his rifle on the ground and drew his two Judges. He wished they had better range, but right now it was advantageous to have something that would go boom when he pulled the trigger.

With the number of metro stops in the city, Kade knew they only had a small window to get away before they would be totally trapped in the tunnels. The men on the surface would only be delayed by Zack for so long.

One of the beams of light crossed over Anquan's pistol, and Kade locked his eyes on it. He waited for the lights to slide to the far side of the corridor and then sprinted into the open. As he moved over the pistol, he used his experience as a soccer player to kick it like a back pass and kept his momentum moving forward.

The pistol ground against the floor as it slid toward Yuzuki. All four lights trained on the pistol until it passed out of their sight. Kade used the momentary distraction to slide across the floor and hide behind the ticket booth.

He squatted with his back to the booth, keeping all four soldiers behind him, while he controlled his breathing so they couldn't hear him. A pair of boots landed on Kade's side of the turnstiles. Tucking his quads to his chest, Kade made himself as small as possible as the light from the soldier's rifle passed just in front of his toes.

"Who turned out the lights?" Mick said, from back where Kade left him.

A second soldier landed on the other side of the ticket booth. Kade held his breath as they scanned for his friends' hiding places.

"Look, a night-light," Jem said.

Kade had to act now. He sprang to his feet and slung himself over the turnstiles. He landed within arm's reach of a soldier. His left hand came down on the rifle, turning the light toward the ground. He placed his right hand a few inches from where he suspected the man's face was and pulled the trigger. The Judge blasted the man, who stumbled back a few steps before falling. A dull thud echoed as the man's skull met the concrete.

Hurrying toward the next light on Kade's side, he opened fire with both Judges. He knew the first shot from each revolver wouldn't do much, but they would inflict some pain, which he hoped would be enough to occupy the soldier. The distance closed, and Kade knocked the rifle away before delivering two close range blasts into the man.

The two men who had already cleared the turnstiles turned their lights back on Kade and opened fire. Throwing himself to the ground, Kade scrambled across the floor and took cover behind the ticket booth. Both lights scanned the floor around him. By the angles, it was clear the soldiers were moving to flank him.

A pistol echoed through the darkness, and one of the lights stopped scanning. A second shot followed, and there were no more lights.

Yuzuki brought Jem and Mick forward, while Kade gathered the rifles with lights and divvied them amongst the group.

"I need to find them food," Kade said, making sure the safeties were on both of his friends' rifles.

"We need to get clear before they pin us in. Then we can get them fed. For now, hope the drugs don't wear off until we get safe. When they realize how much pain they're in, this will get more difficult. Now follow me." Yuzuki dropped onto the tracks and jogged away.

Kade helped Mick and Jem down, then took each of them under a shoulder and hurried as fast as he could after her.

The pack seemed to be up to something. Alpha was being careful to keep his distance, but staying close enough to keep an eye on what his troop was up to. It looked like four of them were communicating about a hunt.

What alarmed him was that, if the pack was hunting, he would have been alerted. Alpha stalked silently through the trees, keeping his eyes on the four of his pack. The four never noticed him. Placing his palms softly on the ground, he crawled to a thick cluster of undergrowth. Once he was concealed, he rose up on two feet to both hide himself better and improve his vantage point.

The four continued patting their chests and the dirt with soft howls. Then a fifth came running up to the council. The new addition was his second-in-command, Beta. Alpha watched as the four opened up their circle to bring in his stocky subordinate.

Beta beat his chest, and the others answered with excited hoots before they went into a low bow of submission.

Alpha huffed and lowered himself to all fours. He put his back to the situation and slinked quietly away.

John had waited in the library long after Emma left. He had tried to seem cool about everything that had just happened, but he thought he may have come off a little too fangirl. It got especially awkward when he had thanked her.

Saying she fled would be like saying the *Titanic* was an okay cruise.

The high of the moment left him on his way back from the library. Somewhere in the dorm was Grace. He didn't know what he would say to her. There had never been a time in his life that he had ever dealt with one woman, let alone trying to balance two. If Grace found out what had happened, he feared that he would have no chance with her ever, but if she heard about it from someone else—especially Emma—Grace might throw him from the roof.

That was a lie. She wouldn't throw him from the roof. That would have implied that she cared about him enough to throw him from the roof. She likely wouldn't even bat an eye.

Each rung of the ladder John climbed, he felt his hope of ever being with Grace plummet. The high he had felt with Emma was replaced with an even deeper sadness at the realization that Grace probably would never want him.

He pulled himself through the window and onto the third floor. Landing on his back, he lay there wondering if he wanted to ever get up. It didn't seem fair to him. The Primal Age had given Kade and X the women of their dreams. Grace was the woman of his dreams, and he'd completely messed up.

John pushed himself to his feet. Maybe she wasn't his dream. It could be possible that he was a romantic and fell in love with the story the others had, and thought he could have that with Grace. There wasn't much about Grace he knew. Despite all the times he tried to get close to her, she didn't want to let him in.

John made his way through the dorm and to his room. He had decorated it with movie posters from films he had always wanted to see, but never had.

There was one thing he could do to brighten his mood: target practice. He was best at archery. No one in the group had close to his skill level.

He picked up his bow and quiver, but when he turned to leave, Grace was in his doorway. John swallowed hard, not sure what to do. The only way out of his room was past her. She wasn't Tiny, but he still had a healthy fear of her.

"I am impressed with what you did," Grace said, leaning against the doorframe.

His brain swirled. He didn't think Emma would have gone straight to Grace. Emma seemed to be sincere when she said she didn't want John's emotion. He wasn't sure why that would make him feel better. There were two women that wanted none of his emotion.

The only thing he could think to say was, "Thanks."

Grace shook her head at him. Fear gripped him as he worried she had laid a trap for him to walk into. "I never thought you'd have the balls to disagree with me."

"Oh, that's what you meant," John said with a sigh.

"What?" Grace snapped.

"Nothing," John said.

"It doesn't make you right," Grace said.

With the amount of emotional baggage John had picked up this morning, Damian's innocence or guilt seemed like the least of his problems. He wasn't so lost in his lovelorn strife to truly believe that the possibility they had a vaccinator amongst them preying on children was less of an issue than his girl problems, but he was feeling egocentric.

"Damian is innocent," John huffed.

Grace cocked her head. "Flip-flopping just because I challenged you. Maybe those balls were too short-lived to be of use."

"Doesn't really matter, does it?" John said.

She crossed the room and took the bow and quiver out of John's hands. She tried to force him to face her, but he kept his gaze away from her. He wanted to say a hundred hateful things, but mostly just wanted to get out of there.

"What's the issue?" Grace asked, grabbing him by the shoulder.

Just a few hours ago, John would have welcomed any contact from her, but as much as he wanted to be with her, he felt his actions with Emma would make that nearly impossible now.

Wright appeared in the doorway. "Did you have a good study session in the library?"

John turned his attention away from Grace. "I studied plants."

"Emma a good tutor?" Wright kept walking and didn't wait for an answer.

Grace pushed away from him, as John's head drooped.

"Did something happen between you two?" Grace asked. She had a fire in her eyes that John had never seen before. She looked like she could burn the whole world down.

"What does it matter?" John asked.

Grace pointed a finger at herself. "It matters to me."

"It doesn't."

"Tell me."

The walkie-talkie on John's dresser erupted with Ashton's voice. "*Stray! Time for the grocery run. Cars. Five minutes. Don't make me come get you.*"

John moved away from Grace and picked up the walkie. "I'll be there."

"I have to go," John said.

Just the distance of the few steps let him see all of Grace. Her form was shaking, like she was silently crying. Her eyes were trained on her feet, and her fists were curled into tight balls.

"If you didn't want me anymore, fine, but you don't have to be an asshole," Grace said, rushing out of the room before he could say anything.

Her words cut him to the core. Not that he wanted to be someone's property, but somewhere in her brain they were something more than he thought. His face felt cold as fear drained him of all composure, and he hoped he could find a way make things right again.

It must have been the dust flying from Grace's dirty clothes that caused his eyes to water as he made his way to meet up with Ashton.

When they emerged into the daylight, Kade's skin felt basted in sweat. He became aware of his odor for the first time. Even though he smelled like a pig that had rolled in its own feces, that was nothing compared to how rank his companions smelled. The president's men wouldn't need anything but their scent to track them.

Instead of heading north as Kade had suggested, Yuzuki had led him south along what was once the Blue Line Metro to L'Enfant Plaza, where they had to evade a small group of soldiers before they continued south on the Green Line tracks to the Waterfront stop. She had explained that this would keep them underground the longest, and right now they needed cover more than anything. Plus, the Waterfront stop would bring them above ground less than a quarter mile from the Washington Channel. It was more important for them to get away from the city than to get away in the right direction.

Once they hit the streets, Yuzuki led them on a quick sprint to a restaurant where she used to waitress called the Cantina Marina. Kade sat Mick and Jem on the floor behind the bar while Yuzuki kept watch outside to make sure no one was following them. Mick and Jem's faces were the dark yellow of a healing bruise, and their eyes had a hollow look, like there was no comprehension behind them. Kade tried to think positively: they had been bloodied and bruised, but neither had a broken bone. Had either of them been hobbled, he would never have been able to get them out of the city. With how weak they were from being malnourished, he had practically had to drag them every step of the way.

Kade scavenged for anything he could feed his two friends to bring them down from their high. A starved stomach was a tricky beast to slay. He couldn't just throw food at them or he could make the situation worse. He found a refrigerator unit that seemed to have been untouched. Even though the power was out, the water inside was still drinkable. He cracked one of the lids and poured the water into two shot glasses. He handed a glass to Mick and one to Jem and told them that if they kept it down they could have more in ten minutes. Then he took an unopened bottle over to Yuzuki, who was staring out over the marina.

"Sorry about your friend." Kade handed her the bottle.

She gave him a nod and took the bottle. "Sorry about yours."

"He was a better man," Kade said.

"Things aren't fair," Yuzuki said. "A year ago I was being hit on in this very bar by rich men who wanted to show me their yachts; a few months ago I was leading raids against the president of the United States; now I am standing here with three people I don't know, unsure of what happens next."

"Next, we get those two space cadets back to Earth, then we get the hell out of Dodge," Kade said.

"Then what?" Yuzuki asked.

Kade's ear caught the sound of glass clinking on the bar and turned to see Jem trying to pour himself another shot of water.

"No," Kade called out like he was disciplining a dog. Jem shot back behind the bar.

Yuzuki waved a hand over the marina where there were all kinds of boats moored. Many of them were worse for wear and looked like they wouldn't stay afloat long, but a handful of them still looked like they could bear weight.

"Any chance you know how to sail?" Yuzuki asked.

"Not something in my skill set, sadly," Kade said.

Yuzuki let out an exacerbated sigh. "I guess we can just float, then. I would like to say let's wait till dark, but they're looking for us. Sooner the better."

"Let me see if I can't get some food in them first," Kade said.

Yuzuki kept her eyes looking out at the water and gave Kade a nod.

Kade spent the next hour coaxing Jem and Mick to eat croutons and drink water in small amounts. They seemed to improve somewhat but were still inebriated. Whatever food Kade could find that wouldn't spoil he packed into an industrial trash bag, along with a six-pack and a handle of vodka.

He had just rejoined Yuzuki at the window and let her know he was ready to go when they heard the *whoop whoop* of rotor blades. A second later, a helicopter flew up the channel.

Yuzuki looked at Kade, her eyes wide with panic. "Promise me you'll kill me before you let them take me back."

"They're not going to get us," Kade said, trying to convince himself.

"Promise me."

"Promise."

"Thank you."

"Which boat are we taking?" Kade asked.

Yuzuki pointed along a pier that was a little ways down from the restaurant. "Those small sailing yachts will be our best bet. We can just let it float until we are clear."

"Won't we be sitting ducks with that helicopter patrolling?" Kade asked.

"It isn't looking for us specifically. That's their once-a-day routine patrol."

Kade didn't feel any more at ease hearing this, but Yuzuki hadn't led him astray yet. He slid open the glass door and crept out onto the deck. Lowering himself to all fours, he crawled to the edge of the wooden steps that led down to the docks. He paused at the top, listening for any unnatural sounds, but the only thing he could hear was the lapping of the water.

The deck was worn and splintered, so he moved with caution to avoid imbedding pieces of it into his hand. When he hit the last step, he repositioned himself into a crouch and scrambled to the first boat. He ducked behind it, using it as cover. He didn't like how exposed he felt, especially with a helicopter flying around.

He sprinted to the next boat and stopped in cover again. Scanning the area, he still saw nothing and decided to make a break for the sailing yacht at the end of the dock. With steps as light as he could make them, he sped down the worn wooden planks.

Kade tossed the bag into the open boat and went around the edge, untying the lines. Having spent the winter in the water without anyone to care for it, the white paint had chipped and cracked while a dirty watermark had marred the outside of the craft. With only one rope to go, the boat had pulled partly away from the dock.

Kade waved in the direction of the restaurant. Yuzuki left the door open and herded Jem and Mick toward the boat. Yuzuki had Kade's rifle with her. Although Mick and Jem were both carrying their own rifles in a way that made them look like they might be able to use them, their hollow eyes showed that they weren't their old selves just yet.

Mick stumbled on the steps and fell to his hands on the deck. Kade couldn't imagine how much a fall on such a damaged body had to hurt. The rope slipped from Kade's hands as he took a step toward his friend but turned back as the boat started to drift away. He recovered the rope and watched Yuzuki grab Mick by the collar like a mother cat and shove him off the dock and into the boat. Jem followed the example and leaped in. Yuzuki climbed in next, keeping her rifle at the ready.

Kade dropped the final rope and grabbed the gunwale. He pushed the boat along the dock until it was clear to float on its own, and he jumped in before it drifted away.

As he landed in the boat, he felt a stab of pain in his back. He reached under himself and pulled out a toy scuba diver. He turned the plastic man over in his hands, remembering what Zack had said to him. Tiny was pregnant.

Kade dropped the toy into the water. The yellow plastic diver sank out of sight beneath the murk. He'd never wanted kids. Huntington's was linked to sex genes, which meant his mom had a 50 percent chance of passing it to her kids. For him, it was much more black and white. If he had a boy, he would be healthy; if he had a girl, she would have it. Any daughter of his would be condemned to death. The day she was born, he would know she wouldn't live past her thirties. He would be long dead before she reached that age, and if he let his own Huntington's run its course, she would have a clear idea of the hell that awaited her. Same as Kade had from watching the disease claim everything he loved about his mother, before it finally took her life.

He was going to die soon. Kade hadn't thought much about that since the Primal Age had begun, but his clock was running low. His mother had died in her midthirties, which meant his symptoms could start any day now.

For the past few months he had forgotten about the impending death waiting for him. After all the struggles they'd had to survive, for the first time since his diagnosis he'd been able to push the idea out of his mind and focus on living.

A kid would change everything, though. In a best-case scenario, he would live to see its fifth or sixth birthday. Kade could hardly remember anything from those years. His own child might not be able to remember him.

Unless it was a girl. His daughter would remember him every single day, the same way he remembered his mother. His daughter would remember every single day that she was going to die young because of the genes she got from her father. She would grow up knowing the same things Kade knew now. His life would end in a slow and agonizing way before he was old enough for a midlife crisis.

The worst part was that having a kid meant the chance of passing on the gene of an untimely death to a person you were supposed to protect no matter what. If he had a daughter, she would have a 50 percent chance of giving the disease to her own offspring. And there was no way to test for the gene markers—those kids would have to live in complete uncertainty until they showed signs or broke fifty.

As much as he had resented his father at times for having him tested, at least Kade knew. When his life had been derailed, at least he had not been an adult, entrenched in a life with a wife, one-point-seven children, a white picket fence, and matching minivans. He'd found out young enough that he would not have time to do anything of merit in his life, and he therefore decided he would not be sad to see it go.

Had it not been for the Primal Age, all of that would have been going according to plan just fine. Now he did have a life that felt meaningful. He had a woman he loved. And she was pregnant. He wanted to feel ecstatic, but the dread was overwhelming.

"No!" Yuzuki said.

Kade's attention turned to Jem, who had dug out the bottle of vodka, unscrewed the cap, and was about to take it to his mouth. Kade lunged and snatched the bottle from him.

"Not yet," Kade said.

"Sorry." Jem drooped his head to his chest like a child.

Kade rummaged in the bag and retrieved a bottle of water for Jem and Mick.

"Slowly," Kade said.

While he watched them nurse the bottle of water, Kade realized he couldn't even take care of these two, let alone a kid.

"You brought vodka?" Yuzuki asked.

Kade shrugged. "The whiskey was gone."

They had floated out of the channel and were picking up speed on the Potomac River. To the south, Kade could just make out a highway crossing the river.

Yuzuki held her hand out, and Kade passed her the glass bottle.

Kade assumed she wanted to toss it overboard, but she took the bottle to her lips and swallowed a shot.

"Never thought I'd be excited to see cheap vodka," she said.

She passed the bottle back to Kade, and he allowed himself one shot so she wasn't drinking alone.

"Not that I don't want to play Huck Finn, but we are floating the opposite direction of where I need to go," Kade said, capping the lid.

Yuzuki pointed at the bridge they were floating toward. "That's Route 95. We should be able to navigate to hit one of the supports or make it to the bank. We'll get out there and cross into Alexandria."

"We just wait?"

"Get some food in your boys. They should be coming around soon. It usually takes about a day for the drug-and-starvation combo to run its course," Yuzuki said.

Kade opened the garbage bag and retrieved a box of croutons for Jem and Mick.

Alpha led the pack across a road to a residential area. They were trying to scope out a future winter home and were exploring areas farther away from their usual hunting grounds. Alpha had six pack members with him, including Pepper, but so far there had been no signs of either others or those like him.

They had broken through a weak door to a basement and were exploring when they heard the sound an other's machines. At the noise, the pack scattered for the stairs, taking off like a herd of deer spooked by a predator.

Alpha was halfway across the road when the foamer in front of him was plowed by a large pickup with a raised snowplow on the front. His pack member's body flew down the road, bouncing with bone-breaking impacts. The pickup continued forward, running the damaged foamer over, then skidded to a stop.

All the doors opened, and four others climbed out. One had a rifle, a second carried a baseball bat, the third a pistol, and the fourth a large metal rod with a sharpened end. Alpha let out a low roar calling for his pack to flee, not fight.

The boom sticks cracked, and another of his pack fell. Alpha picked up his pace, crossed the road, and made it into the trees. Pepper and another of his were by his side, but another crack of gunfire dropped the two foamers that hadn't made the tree line.

Alpha spun back toward the road. His pack members were still alive, but hurt. They struggled toward the trees, crawling on weak limbs, fighting for each step.

The four others closed in on his wounded pack, who were crying out in pain. The others answered with laughter and boots to his brethren. Alpha started toward the others, but Pepper put herself broadside in front of him and rammed her forehead into his chest. When Alpha didn't budge, she nudged him again.

Finally, Alpha gave up. Turning to leave, he saw a bat descend on the back of one of the wounded, causing him to howl in pain. More laughter from the others. Then silence from his kind as the metal shaft went through his packmate's head.

Alpha fled into the trees, unable to watch the monsters anymore, feeling a pain in his gut like he was going to lose the contents of his stomach.

CHAPTER IX

GROCERY RUN

John drove in silence as Ashton guided him north in the black pickup truck that Ashton considered hers. They were traveling slowly, as it was the first time either of them had left the campus grounds since they'd arrived at Houghton College. X had left a detailed map that marked the safest path, but even still, they wanted to be careful.

"Stray, don't mistake this for caring, but who shot your dog?" Ashton said.

"I did," John said, as a small one-street town appeared in the distance.

"That was stupid," Ashton said, turning her attention back to the map.

She was the last person in the world, not just Houghton, he wanted to talk to about his personal issues. He couldn't wait for Kade to get back so his pseudofather could help him make everything right again—especially as he was beginning to doubt Kade's leadership and wished to see him do good again. Ashton didn't need any more ammo to pick on him.

"Kind of exciting, being off the reservation," Ashton said.

"Are you attempting small talk?" John asked.

"What crawled up your ass and died, Stray?"

John let out a long sigh.

Ashton backhanded him in the chest. He glared at her, but the cold stare she gave in response was far more intimidating.

"We all live in this same shit storm. Nothing is perfect for any of us, so if you want to act like you're on outcast island by yourself where no one understands, go for it. But like it or not, we're all struggling, and it is better to struggle together than alone," Ashton said.

Perhaps this was Ashton's version of caring, he thought.

"Make a right," Ashton said, then added, "Stray."

He turned the truck down the main road, and they kept their eyes peeled for the pet store. When he pulled into the deserted parking lot, Ashton maneuvered the rearview mirror and swore under her breath. She cast the door open, and John tried to match her haste, not sure what had propelled her.

"Franklin, get down here right now," Ashton said.

From under a blue tarp in the bed of the truck Franklin climbed down, with Bristle tucked into his jacket.

Ashton turned the kid around and smacked his behind. Franklin jumped forward as Bristle let out a hiss.

"I told you to lock yourself in my room until I got back," Ashton yelled.

"I felt I'd be safer coming with you. Besides, I want to make sure you get food Bristle will eat," Franklin said.

"Goddamn it, kid. I can pick out cat food," Ashton replied.

"She's a king cheetah," Franklin retorted.

"Wouldn't that make her a queen?" John said, surprising himself.

Franklin and Ashton both shot him a stilted look, but both showed traces of a smile.

"Stay close," Ashton ordered, retrieving her hunting rifle from the truck.

John grabbed his bow as they made their way to the entrance of the pet shop. They paused when they came to the formerly sliding doors that were now hanging wide open. Ashton pulled out the map one last time before they stepped inside.

When they had been driving, they'd felt like prisoners who had been given a taste of freedom. Crossing the threshold into the dark interior of the pet store was more like walking into a horror movie.

Bristle leapt out of Franklin's shirt and slinked into the darkness.

"Go get your cat," Ashton said.

"She's a king cheetah," Franklin said as he ran after her.

"Where's your flashlight?" Ashton asked.

John checked all of his pockets, but in his rush to leave he hadn't been thinking clearly and forgot to snag his usual equipment.

"You're a horrible Boy Scout," Ashton said.

"Eagle Scout," John corrected.

"No wonder you can't get a girl."

John tried to fight his growing smile, but it only made him feel more clown-like.

Ashton's eyes went wide when she saw his smile. "No. Grace didn't?"

Turning away to hide his smile, John found himself looking at aquariums full of dead reptiles and rodents. With the exception of the one labeled *rats*—the lid had been slid open enough for a rodent to squeeze through.

"You care about Franklin," John said, trying to change the subject.

"It wasn't Grace. The Brit chick?"

"Kade always calls me kid, the same way you call Franklin kid."

"I won't lie, I am a little impressed."

"I never thought you'd actually care about the kids."

"I'll have to side with Grace in the divorce."

"I can't believe you spanked him."

"Did she spank you?"

"You can't—think—words—darn it," John said scrambling for any response.

Ashton hoisted her rifle overhead like a championship trophy. "Winner!"

"Can we just find the food and get moving?" John said.

"Why? Got a date?" Ashton said, smirking.

John shook his head. "I'd like to try to make things right with Grace."

Ashton led John down an aisle of cat food. "If anything, you forced her to act. I love her to death, but she couldn't expect you to just wait on the sidelines forever."

"Why don't we talk more often?" John asked, feeling the same level of peace he felt talking with Kade.

"Because you're a pansy," Ashton replied.

Well, that settled that. He thought about mounting a defense, but any response he could come up with would only further justify her case. Instead, he looked over the rows upon rows of food for cats. There was dry food, and wet food, and kind-of-dry food, and gourmet food that was supposed to taste like real chicken—the variety went on and on.

"Franklin," Ashton called, as a shadow passed across the entrance.

John grabbed Ashton and pulled her down behind the shelves. He kept his eyes on the entrance.

"What the hell are you doing, Stray?" Ashton said, tearing her arm away from him.

"I thought I saw something move," John said. He could have sworn it was a person that crossed the threshold.

"It was probably just Franklin," she replied.

John stuffed his pockets full of cat food cans. If they had to leave in a hurry, he didn't want to have to come back. He had been trying to keep his ear turned toward Franklin, and John didn't think the boy was anywhere near the entrance.

"Let's quietly find the kid," John murmured.

"I think you just got spooked by a shadow," Ashton said, but he noticed she didn't stand back up.

"If it turns out to be nothing, you can make fun of me. You might want to grab a bag of food, just in case," John said as he nocked an arrow and moved to the end of the row.

The building had a square layout with a circle of aquariums in the center. It was possible that, if someone came through the main entrance, they could circle around the fish tanks and sneak out behind them. But before they moved, John needed to find the kid and determine if they were in danger. The only issue was he thought Franklin was on the other side of the entrance. John led Ashton to the edge of the tiled floor that served as the main avenue of the store. To cross over would expose them to the entrance. Ashton could be right—he might just be spooked.

Then they heard a pair of voices.

"I'm telling you that truck wasn't here last month," a female voice said.

"Why would someone stop at a pet store?" a man said as the two came through the entrance.

With the daylight behind them, John couldn't make out much other than that they were both tall and carrying weapons. Based on how they carried their weapons, John assumed the woman had a rifle and the man had a baseball bat.

Ashton put a hand on John's shoulder and whispered, "We have to find Franklin."

He patted her hand to reassure her he was on the task.

A high-pitched squeak came from a row of shelves beside the strangers, and they both jumped back as a fat rat scurried into the center of the white tile. Bristle pounced from out of nowhere and snatched the rat by the neck.

He could hear Ashton hold her breath, as he scanned for any sign of Franklin.

"Just a cat," the man with the baseball bat said.

"Do you know where the Feline Flu came from? You've got the bat, put it down before the cat spreads more disease," the woman said.

John pulled the bowstring back, ready to strike, when his heart dropped.

"She's a king cheetah."

The small doses of croutons seemed to be working wonders for Mick and Jem. The spark was back in their eyes, and they were filling Kade in on everything he had missed. Kade wasn't sure how strong they were, but at least he didn't feel like the designated driver anymore.

They had managed to run the yacht aground just before the bridge. After that, they shoved the yacht free so it could float away and hopefully draw any pursuit away from them, and Yuzuki led them into the section of Alexandria known as Old Town. Kade wanted to find a car and get on the road as soon as possible, but most of the area had burned down, leaving nothing but the charred remains of the old, mostly federal-style town houses that had once stood in the town.

Kade ran across a cobblestone street and took cover behind a waist-high brick wall. Behind him, the other three were in a staggered line, each safely protected by their own piece of cover. Waving his hand forward, Kade called Mick up from the rear. Mick charged up from the back of the line, taking the lead. Mick then motioned for Jem to leapfrog from the back of the line.

Jem ran up, passing Yuzuki and then Kade, but as he reached Mick he stopped and braced one hand against a metal sign and puked out the contents of his stomach. Kade and Yuzuki hurried to join the other two.

Mick read the sign Jem was holding on to out loud: "*Childhood home of Robert E. Lee.*"

The property was surrounded by a shoulder-high stone wall that had survived without much damage. The former garden that took up most of the interior property had been burned to the ground. The house, which by the foundation looked like it had once been a beautiful antebellum family home, was nothing but blackened spires of wood.

Jem wiped his mouth. "Take that, Confederates."

Kade laughed, glad to see his companions returning to their old selves.

"Doubt he has a car we can borrow," Yuzuki said.

Mick pointed a finger at her. "That would be stealing."

Kade figured some things would never change.

"I have emergency orders from the United States of America. I can take whatever I need," Jem said.

"Think we could ask them to borrow a car?" Yuzuki said.

"I wouldn't want to put them out after they gave us such nice accommodations."

As they resumed their leapfrog, Kade wished he had more of his usual gear. Between them, they had the four rifles—none of which had a full magazine—the pistol Yuzuki had taken, Kade's two Judges and rubber knuckles, duct tape, a lighter, a bottle of water each, a handle of vodka, a six-pack, and enough food for their next meal. Old Town was so charred he doubted they would find much of anything as far as supplies. His major hope was that they would find a car with keys that had enough gas to get them away.

"I've been trying to keep my mouth shut since I don't recall much, but do we have a plan, or are we just wandering?" Mick asked.

"This was your plan we've been following," Yuzuki said.

Mick scratched his head. "Can someone remind me of the details?"

"Kidding. There is a two-block section that survived the fire. I think that is our best chance for finding a car," Yuzuki said.

"I don't remember anything still standing in Alexandria," Jem said.

"When your boys leveled my campus, I ended up hiding out down here for a little while. Trust me," Yuzuki said.

"I apologized to you already. The fact that I was following orders doesn't make my choices right, but at the time I thought the resistance was the bad guy," Jem said.

"Relax, soldier. We're all doing what we think is right," Yuzuki said.

Kade knew they weren't safe, but he did feel much better being in the sunlight after traveling through metro tunnels for so long. He had felt like a rat stuck in its tubes. Even though he was more exposed here, it felt more natural.

They kept to the burned-out ruins and collapsed buildings while they moved toward the area that Yuzuki had told them would be safe. When they were a block away, Kade understood why Jem thought it had been leveled. The square block was outlined with four-story town houses, the top two floors of which were completely burned, leaving behind ragged supports that resembled angry hands reaching toward God. But the first two stories of most the town houses appeared to be intact.

The inner section of the block, which had been a paved area that led to the town houses' garages, was littered with fallen decks and other debris from the fires. Each house had a garage, which meant there was a strong chance each house had a car. If the car was in the garage, the keys would be in the house. Kade would have kissed Yuzuki if it wasn't for the fact that she smelled worse than his socks.

"Jem, you feel up to searching with Yuzuki?" Kade asked.

"Sure thing, chief," Jem said.

"And Yuzuki, you think this place is off the radar?" Kade asked.

"Jem just admitted he didn't know anything was still standing. I was safe here," she replied.

"Then you guys take the right side, we'll take the left. We need all the supplies we can get, and we should take a quick rest before we move on," Kade said, and they split up.

Franklin stood in the center of the pathway before the two strangers, with Bristle in his arms. It didn't look to John like the kid was scared, but he could feel Ashton trembling beside him.

"I can't lose him too," Ashton whispered.

John pulled the truck keys out of his pocket and handed them to Ashton.

The woman squatted down to Franklin's eye level and grabbed him by the elbow. "Look at you. Such a cute thing. Do you need a mommy?"

"What are you doing? The boss is going to want him for the collection," the man said.

The collection. That was enough for John to conclude they weren't the type of people with whom he wanted to exchange pleasantries.

"I was trying to be nice to the poor, scared child," the woman said in an overly sweet tone.

"I'd be scared if I was him too," the man said.

"Shut your trap and go find whoever else is here," the woman barked.

"We found who is here."

"I doubt he drove himself."

The man grumbled but started down the aisle between the shelves. In a few steps he would be right next to John.

He turned to Ashton and whispered, "When I say go, get Franklin to the truck and leave."

She nodded at him, and he stood tall over the shelf of aquarium decorations and found his target.

"Go," he said as he tapped the trigger release. The arrow launched through the air, passing over Franklin's shoulder, slicing through the woman's neck, and skidding off across the floor and through the entrance.

Ashton was off in a blur, herding Franklin out the door. John drew an arrow from his quick quiver and attempted to stab with the broadhead tip the man who had come within reach, but he had already seen him and dodged the attack. The man swung the bat overhead like an ax; John blocked it with the upper limb of the bow. Seizing the opportunity, John lunged forward, stabbing the man in the abdomen. He gave a quick twist and withdrew the arrow.

The man let out a scream as he dropped the bat and clutched his belly. John didn't know how much damage he had done, but he wasn't going to pass on the chance to escape. He spun and sprinted for the entrance, his sneakers squealing against the floor as he went.

He could see Ashton nearing the truck when her body rocked back in the air like she had hit a wall.

* * *

Kade and Mick searched their last town house. The first floor had a window at ground level. Though Mick didn't voice his displeasure, Kade could see it each time he smashed through the glass panes. He tried to keep out of his mind that they were being hunted, instead focusing on being safe. If he gashed his leg on a broken window, he'd jeopardize their situation.

He was careful to make sure he completely broke away any sharp shards of glass before he entered the town house. They had all been set up the same. The first floor had a half bath with a small sitting room, and a door that led to the garage. The stairs led up to a kitchen and living room. On a few occasions they found an undamaged third floor, where there were two bedrooms. None of the town houses had an intact fourth floor.

Mick went into the garage while Kade made his way upstairs. In the last house he had found a suit that fit him, and as strange as it felt, he had traded out his stolen army uniform for the suit. They also came across two children's backpacks. After a game of rock-paper-scissors, Mick won the Marvel backpack, and Kade ended up with a pink *Dora the Explorer* pack.

"All clear," Mick said from inside the garage.

Kade moved up the stairs to the second floor. The white walls of the stairway turned into a vibrant fuchsia as he entered the living room. The walls were lined with bookshelves, a couch, two reading chairs, and a fireplace.

"No keys," Mick hollered.

As soon as he stepped into the kitchen, Kade found a bowl on the countertop that had a janitor-size key ring in it. He snatched the keys and returned to the top of the stairs.

"Mick," Kade said, and a moment later Mick appeared in the stairway. Kade tossed him the keyset and went back to the kitchen.

Like all the other town houses, this one reeked of smoke, but it seemed otherwise undisturbed. He opened the fridge, and the smell of rotten produce mingled with the resident stench. The inside of the refrigerator was consumed by mold. Kade decided it was best to leave anything he found there untouched.

He was luckier with the cabinets. The former owners kept their rice in Tupperware containers, and there were three cans of premade soup. Kade opened the pantry next to the refrigerator and fist-pumped the air, then looked around to make sure he was truly alone. With the potentially embarrassing moment behind him, Kade appraised the full case of purple Gatorade.

Liquid gold.

Calories, electrolytes, and hydration all in one. With this find, he'd be able to keep Jem and Mick from backsliding.

His excitement shot through the roof as he heard an engine start in the garage. He tossed the food on top of the case and hauled it all downstairs with him. The black dress pants made a swishing sound as the legs passed each other. As much as he didn't feel like himself in the white button-down and pants, they were extremely comfortable.

He rounded the corner and stared at the idling beast before him. It was the largest Jeep he had ever seen. There wasn't even enough room in the one-car garage to open the passenger door to the hard-topped monstrosity.

"We're going to need a lot of gas," Mick said, running the car through a driver's training start-up.

"Worse problems to have. Get familiar, I'll fetch the others," Kade said.

He set the food down and brought the rifle back to the ready. Leaving the way he'd entered, Kade swung around the outside of the block. Kade expected the other pair to have made close to the same amount of time that he and Mick had, so he started with the last town house.

A scream came from the town house, and Kade broke into a sprint. He slowed only for a moment to make sure he went through the window safely. His feet pounded off the steps as he rushed to the second floor. He kept his rifle trained on the top of the stairs, then swung his sights across the room as he reached the next level.

Two people were in the room, both aiming guns at him. They were completely naked.

"Chief, you scared the hell out of us," Jem said, lowering his rifle.

"Ever heard of knocking?" Yuzuki wiped sweaty hair out of her face.

Kade glanced from one to the other. He knew what was happening, but his brain was still trying to put the pieces together.

Yuzuki lay on the couch and set her rifle beside her on the floor.

"I was supposed to be executed about an hour ago. What better reason to celebrate?" Jem said, waving Kade off.

"We found a ride." Kade walked backward down the stairs, unsure of what else to say.

To Ashton, time seemed to slow down while she was in the air. Before she had left the pet store, she hadn't checked to make sure the exit was safe. She was close enough to touch the truck when the iron rod struck her like a home run swing. The bag of cat food she had been holding in her right arm lessened the blow, but her arm immediately felt hot and cold, and her ribs hurt so badly she couldn't catch her breath.

As she fell to the ground, she noticed a truck a few spaces down. The landing only impeded her ability to breathe, and her world swam in darkness for a few seconds as her head pinged off the pavement. The bag of cat food exploded and rained kibbles all over the parking lot.

"Stay right there, boy."

Ashton forced her eyes open. She saw two people by the opposing truck, as well as a third standing directly above her. Looking like a butcher appraising his meat, he held the sharpened end of the iron bar to her throat. Her left hand still touched the stock of her rifle, but even if she could get the shot off, the rod would impale her. She didn't want to look at Franklin, but she could hear him crying.

"She's pretty enough to keep. Bring me the chems," the man above her said.

Over by the truck, a man wearing a Red Sox cap and a blue puffer vest set his rifle in the back of the truck as he searched through a toolbox loaded with different bottles of chemicals. When he couldn't find what he was looking for, the woman huffed, then turned to help him.

"Leave Miss Ashton alone," Franklin hollered as he brandished a knife from inside his jacket. The knife looked military grade, like the one Tiny carried, but Ashton had no idea where he'd gotten it.

His shout took everyone by surprise, and he plunged the knife into the groin of the man standing over Ashton. The man smashed the rod into Franklin like a bo staff. Franklin flew back, crashing into the passenger side of their truck. The man stumbled but hauled the rod back, intending to impale Franklin on the sharpened end.

Bristle leapt off of Franklin's chest and landed daintily on the rod, then sprang again to latch herself around the man's face. The cheetah hissed and growled as she bit down on the man's esophagus.

The fight was punctuated by the twang of John's bowstring as an arrow slammed into the man's chest, which caused him to go limp and drop all at once. Before the man crashed to the ground, Franklin withdrew his knife, and Bristle abandoned the falling man, landing gracefully on Franklin's shoulders.

John flipped his bow over his back, then hoisted Ashton to her feet. She roared in pain. Franklin held the passenger door open as John—a little more roughly than she would have liked—helped her inside. John shut the door on them and launched an arrow at the other two people. He kept a barrage up that sent them running to the other side of their truck for cover.

Ashton tried to slide across the seat to the driver's side, but her right arm would not cooperate. She eventually slid past the gearshift, regarding it like an alien artifact she had no idea how to use.

"Miss Ashton, are you okay?" Franklin asked.

Franklin, the little genius, had picked up driving a manual on his first try. He could be her right arm.

"Can you shift for me?" Ashton asked as she awkwardly started the car by reaching under the wheel with her left hand. Franklin nodded, and Ashton realized he didn't have his glasses on anymore. She figured he must have lost them when he'd been hit.

John kept his opponents' heads down as they climbed into the far side of their truck. Without a clear shot, John started to make his way back toward his own truck.

Ashton and Franklin worked in tandem to reverse the truck out of the parking spot, then threw it into gear. John tossed Ashton's rifle into the bed and then rolled over the side wall himself. A second later and he would have been smashed between the two vehicles.

When John had let up his attack, their enemies had jumped into their own truck, which was outfitted with a snowplow that was raised up like a battering ram and now crushed the side of Ashton's truck.

Luckily, any damage was cosmetic, and Ashton and Franklin accelerated away from the postapocalyptic buggy. Their pursuers had to turn all the way around to give chase, and that gave Ashton enough time to put some distance between them, though their maneuverability was limited with the delay in shifting.

This wasn't the first time Ashton had fled an attack in this truck. Last time it had been with X. She hadn't allowed herself to think about him since he'd left. Her dark knight, who she wanted to be mad at more than anything. But right now she just wanted to see him again.

In the rearview it looked like the devil himself was chasing them. On either side of the snowplow were a gigantic set of antlers that Ashton assumed came from a moose. Sticking up in the back of the truck like a scorpion's tail was a winch. Most disturbing were the human skulls that lined the roof of the cab. With their wide-open jaws, it appeared they were laughing at her while the truck from hell gained on them.

John had emptied his quiver and switched to Ashton's rifle, but he was saving his shots for when the man stuck his head out of the passenger window. If they were caught, Ashton couldn't imagine they would be lucky enough to get away again. Her entire right side hurt her just to breathe. Not that Franklin was a major factor, but without his glasses he wouldn't be much use. John was nearly out of weapons. The only chance she had was to lead them all the way back to Houghton and hopefully rally a force to meet them.

She just had to keep the devil at bay.

Kade and Jem lifted a large beam that used to support a deck out of the driveway. Jem's ear-to-ear grin hadn't left his face since he rejoined Kade.

Yuzuki and Mick were grabbing a quick sleep while Kade and Jem cleared the path. That would allow Jem and Kade to nap during the first part of the drive, assuming everything went smoothly.

They dropped the beam into the alleyway. Soot covered Kade's white shirt.

"Might be the most dressed up I've ever seen you," Jem said as they headed back for the next pillar.

Kade just nodded. He couldn't stop thinking about the possible outcome of sex. Tiny was pregnant. He was going to have a kid.

"Did you use protection?" Kade blurted out.

They grabbed opposite ends of the next pillar and hoisted it.

"I forgot my condoms back in the POW camp," Jem said.

Scooting along, they shuffled the pillar clear.

"What if she had something?"

"You're sounding like my mom. I think I have bigger things to worry about than herpes right now," Jem said.

"Herpes is for life, and so are babies."

Jem dropped his end of the pillar. The thud echoed through the ghost town.

"What is up with you? Isn't this the part where you are supposed to high-five me for breaking my months-long slump? This is the first time I had any since my going-away party. I expect this stuff from Mick, not from you."

"Just . . . in your condition, should you even be doing that right now? Look at you—you're like some modern art exhibit." Kade dropped the pillar.

Jem clenched his fists, then slowly relaxed his hands. "Am I in pain? Yes. Breathing hurts. Moving these beams hurts. Everything I do hurts. But hurting is a lot better than being dead. For the past week I've been thinking I was going to die any minute. I didn't think I could be saved. I didn't think I *would* be saved. Now here I am, still living. Yuzuki and I both needed something to remind us we're living. Maybe this isn't what you'd have done, but it's what I needed to do."

"Sorry, bud, I am happy for you. She is more than welcome to stay with us in Houghton."

"Kade, this wasn't about feelings. We were both so grateful to be alive. That being said, she is resourceful, so I hope she stays," Jem said.

"Wasn't trying to push her on you," Kade said.

"And if she did have a kid and I was aware of it, I'd raise it. That's what normal people do," Jem said.

Kade turned his back to hide his face, but made it look like he was going for the next pillar. The only issue was they had just moved the last one. He searched for something to make himself look busy.

He spotted a hose. They still needed to syphon gas. Picking up the end of the hose, he reached for his sword to cut himself a length, but the sword wasn't there. The hose became the scapegoat of all his emotion as he whipped it off the side of the house.

"Shit," Jem said. "She's pregnant, isn't she?"

"That's what Zack said. Tiny hasn't told me yet," Kade said, pressing his forehead against the brick siding.

Tiny should have been back in Houghton by now, where she should have enough medical attention not to be in any danger. He'd have to bring her the bad news about Zack, the man who had saved all of their lives—even harder than telling her that he knew she was pregnant.

Jem leaned his back against the wall next to Kade. "Talk to me, Goose."

"I'm shit-my-pants scared," Kade said, feeling a lump catch in his throat.

"It isn't what you planned, but you're going to be a dad. You've got to be at least a little bit excited?" Jem said.

"Dying aside, who says I'll even be a good dad to her?"

"Her?" Jem asked.

"If it's a girl, she'll have Huntington's," Kade said.

Jem put a hand on Kade's shoulder. "You've taken care of all of us for as long as I can remember. You're going to be a great father."

Kade choked on the lump and tears flowed down his cheeks. "I've got five years left—if I'm really lucky, ten. She won't even remember me."

"Now, that one I have to call bullshit on. You're Jesus, we're the apostles. Even if she doesn't get you for long, she'll still know you. Your legacy will continue as long as any one of us is still breathing. Come with me. I know what you need," Jem said.

Kade followed Jem around the corner and into the town house. They were as quiet as they could be as they passed Mick on the pull-out couch on the first floor and Yuzuki on the couch on the second. Entering the kitchen, Jem turned the small TV on the counter toward the two-chaired breakfast table.

"Sit," Jem ordered.

Kade did as he was told, and watched Jem retrieve the six-pack from the trash bag. He pulled out a bottle and positioned the cap on the granite countertop. With a swift hit he knocked the cap free. He repeated the process with a second bottle, then brought both of them to the table. Kade took one of the beers, and they clicked bottles before taking a swig.

"My favorite kind of beer—the type with alcohol," Kade said.

"Shhh, you're going to miss the movie," Jem said.

Kade stared at the blank TV screen. They had no electricity. He looked at Jem, who was leaning back in his chair watching the TV like it was magnetized. The possibility that Jem wasn't recovered from his drug trip crossed Kade's mind.

Then Kade smiled. He understood. They were watching their favorite movie that had marked every important occasion of their lives. The same one with the alien robots they had watched the day Jem left with the National Guard. The same one that Kade had finally understood after his fight with Sarge.

He knew they should be preparing to leave, but Jem was right. This was what he needed. Taking a swig of his beer, he watched the opening titles.

Ashton was getting them close to Houghton. On two occasions their pursuers had rammed their rear end, but John was able to deter them with a bullet through the windshield. Sadly, he hadn't been able to hit the people inside. Ashton was getting the idea that their pursuers were just waiting for John to run out of bullets, which wouldn't be much longer at this point.

"Franklin, I'm going to need you to call for help," Ashton said, and the kid pulled the walkie from her belt. He kept his left hand on the gearshift and used the walkie with his right.

"Ashton, John, and I are in trouble."

"You could make it sound a little more dire," Ashton said, amused by the kid's matter-of-fact delivery.

Her amusement disappeared as the plow rammed into them again. Judging by the absence of gunshots, John's gun must have been empty. She was beginning to wonder why no one had answered them yet when the walkie chimed.

The voice belonged to Emma. "*What's wrong?*"

Emma, Grace, Victoria, Damian, Wright, and an unconscious Meredith. Ashton was leading two lions straight to a flock of lambs. Grace was tough, but she wasn't a warrior like Tiny. Victoria was the most threatening of all, and she was hardly someone Ashton wanted to take into a fight.

"We're being chased by two people in a truck. We are out of ammo, and I think Miss Ashton has a broken arm," Franklin said.

"How far away are you?"

Franklin looked to Ashton for the answer and then relayed that they had about four minutes until they reached the last bridge. Emma told them to stay their course. When Ashton tried to pass more details to Emma through Franklin, no one responded.

She gave up trying when John tapped on her window. Propping the wheel with her knee, she lowered the window.

"Next time they get close, I'm going to board them," John shouted over the rushing wind.

"You're not a pirate. Just stay down. Home knows we're coming," Ashton replied.

"I think we have a better chance if I board them," John shouted back.

Though Ashton didn't disagree, she didn't see that plan working out for John. Back on campus, they would have more options and could get their pursuers to make a mistake.

"Hang tight," Ashton ordered as they approached the slalom of cars.

Their fate now rested solely in her hands since they wouldn't need to shift through the slalom. She swung the truck side to side, dodging cars and keeping a steady rhythm.

They emerged out of the first set of blockers, and she swung the truck as close to the bridge as she could before they entered the second obstacle course of cars. Just passing the first car in the second set, she saw sparks fly all around the devil car as it skidded out of control, plowing into the car Ashton had just passed.

When she saw a man wearing a black cowboy hat heading for the hell-spawned truck, she lost all focus on driving, and even though Franklin attempted to keep them downshifting, she was no longer using the clutch. They sputtered to a stop.

She threw her door open and hopped out, and was immediately reminded of her injuries. Catching her breath, she hobbled toward the wreck. John landed beside her and looked torn between helping her and getting into the fight.

There was no mistaking the cowboy. Xavier, her dark knight, had come to rescue her again.

John put a shoulder under Ashton's good side and helped prop her up.

"Oh no," John said as his face went white. Ashton followed his eyes to where Emma was perched on the bridge with a rifle. John's eyes never left the end of Emma's gun. Emma fired at the truck, and the windshield exploded in a spray of blood and matter.

The passenger door flew open, and the man with the Red Sox hat ran out, trying to put distance between himself and X. It was no use. X leapt onto the back of the truck, used the winch as a swing, and landed right behind the man. John moved Ashton to cover behind the car, but she made sure she could see X. His bladed knuckles were already donned when he lunged for the man, sinking the curved blade into his back. The two toppled to the ground, and X pulled the bloodied blade clear. He turned the man's head to the side and delivered a solid blow with the spiked knuckles.

"You. Do not. Fuck with. My girlfriend."

The final blow ripped the flesh and shattered the bones in the man's face, leaving no trace of his features. X left the body and rushed over to Ashton.

"Was that all of them?" X asked, taking Ashton from John.

"Yes," John replied.

"I'm going to take her back. Can you clean this mess up?" X asked.

Ashton wanted to protest, but she needed to be examined. Even if he did just save her, she wasn't ready to forgive X. He had left her, after all.

"Yes, sir," John said.

"Thanks. When you finish, come find me." X helped Ashton back toward Lambian, while Emma went to help John and Franklin.

The entire way back X tried to talk to Ashton, but she ignored him. Giving him the silent treatment was difficult since she wanted to know what had happened with his mission but, she thought, she could find that out from someone she didn't want to harm.

X was persistent, trying to talk to her until she was laid in the gurney. Ashton hoped she might be able to get the information she wanted at the top of the pulley, but when she was hauled through the window, it was by Grace and X, and she intended to keep her vow of silence. Grace and X each took a shoulder and assisted her to the medbay while Fenris and Rex stood in the doorway, watching the procession.

"Did you get your tongue cut out?" Grace asked after X concluded his one-sided tirade of apologies.

"No, I'm just not talking to X," Ashton said.

"Then X, can you stop trying until she forgives you? It's annoying," Grace said.

"Can you just tell her—"

"No," Grace replied as they entered the room they used for their medbay.

Ashton's excitement made her forget about her pain when she set eyes on Tiny. She pushed away from Grace and X, hoping to get answers, but then realized Tiny was a patient, not the doctor. Tiny was sleeping heavily on one of the white-sheeted beds, her chest clad in just a sports bra. Her side was covered with a reusable cold compress, but all around it was a deep purple bruise that resembled a blooming violet.

"What happened?" Ashton asked. Her injuries struck back with more pain than she'd ever remembered. The shock caused her to stumble forward, but X, her ever-watchful guardian, caught her under her good arm and supported her.

Number Five, who had been making up the second bed, was the one to answer her in a whisper. "She has a concussion. It would be best not to stimulate her."

X guided Ashton to the second bed, and she remembered the last time the two of them had been in this room. It was the first time the man she loved had informed her of his feelings. Ashton felt bad about her chilly resolve, but she had told him when he left he couldn't expect her to just be waiting for him upon his return. If she caved in now, it would prove the threat empty.

He helped her get situated, then went to the doorway. "Can you let me know what her injuries are?"

"I'll keep you updated," Number Five said.

X tipped his hat, took one last look at Ashton, and then left the room.

"Would you like me to stay with you?" Grace asked, but Ashton shook her head.

Grace followed X out the door, leaving Ashton alone with Number Five and Tiny.

"Is Kade back? Did they save Jem and Mick?" Ashton whispered.

Number Five went over to the dresser and jotted something down on a notepad. "Why don't you tell me what happened to you?"

She showed the notepad to Ashton. *Drew dead. Zack captured. Tiny shot. X and I sent back with her. Kade still trying. Don't say anything.*

Ashton looked up from the paper wanting to ask more, but Number Five turned her eyes across the room to Tiny. Fury boiled inside Ashton. If she hadn't been so stubborn, X could have filled her in before she was in the room with Tiny. Now she was stuck in silence, with more questions than answers. The only thing she could do was get her wounds mended.

"I got hit with a metal bar. I think my arm is broken, and a few of my ribs aren't feeling friendly," Ashton said.

Number Five inspected her and went about testing the damage, all while Ashton wondered where her brother was and if he was still alive.

Alpha lay with Pepper in his normal hiding spot under the deck of his winter home. Between defending his spot and the run-in with the others, he had lost nearly half his pack. Fewer members meant they needed to find less food, but they also only had half the hunters.

He needed to strengthen his pack, which would be dangerous.

He'd soon have to patrol a larger area looking for small packs to induct—which was a risk because it would involve leaving Beta behind and in charge. The one thing he did have going for him was Pepper. He knew he could count on her loyalty and, occasionally, her judgment over his own. The feelings he had for her were very different than they were for any other pack member. She was different to him, but he wasn't sure how.

CHAPTER X

VANESSA P.

K ade wanted to sleep, but the seat in the Jeep felt worse than a bed of rocks. The Jeep looked large from the outside, but the seats had almost no mobility and were tightly cramped. Jem didn't seem to have the same problem and was snoring in the next seat over.

After they finished the movie, the two had salvaged as much gas as they could from the other town houses. Their main issue wasn't the gas, but a lack of containers. They had a total of six gallons stored among a five- and a one-gallon container. They debated whether or not to use containers not suited for carrying gas, but in the end they decided it would be safer to find a refilling area than risk destroying the engine.

They had a dinner of soup, rice, and Gatorade. Kade hadn't realized that he hadn't eaten since he started his walk-up-to-the-front-door plan. They ended up eating every ounce of soup and the last grain of rice. He knew that, in all of their states of deprivation, eating that much was a risk, but they would likely have eaten him for dinner if he'd tried to stop them.

The trip had been slow so far. The entire city had been wrecked, so they were constantly avoiding debris and having to find ways around blocked routes. Their gas supplies were hardly enough to get halfway home without detours.

"Stop the car," Yuzuki said.

Mick did as she said and parked the car in the center of the road. That's when Kade heard the whooping of the helicopter.

"I thought you said that was a once-a-day thing," Kade said.

"The patrol is, but if you didn't notice they lost a few prisoners recently," Yuzuki said.

They watched as the helicopter passed above the city.

"I can't believe they'd waste this much fuel on us," Jem said, having been awakened by the quick stop. "They are doing low, fast passes—means they have an idea where we are, but not exactly where. We can wait it out and hope they don't stop, or we can give them something to look at."

"What would draw their attention?" Kade asked.

"Sound and motion do a pretty good job," Jem said.

"I know just the trick. Jem, Kade, with me. Mick, keep the car running," Yuzuki said.

"You're aware I am burning a ton of gas not moving," Mick replied.

"Keep it running," Yuzuki repeated as she drew the bottle of vodka out of the bag. Kade grabbed his Dora pack, and the three got out of the Jeep.

Yuzuki took off running; Kade and Jem chased after her. They rounded a block and cut through a burned-out building, then emerged into an open lot that housed a two-story cinder block building. Half of it was nothing more than strewn rubble, but the half still standing had two large bay garage doors.

Yuzuki took them through the rubble and into the still-intact garage of what was once a firehouse. The entire garage looked like it had puked all of its contents inward.

"Sound and motion," Yuzuki said, pointing to the fire engine.

The gleaming red truck looked so pristine it didn't appear to know the end of the world had come. Jem walked over to the vehicle and ran his hand over it like they were old friends.

"When you were in one of your dazes, you told me you used to be a firefighter—as well as a helicopter pilot—and had a dog, then asked if I wanted to sleep with you. So, Casanova, can you drive her out to the street, aim her away from us, and drop a block on the gas?" Yuzuki asked.

Jem smiled ear to ear as he retrieved a piece of rubble and climbed into the cab. He looked like a kid with a brand-new toy.

"Up for some arson?" Yuzuki asked. She went over to the vehicle bay that was closer to the destroyed half of the building. There was an emergency pickup, but the truck had been crushed by debris. She opened the vodka and poured some on each of the four tires.

Kade reached into his Dora pack and pulled out his lighter. He followed her path, setting flame to the rubber.

Jem drove the engine forward, nudging the garage door. The engine pushed the door off its tracks, and the door fell flat, kicking up a cloud of dirt. As Jem drove over the door, Kade and Yuzuki took off running.

Thick black smoke was rising in a constant plume from the fire station. Kade kept running and hurried toward the waiting Jeep. He opened the door and threw himself inside, feeling like a kid out for some summer mischief. A sheen of nervous sweat coated his body.

"Is that sirens?" Mick asked as Yuzuki climbed into the passenger seat.

"Yes, sir," Kade said.

"Did you guys steal a fire engine?" Mick asked.

"No, we're just parking it somewhere else," Kade replied.

"But we did start a fire," Yuzuki said, pointing toward the rising smoke in the direction from which they had come.

"That's arson," Mick said.

"I don't think anyone will press charges," Yuzuki replied.

Jem opened the back door and climbed in. "Why are we sitting still?"

"Mick wants to arrest us," Kade said.

"This is why you never get to do the fun jobs. Now drive," Jem said.

Mick drove them away from the scene of the crime. The sirens blared in the distance, and the smoke grew smaller as they continued on.

* * *

X drove the black pickup north, with John in the passenger seat directing him. The truck had taken a beating in the pursuit, but it was still running. The one thing X had always made sure to do on grocery runs was to cover his tracks. He couldn't leave a bunch of bodies lying around for someone else to stumble across.

John sat beside him with a full quiver of arrows, a machete on his hip, and enough loaded cargo pockets to hold all the tea in China. He was surprised by how eager John had been to come with him on the return trip, but he wasn't going to turn down the help. The two exchanged stories of what happened on the mission and at Houghton.

X hated to admit he wasn't sure which kid was Scott, but it didn't make it any less of a tragedy. In the long run, they were necessary to the survival of the cohort. Eventually, X probed to see if he could learn anything about how angry Ashton truly was.

"She scares me way too much to ask about anything that personal," John replied.

X laughed. "She scares me too."

"Slow down," John said as they neared the pet store. "I forgot. I stabbed a man, but I didn't kill him."

X pulled the truck over and parked it along the street. "We'll sneak up on foot."

They climbed out in front of a jewelry store and stalked toward the pet store. X pushed Ashton out of his mind, focusing his attention on the task at hand. The man may have been wounded, but he could still be waiting to blow their brains out.

The shadows of dusk were playing tricks on X's eyes, so he let John take the lead. They took cover a few doors down from the pet store. John nocked an arrow and informed X that the one body in the parking lot was the person who had attacked Ashton. It crossed X's mind to desecrate the man's body, but he decided that death might be enough of a punishment for him.

They closed the distance, and John peered inside the pet shop.

"The one I killed is where I left her, and so is her gun. I don't see the guy I stabbed, but he should have left a pretty clear trail," John said.

X clapped him on the shoulder. "You've come a long way from the kid I met last fall."

"Just stay alert. He could be anywhere in there."

John led the way into the dark pet store. X was used to operating in darkness, but he still didn't like waiting for his vision to adjust. Or that someone was in here and could see him. Letting his sight drop to second fiddle, he focused on listening for anyone who might be lurking.

John stopped in the middle of the walkway to inspect a wet puddle on the floor. He stayed low and followed the drips. X did his best to emulate John's posture. The blood led them to the back of the store, where the restrooms were located. The trail led into the men's room. John slung his bow over his shoulder and pulled a crank-charge LED flashlight out of his pocket.

"I'll light it up. You make sure he's dead," John whispered.

With a gentle finger, X pushed down on the door handle. When the latch retracted from the slot, he kicked the door open and turned the light on. There was a flurry of movement, and X fired once. The shot rang out, deafening him from any other sounds in the small space. John brought his hands to his ears, drawing the light away from the bathroom.

A pack of rodents charged through the open door, stampeding away from the sound. The one thing X was sure of was that there was no one in the bathroom. He felt like a fool for firing without confirming his target.

The women's door, which was directly behind John, flung open, and a baseball bat descended toward John. X tried to take aim but couldn't get a clear shot. The bat collided with the bow on John's back, dropping him to one knee. Pieces of plastic from the bow clattered against the floor. Before X could find a target, John spun around, drew his machete, and swung hard. There was a wet thud, followed by the crack of a skull on the tile.

John was rigid in the final position of his follow-through, as if he were posing for his first home run. "I'm worried that this keeps getting easier," he finally said, his voice wooden.

"It is part of the world we live in now. You physically okay?" X asked.

"Going to have to fix my bow, but I'm fine," John said.

If the Old World John met the Primal Age John, X doubted they would recognize one another. He only hoped that the changes would be more positive than negative. But X didn't consider counseling one of his strengths, so he would wait for Kade to return and relay his concerns about John then.

They still had tracks to cover.

Kade took his turn at the wheel. They were almost in Pennsylvania, and it seemed like their diversion had worked. Yuzuki was using Jem as a pillow in the backseat. Despite Kade's suggestions, Mick refused to sleep and kept checking to make sure the other two were sleeping.

"I have a hazy memory of telling you something important," Mick said.

"You did," Kade replied.

"Well, I wanted to consciously tell you. I'm gay," Mick said. Kade could see Mick's muscles tense up as the words escaped his mouth.

Kade shrugged. "Okay."

Mick's head snapped around, and his face flushed as bright as his hair. "That pisses me off so much. None of you care."

"I'm sorry?" Kade said.

"Years I've held this in. I thought you guys would judge me," Mick said.

"I'll judge you the same as I used to. I'll still make fun of you when you sleep with people like Vanessa P., whether they are men or women," Kade said.

"I never slept with Vanessa P."

"That was a stupid thing to lie about. Think about how much ridicule you could have saved yourself," Kade said.

"She slept with Jem that night."

"Jem doesn't get fazed if we make fun of his partners. So, back when we were in the same locker room, did you ever . . . ?"

Mick laughed. "You're not my type."

Kade put a hand on Mick's shoulder. "Lucas was, though, right?"

Mick nodded and stared out the passenger window.

"I'm sorry. I wish I could have been there for you properly after that," Kade said.

"Probably best you weren't. You might have cast Grace out then, and think about how cold this winter would have been without her."

"She has been a lifesaver, but I still wish I'd have known," Kade said, returning his hand to the wheel.

"Who would have thought the Primal Age would be the land of opportunity? You're getting below half a tank. Exit in two miles," Mick said.

Kade took Mick's sudden change as his way of saying he was done talking about this, so he let the conversation close. Mick had it right—the Primal Age was a land of opportunity. Mick had been able to let go of his secret, and Kade had been able to find a reason to live. Kade doubted Mick would have been able to come out had the end of the world not befallen them. During their years of friendship, Kade had only suspected Mick was gay on a few occasions, but he had not given it serious thought. Now, looking back, all of the bread crumbs were there. Mick had never had time for a girlfriend. In high school, he had said they would ruin his concentration on soccer, and after that, he had dedicated himself to the police force. There had been a number of women who had practically undressed and thrown themselves at Mick over the years, but Mick had found something wrong with each of them. The few members of Mick's family Kade had met weren't the most liberal of thinkers. Mick had never spent much time at home and was one of the many who spent weekends at Kade's house. With those pressures, Mick could have gone on carrying his burden until the end of time.

"I can't wait to get back. I feel like I've been gone a year," Mick said.

Kade was terrified to go back. He would have to face Tiny and his fate as a father. He had great role models in his own parents, but he didn't know if he could live with himself, knowing he had passed on Huntington's. There was a slim sliver of hope in his mind that Zack had lied to him, but he couldn't imagine that Zack's last decree would be a joking matter, just to get a rise out of Tiny.

"The relativity of time has always amazed me," Kade said.

Mick rubbed his arms as if the cabin had suddenly gone cold. "It's been a really long week."

Kade had no idea what Mick and Jem had been through, but based on their condition when he arrived, it hadn't been a five-star hotel stay. Part of him was worried that they had given away the location of Houghton, but he would give them more time to recover before he put them through another round of questioning.

Kade put his turn signal on to appease Mick and turned up the exit ramp. He checked the signs to see what options he had, and made a right where there was supposed to be a restaurant as well as a Sheetz gas station. The hope was they could find a few parked cars. The odds of them actually running were slim since they had been weathering the elements, but if they could trade out the Jeep for something with a little better gas mileage, they would be in good shape. The main goal was to syphon some gas to finish out the trip.

The gas station came first and there wasn't a single car there, but Kade made a mental note to go back and steal as many Snickers bar as he could carry. It might help speed Tiny's forgiveness.

"Looks good," Mick said as the headlights illuminated the darkened parking lot of the restaurant. There were three cars in the lot.

Jem and Yuzuki were still entwined in the backseat. Kade hated to wake them, but he needed all four guns. He patted Jem's leg, and they started the awakening process.

A few minutes later Kade stood in front of the Jeep's high beams, while Jem stood behind the Jeep keeping it guarded. Yuzuki slowly drove the Jeep toward the parked cars with Mick in the passenger seat.

Kade kept his eyes focused forward to keep his night vision as they scanned the parked cars to make sure there was no one occupying them. Each car was missing the two things they were looking for: life and keys. They wouldn't be able to trade out vehicles, but they could at least fill up.

When they started syphoning, Jem suggested they check the restaurant to be sure none of the owners were inside. Since they only had one hose anyhow, Kade agreed, and the two kicked in the back door.

They entered through the kitchen and scanned the darkness using the lights on their rifles. The shadows cast by the pots, pans, and utensils looked like crooked arms snaking along the walls. The building seemed empty, but still had a language of its own. It groaned at the intruders and hissed in time with the wind.

Kade did a pass through the eating area and returned to Jem in the kitchen. Jem stood before a large metal door like it was an Earthbound god. Kade stared at the door to the freezer, feeling the same reverence.

"If it hasn't been opened, there could be food in there," Jem said. Not just any food, but super-fattening, greasy, lard-filled, chain restaurant food that could sustain them for a while.

Jem kept his rifle trained on the door as Kade swung it open. Kade jumped back as the walk-in freezer lit up. There were two bodies on the floor, and it didn't appear as if the cold had killed them. There was a gaping hole in the neck of one body that was the perfect imprint of a mouth. Kade shut the door.

"I got excited for nothing," Jem said.

Three sharp blasts of the horn sounded from outside. Jem and

Kade sprinted through the exit, where the Jeep was waiting with open doors. Without any questions, they threw themselves into the backseat, and Yuzuki accelerated before they had time to close the door.

Kade didn't have to ask what the emergency was—there were three pairs of headlights coming for them. He didn't know if they had stumbled into someone else's territory, or if they were being pursued by the president's men.

"Cunningham?" Jem asked, looking out the back of Jeep.

"Judging by the height and separation of the lights, they have to be military vehicles," Yuzuki said.

"I thought we lost them," Kade muttered.

Jem was perched like a little kid with his knees on the seat, looking out the back. "Cunningham has a hard-on for us—for me, to be exact."

"Former CIA. Has a real knack for torture," Yuzuki added.

"Apparently, when I stole that helicopter, I pissed off the wrong people. Cunningham will track us to the end of the world," Jem said.

Yuzuki cut the lights and swung the Jeep onto a turnoff in the woods. She repositioned them so they faced the main road.

"Let's hope they blow by," she said.

A minute later the first set of lights flew past, then the second, and finally the third. Kade let out the breath he didn't know he had been holding.

"Did you offer to give the helicopter back?" Kade asked.

"Of course I—go, go, go," Jem shouted.

The last vehicle had reversed back to the place where they had turned off. Yuzuki slammed on the pedal, and they lurched forward like a plane at takeoff. The trees whizzed by as the vehicle tried to block off their escape. Yuzuki cut the wheel hard, trying to avoid the enemy, but ended up catching their back corner with the front of the Jeep.

The passengers of the Jeep were tossed around as Yuzuki fought to remain in control. They had spun the back end of their blocker out of the way. They resumed motion and sped down the road toward the highway.

Jem grabbed Kade and forced him into the footwell, then threw himself on top of him. The back window exploded as a bullet passed through the cabin and out the windshield. Yuzuki swerved the wheel side to side as the gunfire continued.

"Something isn't right," Jem said, getting back into the seat.

Kade felt the same way. If the first vehicle had stopped, it would have made sense that they'd seen them turn off, but the third one reversing to them was something else.

"What if they're tracking us?" Kade asked.

He had been devoid of technology for so long that he had begun to forget what technology was capable of doing. Every single phone in the Old World was capable of GPS tracking. The president was sure to still have some equipment in working order.

"Or someone is communicating with them," Jem said.

Yuzuki took the on-ramp so fast that the tires squealed, and Jem slammed into Kade. Barreling onto the highway, Kade realized that the impact had knocked out the right side headlight.

"If you're saying what I think you're saying, that torture must have really screwed your brain," Yuzuki said.

"I'm just saying one of these things is not like the others," Jem said, lifting his rifle.

Kade grabbed the barrel and aimed it down.

"Yeah, one of these was tortured for months, and if you haven't noticed I am driving us away from the bad guys," Yuzuki said.

Mick kept his attention out the window, like a child ignoring a parent fight.

"Our asses might be your ticket to freedom," Jem said.

"And the sex?"

"You could just be trying to gain my trust. We both know that bitch Cunningham wants me back alive," Jem said.

"Hold the wheel," Yuzuki said to Mick, then contorted herself around and drew her pistol on Jem. "Take it back."

Jem tried to lift his rifle, but Kade kept it pointed at the floor.

"Yuzuki, relax. You wouldn't have asked me to kill you before I let them take you if you were one of them. That would be terrible planning on your part. I know you're with us," Kade said.

"Make him take it back," Yuzuki growled.

Kade shot Jem a look, but he shook his head in response.

"Take it back," Yuzuki said.

"Go ahead and shoot me. Prove me right." Jem dropped his rifle and held up his arms to give her a clear shot. Kade thought about reaching for Yuzuki's pistol, but he was worried she would take any action as a threat and didn't want to spur her on.

"Guys!" Mick blurted. Everyone's attention turned. The lights of their pursuers were still in sight, but besides that, Kade couldn't find anything.

"I think it's me," Mick said. "I'm what they're tracking."

Yuzuki took the wheel. Jem shook his head. "They were supposed to execute you. That wouldn't make any sense."

Mick ran a hand through his hair. "During my last session they told me they were going to let me go once they executed you. They didn't need me for anything, and my only crime was knowing you."

"And you didn't tell me this because?" Jem snapped.

"I was so out of it, I didn't know if it was true or some delusional dream I had while they were working me," Mick replied.

"You didn't tell me."

"They stitched up a wound on my back. I'm guessing they put something in first," Mick said.

Yuzuki aimed her pistol at Mick. "I'll give you two choices: I shoot you and then roll you out of the car, or I'll slow down enough for you to bail out."

Mick popped his seatbelt and hung his head like a whipped dog. "Mind getting me closer to the grass."

He grabbed the handle as Yuzuki moved the car closer to the berm.

"No. Yuzuki, don't slow down," Kade said.

"You want me to shoot him?" she asked.

"Jesus, no. Tiny got shot. Zack and Drew gave their lives. We're not losing anyone else," Kade replied.

"Drew's dead?" Jem asked.

Kade ran a hand over his buzzed hair. That probably wasn't the best way he could have told Jem—he had completely forgotten that Jem didn't know. He had been so wrapped up in the tragedy of his impending fatherhood that he'd neglected to mention to Jem that someone he had freed had died trying to save him.

"We were ambushed. I'm sorry," Kade said.

Jem shook with anger while pointing a finger at Kade. "I told you not to come. I told you not to come. How is it fair to trade those lives for ours? We made our choice knowing the risk. First my dog, now my friends. Can't I trust you to keep anything I love safe?"

"I told you not to go. If you hadn't gone, no one would be dead. No one," Kade snapped back.

"I gave my word, like you did to watch Argos. I keep my word."

Kade wasn't sure who this person was, but he didn't like him. Jem had always been a calm and collected person. This was not the person he knew.

"You want to have this out, we can don some gloves when we get home. Right now, we need a plan," Kade said.

Jem's eyes narrowed, like he wanted nothing more than to rip into Kade's chest at that moment, but he settled back into his seat. "It's not my home."

Kade pulled the magazine from his rifle and slid the shells out one by one. He split them in half and handed a pile each to Jem and Yuzuki.

"Does this plan involve you charging an armed convoy yelling *bang, bang, bang?*" Mick asked.

"Yuzuki, trade seats with Mick," Kade said.

The two looked like a pair of mating snakes while they jostled to trade positions without losing speed or control. Kade dug into the bag of food and pulled out the bottle of vodka, then tore his sleeve off. Jem and Yuzuki loaded Kade's rounds into their rifles.

"Going to tell us what the plan is, or just gonna yell *surprise?*" Yuzuki asked while Kade stuffed his sleeve into the bottle.

"Same movie, different actors," Kade said, then proceeded to explain. Mick would slow down enough for Jem and Yuzuki to bail out. Kade would hit the lead vehicle with the Molotov cocktail, then they'd start a fight. They were outnumbered and low on ammo, but Kade hoped as long as their eyes were set on chasing Mick, they could use surprise to their advantage. Then, if they won the fight, they could get around to removing the tracker from Mick.

Mick had slowed down, and the other two were getting ready to bail.

"If this plan goes to shit, just get away on foot," Kade said.

Jem tossed his rifle, then himself, out of the Jeep.

Yuzuki pulled Kade to her and gave him a kiss on the cheek. "Good luck." Then she followed Jem.

Kade climbed over the backseat and opened the half door. He held the Molotov cocktail in one hand and the lighter in the other.

"Can I protest this idea?" Mick asked.

"Ruling on the field stands," Kade said, watching the headlights as they approached.

When the headlights were about fifty yards away, he leapt from the back of the Jeep, hitting the ground at a run to keep his balance. As he charged into the blinding light, he lit the alcohol-soaked fuse. Three more steps and he hurled it against the windshield of the oncoming vehicle. The bottle shattered, and flames spread over the hood. Kade dove to the side as they skidded past. He pulled the two Judges and rushed for the burning vehicle. Between the two pistols he had five shots left.

The other two vehicles in the convoy squealed to a halt. Kade met the flaming vehicle at the same time as the driver's door flew open. Kade rounded the door and slammed a knee into the person exiting. As they both fell back into driver's seat, Kade delivered a point-blank shot from the Judge into the person's face. The blast splattered blood and bone all over Kade.

As he moved toward the back, the passenger door rocketed open, catching Kade in the side and sending him sprawling toward the ground. While he fell, he didn't fight his body's momentum but kept his focus on his sights. Before he reached the ground, he popped off one shot. He hit his target far lower than he had planned but ended up shooting the man in the groin.

The man collapsed to the ground with an ear-splitting scream. Kade wasted no time delivering a second blast that silenced the soldier. He holstered his empty pistol and retrieved the man's rifle.

Two soldiers rounded both ends of the vehicle at the same time. Kade sprang over the dead body and into the backseat as the two opened fire. Judging by the yelling, they might have saved him a bullet. But Kade didn't take time to check and launched himself out the open door on the other side.

The convoy had stopped in a triangle formation, with the flaming car in the lower left corner. When Kade emerged out the other side, he found himself in the center of four soldiers taking cover between the vehicles. One of the four was dressed in what appeared to be Navy whites. The woman in white's long hair gleamed in the headlights.

Kade scrambled to his feet, unloading his last three shells from the Judge and firing poorly from the hip with his rifle like he was in some sort of Schwarzenegger movie. He doubted he'd hit anything, but he used the volley to cover his escape as he fled the triangle. Clearing the cars, he saw the bodies of every soldier that had tried to exit on that side.

"It's me, it's me, it's me," he hollered as he ran toward the side of the road.

Kade threw himself to the ground, using the natural runoff grade of the road as cover. A shot came from a few yards up the road, and Kade wormed his way there. Jem and Yuzuki were lying side by side with their rifles trained on the convoy.

"How are we doing?" Jem asked, not taking his eye off his sight.

"Four or five to go," Kade said, bringing his rifle up.

"Anyone dressed in white?" Jem asked.

"Yeah," Kade replied.

"That'd be that bitch Blaire Cunningham. I'm going to see if I can't get downroad of them, keep them occupied," Jem said as he scrambled away in a hunched form that resembled a foamer.

Kade and Yuzuki fired irregularly at the convoy. Since Kade couldn't see anyone, he aimed for the windows to get an extra burst of glass to keep people down. Jem must have reached his position, because a volley of shots rang out through the darkness. Kade couldn't tell if Jem was even aiming, or if he was just emptying the magazine. The front vehicle in the convoy began to move.

"Don't let them shoot me," Kade said, jumping over Yuzuki and running toward the moving truck. The passenger door was flapping back and forth as Kade closed the distance. Through the broken window, he grabbed the frame of the door and pulled himself onto the running board as the vehicle accelerated.

Kade hoped the driver hadn't yet realized they had an extra passenger. His rifle swung around his shoulder as he clung to the door and the truck to keep himself from falling. Wind whistled by as they reached sixty miles per hour. Kade was trying to figure out how to lift his rifle, but he couldn't give up either handgrip without ending up as roadkill.

A bullet tore through the door, swinging it open wider and pulling Kade off the running board. He lost his grip on the car and threw all of his weight toward the door, clinging to it with both arms and legs like it was a vertical mechanical bull.

The road whizzed by under him. The door flapped in the wind, and Kade kept his focus on the inside of the car, hoping he would swing back within reach. While he swung toward the cab, he got a look at the driver, all dressed in white. Cunningham held a pistol across her right driving arm, but she was focused on the road. A beep that reminded Kade of a radar in a bad submarine movie sounded, and her eyes snapped toward Kade. Her eyes made Kade wish he was staring at the devil instead. They carried such hate he was sure they could eat his soul.

Her finger touched the trigger, and Kade did the only thing he could: he let go of the door. Kade put his arms protectively around his head and tucked into a ball as the bullet missed him by a millimeter.

Kade landed not on the ground, but on his rifle. The metal sparked and shrieked as he slid along the road. The strap broke, and Kade rolled down the road. The pavement tore at his arms and legs, shredding his suit and skin indiscriminately. Kade didn't know how far he rolled, but by the time he stopped he felt like he had been run through a washing machine filled with cheese graters. He tried to get to his feet, but fell to his knees.

Blood dripped from his body as he crawled toward the side of the road. His body was illuminated as Cunningham turned the truck and came back toward him. Kade never looked at the truck, but focused on the trees off the side of the road. He put one painful hand in front of the other. One knee, then the other. He fought for each painful inch.

He never even made it to the berm, let alone the trees.

The truck came to a halt a few feet away. The door slammed as Cunningham exited. Her high-heeled leather boot, the type a dominatrix would wear, smashed into Kade's face, flipping him onto his back. His appendages searched for a hold, but he was as helpless as a turtle on its back.

The sharp heel came down on his chest, and he felt the same impending sense of death he'd felt during his fight with Sarge. Maybe Alpha would appear and save the day again.

She looked down at him, her raven eyes alight. A coy smile spread across her face. "If you ask me nicely, I will kill you now. Just say I am a traitor terrorist who deserves to be put down like a dog with rabies for the crimes I committed against the US of A."

Kade thought this must have been what a gazelle felt like when a lion sank its teeth in.

"If not, you will find I am very skilled at dragging every moment of pain into a millennium," she said.

The radar beep sounded again.

She aimed her pistol at his head. He didn't know if it would be that bad if she pulled the trigger. He'd never have to face fatherhood. His child could grow up believing whatever it wanted about him.

His child. He was going to be a father. Fatherhood was a duty, a privilege. His child deserved to know him, if only for a few years. Tiny deserved to have someone share the burden. He didn't want her to pull the trigger.

So he gave her the same answer he'd given Sarge: a nice, wide, happy smile.

"You'll be a fun one, won't you?"

Another beep. Then another. And another. They kept coming faster and faster.

Her coy smile turned to bared fangs as she spun and opened fire. The Jeep barreled toward her, and Mick must have seen Kade lying across his path at the last moment, because the Jeep locked up into a skidding slide. The Jeep slammed into Cunningham, sending her flying over Kade. But it stopped so close to Kade's face he could lick the tire.

His white shirt was flayed and covered in blood. His arms were rubbed raw from using them as a helmet, but his head was still swimming. The front bumper of the Jeep became his focal point to control his swirling vision.

The black flashes of spinning tunnel vision dissipated, and a pair of hands grabbed Kade's ankles and hauled him out from under the Jeep. Kade screamed as his wounds were once again dragged across the pavement.

"He's alive. You can relax, Mick," Jem hollered, setting Kade's feet down.

Mick relinquished his grip on the steering wheel and put the Jeep in park, which caused it to roll two inches forward. "I didn't want to hit him with the lurch."

Kade was caught in an undertow, being dragged out to sea. He fought to stay where he was, but he could feel his strength conceding to the force of nature. His mind swirled chaotically, so much so that he was glad to have his back to the ground, or he wouldn't have been able to figure out which direction was up.

The chain holding his knuckles lifted off his neck, and Kade feared he was being thrown into the sky by his own momentum. With a tight jerk, the chain was free of his neck. His arms flailed as he tried to find the chain, but not even a pinky would move where he told it to go.

Jem put a hand on his chest. "Relax. You're pretty shaken up. I'm just borrowing your knuckles. You'll get them back."

Nodding for Yuzuki to approach, Jem walked toward a white pile on the ground.

Chapter XI

Long Way Home

X and John had buried the bodies by the light of the truck, behind the only church in Houghton. The church was across the stream from Lambian Hall. It looked like an old square schoolhouse, except with a steeple and stained glass windows. The white paint had pealed so badly X doubted the structure would be safe by next winter.

John tossed a shovel full of dirt on the mass grave they had dug for their attackers. "This was the church I had to go to when I was at prep."

X had been to church a few times in his life. Before X's mom was comfortable leaving him home alone and whenever she couldn't find someone to watch him while she worked, he would end up at church. He could sit through an entire day of mass without anyone knowing he was there, a little boy by himself. Though he'd listened to hundreds of sermons that way, the thing he learned from church was how to lift money from the collection plate without getting caught. Some days he could make more than his mom did at work. His churchgoing days ended when she caught him with his pockets full of offerings.

"I'm sorry. That should be classified as cruel and unusual punishment," X said.

The light from the truck cast their shadows across the stone wall of the church graveyard. "I hated it then, but I think I miss it," John said.

"You think?" X added another shovel to the grave.

John tapped his chest. "Something's been missing. I just killed three people because I believed they were a threat. I don't feel bad, but I don't feel anything. There's an emptiness."

"You did what you felt was right. I can imagine whatever supreme being there may or may not be would understand your actions." X patted the earth down on the grave, then the two got into the truck.

"I'm not worried about how my soul will be judged. I'm worried about what I believe anymore," John said.

X wasn't sure what to say. There wasn't a modicum of religion in X. A crisis of the mind he may have been able to assist with, but over a crisis of the soul, he had no jurisdiction. The best idea he had was a distraction.

He pulled a small square box out of his pocket and handed it to John.

"What do you think?" he asked.

John took a look inside at the massive engagement ring and let out a laugh. "I never even saw you take this."

"It was a quick detour," X said.

"I think you did good," John replied.

Doing good was something that unsettled X. Doing bad was something he was good at, but doing good always made him suspicious of his own motives. He wanted to earn his white hat back, but he didn't know if that would ever be possible with the trail he had left behind. Maybe the best he could hope for would be a gray hat.

John climbed out of the truck to move the blocking cars out of the way. They traveled through the defenses, then parked the car with the rest of their motor pool at the student center.

"We'll come back for the food in the morning. I don't want to push our luck and run into a foamer tonight," X said as they walked toward Lambian. X had his .357 at the ready; John kept a hand close to his machete.

"How damaged is the bow?" X asked. He was great at keeping his nerve in dark buildings and civilized areas, but he still found the vast openness of a country night unnerving.

"It'll take a lot of work, but I'll be able to put it back together," John said.

X scanned the darkness as they crossed the road leading up to Lambian. "Why not just take another one?"

"This one has been mine since I got here, and I was told it was Lucas's before me. It only feels right to keep it," John said.

"I can understand that. I'd be heartbroken if I lost either of my weapons."

They approached the entrance side of Lambian, and John walkied for the ladder.

"Can you think of anything else I can do instead of going up?" John asked.

"Who are you avoiding?" X asked as the ladder clanged down the side of the building.

"You're not the only one with girl problems," John said as he began his ascent.

While he braced the ladder for the lanky teenager, X realized how little he knew about not just John, but the cohort in general. He had never been close to anyone but Kade in the Old World, and since then he had only gotten to know Ashton. So much of his time had been spent away from Houghton, he hadn't really had a chance to get to know the rest of them.

As he began his own climb, he decided that he would attempt to be a better follower. Even though he'd always felt like a loner, it couldn't hurt to learn how to interact with his end-of-the-world family. Most importantly, it would make things easier on Ashton.

He hauled himself through the window, then John helped him pull the ladder up. Emma was in the entrance room, roughing around with Fenris.

"Brit chick, I wanted to say thanks for the assist earlier," X said.

"Thank John—he taught me how to shoot," Emma said.

"And I appreciate you not shooting me in the face this time," John said.

As soon as the ladder was pulled in, X clapped both of them on the shoulder and set off to find his firecracker. He made his way through the dorm until he came to the medbay. Quietly, he opened the door in case one of the inhabitants was sleeping.

Tiny was sound asleep in her bed, while Ashton's green eyes were locked on him the moment the door cracked open. Ashton's right arm was splinted, wrapped, and slung. Entering the room, the latent instinct in his genes told him a predator was getting ready to strike. He lifted his black hat and brushed his hair back before returning the hat to his head.

"What do you want?" Her words came out as a growl.

"To see how you're doing," X said.

"Arm is fractured. Ribs are bruised. Don't you have another grocery run to go on?"

"Not at the moment," X said, approaching her bed.

"Sorry, I forgot you just got back. It'll be a few days. You should go find someone else to spend them with," Ashton said, sliding as far against the wall as she could.

"I want to spend them with you," X replied.

"You don't get to leave and come back, leave and come back," Ashton said.

"I'm sorry I volunteered to go," X replied.

"It's bad enough when you go on your damn grocery runs, but do you have any idea how crazy it makes me when you leave? No, probably not, 'cause you're a selfish asshole."

X took off his cowboy hat and held it over his chest. His hat-holding hand began to shake. The shakes—this girl must have turned him into a loser.

"I'll never leave you," X replied.

"And how can you promise something as asinine as that?" Ashton rolled her eyes.

X dropped on one knee and pulled the small box from his pocket. Opening the box like a clam, he revealed the pearl inside: a two-carat, princess-cut diamond engagement ring, offset by two half-carat oval cuts, mounted on a white gold band sprinkled with more diamonds—a ring that would have cost a fortune in the Old World.

"Ashton Zerris, I promise to never leave you, if you will be my wife."

Ashton crossed her good arm over her chest. "Put your hat back on."

X looked up at her, fear gripping every inch of him. His composure was tested as he fought the water that wanted to well into his eyes.

She slapped the box out of his hand, sending it clattering under Tiny's bed. "I said, put your hat back on."

X glanced at the discarded ring, then back at the woman he loved. He let out a long sigh, feeling his shoulders slump in defeat, and situated the hat back on his head.

"Yes, you stupid cowboy, I'll be your wife," Ashton said as she threw herself on X, knocking him flat on the ground. As she sat up, straddling him, she pulled the hat from his head and put it on herself. X grabbed her behind the neck, making certain to avoid her injuries, and pulled her in for a kiss.

This firecracker was his from now until forever. All the fear in his body dissipated, and the only thing he could do was smile his stupid smile.

"Kade is so going to kill you," Tiny said with her eyes half-opened.

Ashton put her good hand on the side of X's face. "Please tell me you aren't such a pussy you asked Kade's permission for my hand?"

"Of course not," X said, now wishing he had asked Kade's permission. He hoped this would come as less of a shock to his friend than the last time, when X had sprung on him his love for his little sister.

"Great. So, where to for the honeymoon?" Ashton asked.

"I was thinking Bermuda or the Bahamas," X said.

"I hear they're lovely this time of year," Ashton said, kissing X again.

He held her tight, feeling her beating heart. She had become the sun of his existence.

* * *

Mick's adrenaline was de-escalating when Jem took Kade's knuckles. Yuzuki sat with Kade, and a few feet away lay the red-and-white heap of Cunningham. Opening the glove compartment, Mick pulled out a basic first aid kit that had belonged to the car's previous owner. It was basic to the point he didn't think it had much more than Band-Aids and antibiotic ointment, but it was better to do something than nothing.

Mick got out of the Jeep and joined Yuzuki. At seeing Kade, he tried to hide his shock, but he was sure his face gave him away. Luckily for him, Kade was in no state to notice. His friend looked like he had been run through a meat grinder.

Yuzuki tapped Kade's face, causing his eyes to shoot open.

"No sleep," she said.

"We win?" Kade asked.

A crack that resembled a tree branch snapping echoed down the road. Mick's attention would have been drawn to the trees if the sound hadn't come so clearly from the center of the road.

Cunningham was on her stomach, one arm stuck crooked at her side while the other reached out, trying to pull herself away. Jem kicked her onto her back, then hoisted her up by her neck and landed a fist into her face, knocking her out of his grasp.

She slammed into the ground, but instead of screaming, she laughed. "Is this the foreplay?"

Jem lifted her by the hair and landed another punch into her face, sending her crashing to the pavement. She scooted herself back with her leg and propped herself up on her good arm. "That all you've got, big boy?"

Mick tossed the pouch to Yuzuki and rushed toward Jem, who landed another fist into her face. Her head rolled back like she was going to go unconscious, but snapped back with a bloody smile.

She had tortured him, and Jem, and countless others. She took great pleasure in her task. There wasn't a single second of the entire ordeal that wasn't rapture for her. Every cut, every impact, every action, was born of pleasure. He should want her dead.

But he didn't.

Like every human being, she didn't just magically appear as a complete person. She may been evil, but she wasn't the devil. She had been made into who she was and had been influenced to do what she did.

Mick intercepted Jem's cocked arm.

"You better have stopped me because you wanted some for yourself," Jem said.

Mick shook his head. To a lesser degree, he had seen this in the Old World as a police officer. Criminals had a history that led them to become the people they were. Occasionally, you would have a true psychopath, but most of them had been formed in their youth by terrible experiences that they recreated in their adult life. It was the nurture side of the nature yin-yang.

"Does the faggot not have the stomach for violence?" Cunningham spread her knees open and closed. "Or doesn't this do it for you?"

His eyes never left Jem's. Cunningham wasn't just a product of her youth—she had likely been recruited by the government because of her disposition, her traits turned into a tool. On top of that, the president had spread so much propaganda that the entire DC group was brainwashed into believing anyone who wasn't with them was a terrorist who had caused the fall of America.

"We're better than this," Mick said.

"Maybe you are," Jem said, and added a swift kick to Cunningham's ribs.

Mick knew Jem's pain. This wasn't about the torture. It was about the woman he had loved, whom he had lost because of the president's men, just like Grace had become the target of Mick's pain when he lost Lucas.

"You're better than this," Mick said.

"I won't help you remove the tracker," Cunningham said.

"Bitch, will you shut up?" Mick snapped. Maybe he wasn't that good of a person after all, he thought, but he wasn't going to let Jem kill her.

"We should just let her go and hope she decides we were nice enough to leave us alone? Oh wait, you hit her with a car. We leave her here, she is as good as dead anyway," Jem said, yanking his hand free of Mick.

"We bring her with us," Mick said.

The words sounded much crazier aloud than they had in his head.

Jem scratched his forehead with the knuckles. "Is this some kind of inside plan we made up that I'm not remembering? You lull her into a feeling of safety, and then we kill her?"

"She's got months until she's fully healed. We patch her up, show her we aren't the bad guys, and then see what she does," Mick said.

"What she will do is go back to DC and bring the full force of the president to our doorstep," Jem said.

"I will," she confirmed.

"She won't. Let's take her with us for now, and get moving before they're after us again. When Kade is functional, we can discuss it with him. Not like you can't kill her later," Mick said.

"Better kill me now. You'll regret it if you don't," she said.

Jem looked from Mick to Cunningham, then back. Mick thought Jem finally saw her the way he did: with pity. He slid the knuckles off of his hand and gave them to Mick.

"I'll get the duct tape," Jem said.

"I'll get Yuzuki to do that. I need one more favor from you," Mick said.

"You really are pushing it today," Jem said.

"We need to cut the tracker out."

Cunningham let out a shrill laugh. "Good luck."

"Would you just shut up," Mick said.

Jem gave him a nod. "I'll go find a knife."

Mick called to Yuzuki to get the tape and then traded places with her. Yuzuki seemed just as mad at Mick as Jem was, but if Mick didn't hold on to who he was, there wasn't a point in going on.

Kade gradually became more coherent as minutes passed. He would need to rest for a few weeks. Mick scoffed at the thought—like he could ever get Kade to rest for a day, let alone weeks.

By the time Jem came back, Yuzuki had used almost all of the tape on Cunningham, who was bound so many different ways Houdini couldn't have escaped. Jem didn't just return with a knife, but also with weapons and gear from the soldiers. He explained that he didn't want to let it go to waste.

Mick took his shirt off and placed his hands on the hood of the car as he was used to making people do when he arrested them. Jem stood behind him, wiping down the blade of a combat knife with an alcohol swab. Yuzuki had moved Cunningham closer to Kade so she could watch both of them at the same time.

"I'm not a surgeon, but if I was I would tell you I couldn't operate on this," Jem said.

Mick couldn't see his own back, and with the number of wounds and bruises he didn't know where the tracker was.

"Why not?" Mick asked.

"I think it's under your spine," Jem said.

Just above Mick's tailbone were two incisions, one on either side, each about an inch long. The cuts oozed yellow pus.

"I can't go home unless you cut it out," Mick replied.

Mick felt the tip of the knife push against the stitches. He didn't know if it was blood or pus, but something warm soaked into his pants. Pain seared up his back, and his body shot forward, as if trying to run away.

"Mick, hold still. I don't want to stab you," Jem said. Mick thought that he might like to stab Jem at the moment.

Yuzuki took the knife from Jem and disappeared into the Jeep for a moment. She came back with a strip of seatbelt, which she folded and held for Mick to bite. Mick bit down and put his forehead on the hood.

Jem must have gotten the knife back because the pain resumed.

Mick tried to take his mind somewhere else, but he still couldn't find a memory to hide in. There was so little in his life that didn't have some tarnish on it. The hood felt like it would crumple under his hands, he was pushing so hard.

There was a strong pull, followed by a quick slide where the tip of the knife reentered the wound. One after the other Jem worked through the stitches. By the time Jem finished with the stitches, Mick was screaming his throat raw, even with the belt between his teeth. The pain was only just beginning.

Jem had to part the swollen incisions to look for the device. The entire procedure was accompanied by Jem's apologies and Cunningham's cackling—at least until Yuzuki taped her mouth shut.

Finally, the pain subsided.

"I think I've found it. I don't really know what else to do besides use the knife to get it out," Jem said.

Mick spit the saliva-soaked belt onto the hood. "Get it over with."

"I just wanted to say sorry if I paralyze you or something," Jem said.

"Do it," Mick said, and once again bit down on the belt.

He felt Jem peel an incision open, then two fingers push inside his body. The knife fished around until the blade trapped something solid. Then there was a quick yank as the object slipped out of his body. A blinding pain rose through him, and he collapsed to the ground.

John's bow lay across his bed, along with three other compound bows. Fenris had found her way into the room at some point, but since she was content to lie and watch him work, he let her stay.

The good news was the cams and strings had survived the blow without damage. The bad news was his whisker biscuit—the part that guided the arrow—as well as his sight and stabilizer had been snapped, shattered, and otherwise removed. The fixes were simple. All he had to do was remove a few pieces of hardware with pliers.

The issue was with the pieces themselves. None of the other bows had identical parts on them, and though they would fit his bow, they wouldn't fit in the same way. For the last few months this bow had become an extension of himself. He put the new whisker biscuit into place, and compared to the black ones he was used to, the brown whiskers of the new piece stood out as if they were hot pink. The new sight had an extra pin, which would allow John to sight it at farther distances, but it still felt strange to get away from what was comfortable.

When he finished screwing the stabilizer into place, a knock came from behind. Grace stood in the doorway.

"Mind if I come in?"

John waved her in and cleared the bows off the bed so she could sit.

"I just wanted to see if you were okay. I know you were pretty beat up last time you killed someone." Grace took a seat on the bed.

John stood and paced while Fenris tracked his movements with her eyes. "I feel okay, but I feel different."

"Please, don't shut me out," Grace said.

John stopped pacing and leaned against the dresser. "I didn't even think about the fact that I was going to kill that last man. He was dead before I knew what I was doing. That scares the shit out of me. I know I'm changing, but I want to be in control of myself."

Grace got up and closed the distance between them. His hands began to sweat as she drew closer. He became fully embarrassed as she took his now sweaty hands in hers.

"You'll always be a good guy. At heart you're always going to be a goofy kid who trips over himself," Grace said.

"I don't always—sometimes—usually—trip over my feet," John said.

"I'm not just talking about your feet." Grace pulled herself up to his height and gave him a peck on the cheek. "Are you done fixing your bow?"

John couldn't find words, so he nodded.

"I have a project I could use some help with. I want to get it done today, if you'll lend me a hand," Grace said.

"Sure!" he squeaked.

"Get cleaned up and meet me in my room." Grace released his hands and stepped back into the hallway.

John picked up the bows he had used for parts and headed for the armory. Grace didn't seem mad at him about Emma, which John fully expected. Then again, maybe she was just hiding her anger from him. Perhaps even the job she wanted help with was just a cover to hurt him—or kill him.

He wrangled in his imagination and came to the conclusion that she wouldn't kill him. Hurt him, maybe. But she wouldn't kill him. Maybe she could forgive him eventually, but then he'd have to think about Emma. Emma had said she only wanted to be friends. She could have been lying. Then he'd have his hands full.

His head hurt.

He put the bows in the closet of the armory and tried to clear his mind before he went to see Grace.

The walkie on his belt rang, followed by Victoria's voice: "*Everyone available to Meredith.*"

Grace would have to wait. John ran down the corridor to the living floor.

When he arrived, Victoria and Wright were still there, as well as X and Emma.

"Sorry, guys. Dr. Wright said everyone should be present when she wakes up to see what she has to say," Victoria said.

"And as you can all see, the guilty doctor is not here. Probably planning to make a run for it," Wright said, putting his fingers into his vest pockets.

Meredith was still unconscious, but she was showing signs of waking. Her breathing was becoming regular.

"He isn't planning to run," Victoria said, glaring at the psychiatrist.

"Human behavior is my specialty," he said.

X tipped his hat. "And last I checked none of you are in charge, so I'm going back to the medbay."

X disappeared through the door at the same time Grace came running in, out of breath.

"What's going on?" Grace said, huffing and puffing.

"We're waiting for Meredith to wake up and pronounce Damian guilty," Wright said.

Grace crossed her arms over her chest. "That's what interrupted my—project?"

Victoria tapped her foot on the floor. "I know. Blame the quack. Highest probability even if she wakes up is that she'll be a foamer."

John realized that he didn't have any of his weapons on him. He wasn't sure if a foamer version of Meredith would fall into Kade's no-kill policy or not, but he'd rather be able to defend himself.

"And if she does, then the doctor is the most likely suspect and should be tried all the same," Wright said.

Meredith's breathing picked up its pace.

"He should be here for this. I'm going to get him," Wright said, rushing to Meredith's bedside and putting a hand on her forehead.

John looked at the scarred girl. Her face was scrunched up in a terrified contortion, like she was standing in front of the boogeyman. No kid deserved to go through something so terrifying. He just hoped her brain didn't know the war it was waging. She would either die, submit and become a foamer, or live to see another day.

"I'll go with you," John said.

Grace put a hand on John's chest. "John, you know he didn't do it."

"I don't know Damian," John replied.

He wanted to believe Grace, but he had no evidence to support her case. Damian was in fact the man that had invented the Feline Flu vaccine and created the Primal Age. There was nothing to say the man wasn't capable of experimenting on the cohort.

"The easiest answer is usually the right one," Emma said.

Grace turned away from John and glared at Emma. The two women stood poised like cats ready to pounce on each other.

"John, I need a friendly person here. I'll take Emma with me," Wright said.

Wright left the room with Emma just behind him, but she didn't leave without shooting one final glare at Grace.

"I see Kade has done a splendid job making one big happy family out of you," Victoria said tightly.

They had been tight-knit, but all it took was a few outsiders to tear a rift in their foundation. That probably meant they weren't as strong as he had thought.

Meredith's eyes opened wide, then snapped shut, as her body rolled to the side and her breathing stopped. Victoria dropped to her side.

John couldn't help but feel sorry for the poor girl.

All of a sudden, Meredith's chest lurched and she began breathing again. She had a slow but steady breath as her eyes opened to slits.

"Hey, honey. Can you hear me?" Victoria asked, running a hand mechanically over the girl's hair.

"Can't we give her a chance to wake up first?" John protested, but was silenced by a snakelike look from Victoria.

"I feel funny," Meredith replied.

John was shocked and thrilled. She wasn't dead or a foamer. The little girl had beat the odds.

"You were a little sick, but you're better now. Can you tell me what you remember last?" Victoria asked.

"It's a secret."

Victoria took the girl's hand. "Honey, it is important to help you get better."

Meredith looked around the room like she was searching for someone, then settled back on Victoria. "The doctor examined me."

John clenched his fists so tight he thought he might break his own hands, but he couldn't imagine what type of monster would give a little girl a secret examination before sending her to her death.

"He examined you?"

"A physical. And then he gave me a shot to keep me healthy," Meredith said, her eyes blinking closed again.

"This is all the evidence we need. I'm sorry, but this condemns Damian. We can hold him until Kade gets back, but we need to remove him from the lead position," John said.

"And if Kade doesn't come back, are you going to be the executioner? And who would you suggest takes the lead?" Grace said, squaring up to John.

"If I have to, I will. And I think we should put the leader to a vote, but Dr. Wright has a lot of years and experience to bring to the table."

Victoria cleared her throat, getting both of them to stand down.

"Dear, which doctor gave you a shot?" Victoria said, her voice ringing with fake sincerity.

A sleepy yawn stretched across Meredith's face. "Dr. Wright."

Chapter XII

Hitting Bottom

After the surgery, as much as they had wanted to cleanse the scene of the fight and leave a false trail, they had to get on the road. With only two fully functional people left in the group, they didn't have the manpower to do anything but run.

Kade was more awake now, but his head pounded so loudly he had trouble even joining a conversation. From what he had been able to hear, they'd brought the torturer with them—she was sitting behind him, but was taped silent. Yuzuki was in the seat guarding her, and Mick was laid out across the floor.

Jem had been trying to explain the situation to Kade, but he was only catching about every third word and spent the rest of the time fighting not to puke. Kade put together that Jem wanted to kill Cunningham, but Mick had stopped him. Also, Mick wanted to bring her back to Houghton to try to change her ways.

If someone asked him his name right now, he wouldn't have known the answer. The idea of deciding if someone should live or die seemed like something he shouldn't be contemplating. The best answer he was able to give Jem was if it was keep or kill, it could wait until they got back to decide.

Which wasn't far off now. Between his long blinks Kade could see the stadium lights in the distance. They were finally home. By the time he blinked again, they were sitting at the bridge across from campus with just two cars separating him from Tiny.

* * *

John couldn't believe how wrong he had been as he ran across the grass to the science building. After Meredith had spoken, John took off. He was going to get to Wright first. The man had played him for a fool. John hadn't even felt his strings being pulled.

He plowed through the front door of the science center and took the stairs two at a time. Besides being manipulated, Wright had molested and attempted to kill Meredith. Though he didn't have the evidence yet, John could only assume Wright was responsible for Scott as well.

John reached the third floor and slowed as he went through the door. He didn't want to give Wright any warning he was coming. John put his shoulder against the solid classroom door, which had once held off an entire pack of foamers, and inched it open.

The lab looked like a tornado had hit it. The room was covered with papers, broken glass, and strewn microscopes. Emma's body lay like a rag doll just inside the door, and in the center of the room Wright stood over Damian with a pistol in hand. Judging by the bloodied condition of Damian's face, Wright had pistol-whipped him more than a few times.

At the same instant John drew attention to his presence, he realized he had left without his weapon.

"John, I came to tell him what was going on, and he freaked out. He knocked out Emma, and then attacked me. I was lucky I was able to disarm him. Did she turn? Is she—is she a foamer?" Wright asked.

John fully understood Wright's plan now. He had expected her to either turn or die, leaving the evidence to fall on Damian. Wright had cast enough strife to divide the group. This would give him the chance to take control of the campus. John realized how stupid he had been to let the man manipulate him so easily. Maybe he wasn't as strong a person as Kade believed he was. John cursed himself for being so stupid. But this time, he would pull the strings.

He put on his best sad face. "She turned."

Damian used the diversion to get to his feet, but kept his hands up. John bent down and checked Emma's pulse and was glad she was still alive. There was a small spot of blood on the back of her head, but she would be okay.

"They have her contained. We still need to try Damian. We aren't barbarians." John moved toward the center of the room.

The pistol swung away from Damian and focused on John, who stopped with his hands up.

"You're a terrible liar," Wright said.

John took a deep breath to compose himself. This was not the position in which he wanted to be. Wright was trapped in a corner now, and the only way he could get clear would be to go through everything in his path.

"Look. We don't want you dead. There are enough dead. We just want you to leave," John said.

"A man without a country is no man at all." Wright's finger twitched on the trigger.

Someone slammed into John, knocking him to the floor. He tripped over his feet and fell to his back. Grace lay on the ground where he had been, her double-barreled shotgun still in hand.

Wright fired, and the bullet smashed harmlessly into the cinder block wall. Before he could get off another shot, Damian threw himself on the man, trying to wrestle the pistol free.

Damian's hand curled around the pistol. Wright pulled the trigger. There was an explosion of blood as the bullet tore through Damian's finger. He screamed as Wright knocked him away, but Damian refused to let go of the pistol and carried it with him to the floor.

Grace got to her feet and attempted to bring her shotgun up, but Wright was already upon her. He knocked the shotgun away and slid behind Grace.

John was on his feet preparing to charge when he froze. Clutched in Wright's hand was a vaccine. The needle was in Grace's neck. All he had to do was push.

Bile burned in John's throat. This man was threatening the woman he loved. His eyes darted to the shotgun, but there was no way he could get there before Wright finished the job. He was in a place he feared, a place where words were his best chance.

"Good doctor, please drop the pistol," Wright said.

Damian, who was now missing the better part of his left ring finger and bleeding like an exploded ketchup bottle, set the pistol on the ground and focused on tying off his finger.

"It isn't too late to stop this," John said.

"It *is* too late. It's too late for my family who had no choice in the vaccine. How is it fair that this family, this family that caused it, gets to walk away free and clear?" Wright said.

"Whatever happens, make sure he dies," Grace said and slammed her heel back into Wright's groin.

As her foot struck, he injected the vaccine. Crouched over, he ran for the door. Grace held a hand over her neck where the needle had punctured her skin. Her mouth hung wide open. John rushed over to her side.

"Are you okay?" was all he could think to ask.

"Don't let him get away," Grace said.

She picked up her shotgun and handed it to John as she went to help Damian stop his bleeding. Through the hall and down the stairs John sprinted. He burst into the daylight, trying to track his quarry.

Wright couldn't be that far ahead of him, and there was nowhere nearby to hide. The man always wore dress shoes, so it wasn't like he was about to turn into an Olympic sprinter.

Then John caught sight of him making a direct line down the main road that looped the campus. John took up chase, feeling like he would close the distance before long. The wall of cars came around the bend, and John stepped up his pace, not wanting to take their scramble into foamer territory.

Then Wright cleared the gap in the cars. John put everything he had left into closing the twenty yards between them. The soles of his shoes hardly touched the pavement as he flew toward Wright. He came through the pass and searched for Wright, but his legs flew out from under him and he skidded down the road, losing his grip on the shotgun.

Wright had ducked behind the cars to lie in wait, and where he had apparently stashed a go-bag. John scrambled for the shotgun, amazed at how well Wright had laid out his plans. Before John could reach the shotgun, Wright was able to pull a pistol from his bag. His hands were shaking badly and he missed his shot, but it was close enough that John threw himself flat in the road.

Wright's attention was drawn for a moment by what sounded like a metal drum. A roar came from on top of the wall of cars as a blue-faced monster launched itself at Wright. Kade, wearing his blue ballistic mask, crashed shoulder-first into Wright, who stumbled across the road before falling into the grass and dropping his pistol. Kade beat his chest and charged Wright.

By the time John got to his feet and recovered the shotgun, Kade had Wright hauled up by the shoulders and slammed him headfirst off a car door. Wright reached for his pistol, but Kade drew his katana and placed the tip in Wright's path.

Kade kicked Wright over, then grabbed him by the collar of his dress shirt and pinned him against the car.

Wright opened his mouth to speak, but Kade drew a Judge and pushed the barrel into the psychiatrist's mouth. Wright tried to talk around the barrel. In response, Kade cocked the hammer.

"You okay?" Kade asked John from behind the mask.

John shook his head. "He vaccinated Grace."

There was a quick flick of the whites of Kade's eyes before he pulled the gun out of Wright's mouth. Wright's body relaxed as he leaned back against the car.

A smile crossed Wright's face. "All your chambers are empty."

"If you have anything to say, now would be the time," Kade said.

John picked up the pistol from the ground and moved in, shoulder to shoulder with Kade. "He doesn't deserve a trial. Let me put this monster down."

Kade holstered his empty Judge and put a hand on John's chest to keep him back. "You're not a murderer, kid."

"That's right, John," Wright said. "You're just a very malleable young man. I knew that pinning Scott's death on the foamers would have to shake someone's foundations, but I didn't expect you to be the one."

"This was all to get control?" Kade asked.

"Not at all. But all you little warlords are so concerned with your position that you are blinded to everything else. My children were fed on by my wife." Wright locked his jaw and clenched his eyes shut. "Monsters."

"Everyone's suffered loses," John said, fighting his urge to put a bullet in the man.

Wright shook his head. "Not this little happy family here. They haven't suffered enough. I started with Scott, then Meredith. I was just going to vaccinate them, but I figured why not enjoy them a bit before I killed them? I figured by the time I got through Franklin you'd be tearing each other limb from limb."

"We're stronger than that," John said.

"Are you? That animal who created the vaccine in the first place would have been put down if Meredith hadn't woke up. How much longer would it have taken for the fissures in your faith to break?"

John raised the gun and took aim, but Kade grabbed the pistol and pulled it from his hand before he knew what was happening. Kade tucked the pistol into his pants and held up a hand for John to wait.

"Sit, boy," Wright said. "And you should be thanking me. I've given you an easier choice—unless you're into foamers."

John rushed forward and slammed Wright against the car. He smashed an elbow across Wright's face before Kade wrapped and arm around him and pulled him back. John dug in and kept fighting his way toward Wright, whom he could have beaten to death. Wright dashed forward and grabbed the pistol from Kade's pants.

Kade shoved John away, then spun in a circle, bringing the katana around and cleaving clean through Wright's neck. A spray of blood splattered the cars. Wright's body dropped to its knees before the head fell away and the two pieces of the man landed on the ground.

John could hear nothing but his own heart beating. Kade stumbled, then dropped to the ground, his katana settling beside him. John rushed to his side and noticed how badly injured Kade was—most of his body was covered in cuts.

"I'm all right, kid," Kade said, putting John at ease.

John moved over to the body. He had one question that needed answering.

"Leave him for the foamers. He doesn't deserve a burial," Kade said, tipping his mask back.

Undoing the buttons on Wright's vest, he found what he was looking for. The internal pockets of the vest were lined with vaccines, which were cool to the touch. Wright had to have more stashed somewhere. John removed the vest, hoping the vaccines would somehow be able to help Damian save Grace.

The damage was almost too much for Kade to fathom. They had to expand the medbay. Tiny, though still sore, was now up and moving to help Number Five treat the wounded. Scott, Drew, Zack, and Wright were dead. Meredith had barely survived her bout with the vaccine. Grace was going to enter her coma at any point. Mick was still laid up from their makeshift surgery. Jem's psyche seemed damaged. Ashton had broken her arm, and X wasn't leaving her side. Damian had lost his left ring finger, but showed his Zerris side by rushing to research the vaccine to try to save Grace the moment they cauterized his finger. Emma had been knocked out cold, but was coming around. Yuzuki was being rested and hydrated to recover from her months in captivity. Cunningham was locked up in one of the rooms, waiting for Kade's verdict. Kade himself was one big piece of tenderized meat.

Franklin and John seemed to be the only two to have weathered the latest round of misfortune without a scratch. Had X not been on his way to meet Kade's Jeep on the bridge when everything went down, Kade doubted John would be counted among the living.

He hadn't even gotten a chance to talk to Tiny since she was so busy tending to everyone, and Kade's road rash was not a top priority. She didn't even ask him about Zack, which made him believe she already assumed the worst.

The only people not occupied by the medbay were Jem, Yuzuki, Franklin, and Meredith, who were all playing Monopoly in Jem's room. Damian and Victoria were buried in research; Grace and John were simply waiting. Kade wanted to get a chance to say goodbye to Grace, in case she didn't make it through her coma.

When he came to John's room he knocked on the door, and Grace's voice told him to come in. John was sitting against the head of the bed with Grace lying back between his legs, resting her head on his chest.

Kade tipped his chin in greeting to John, then said, "Grace, I'm sorry for ever bringing them here. You've been—"

"Stop it now," Grace commanded. "I'm not saying goodbye to anyone. Either Damian is going to pull out a miracle, or I am going to beat this. If a little girl can do it, so can I. I will see you tomorrow, big brother."

Kade had so much he wanted to tell her—how grateful he was for everything she had done for the group. They would never have made it this long if it wasn't for her. But if she didn't want goodbyes, he wouldn't make her face them.

"Get some rest, little sister," Kade said.

His eyes locked with John's and he could see the terror in the teen, but he was impressed by how little emotion he was showing. He wished there was a way he could lend him some strength.

Kade left the two and set off through the dorm. He ran his hands along the walls to remember how they felt. It seemed like an eon since he'd last walked the dorm halls. The last thing he wanted at the moment was to be alone—there was too much to process, and even more to worry about.

"Was it worth it?" Jem said from behind him.

Kade turned and faced his old friend. Jem's eyes were beet red, and he looked like he had aged a decade. "Where are the kids?"

"I lost already. Was it worth it? Scott. Drew. Zack. Grace. All of them would still be alive if you hadn't come for us. Four lives. Four innocent lives that had nothing to do with any of this, and they paid the price so Mick and I could live—Mick and I who knowingly put ourselves into that position and explicitly told you to leave us in it." Jem closed the distance to Kade.

They were nearly forehead to forehead when Kade spoke. His voice was low, and he kept his eyes down. "If I knew what the outcome would be, I'd have left you two."

With his hands Jem mimed his head exploding. "What did you expect to happen? You walked into a military compound. You accepted an enemy's prisoners in exchange for help. I don't see the world where you thought this could have ended well."

"After a couple months of everything falling my way, I felt like Superman, all right? I thought for a moment it would be okay. I figured our transfers would be happy for a new home. I hoped we could just pop in and save you."

Jem shoved Kade hard, knocking him back a few steps. "My kids' caretaker is dead. Scott is dead. Meredith is . . ." His voice lowered. ". . . scared. I'd have told Drew to have you come get us if I thought it would be safe."

Kade regained his footing and held his arms out at his sides. "Swing if you want. I know I can't make this right."

"No. You can't. Argos, Scott, Drew, Meredith. You can't make any of that right. I've been trying to think of somewhere to go with Franklin and Meredith that would be safer for them, but for now this will have to do."

Jem pulled back to swing. Kade titled his head to absorb the incoming blow.

"James!" a small voice yelled.

Jem tucked his swing, avoiding Kade. His momentum spun him in a full circle. The two grown men stared down at Franklin, who was adjusting his new pair of thick-rimmed glasses.

"Bad things happen. Coach Drew used to always tell me before a swim meet that he'd never be mad as long as I did my best. Mr. Kade, did you do your best?"

"It doesn't look that way," Kade responded.

"Did you do your best?"

Kade gave the kid a single nod. The outcome was horrendous, but Kade did believe he'd given his best. He might have failed in his assessment of the risks, but he had given it his best.

"James, apologize to your friend," Franklin ordered.

Jem faced Kade and had the look of a dog with his tail between his legs. Kade felt the same way after being corrected by the child. They embraced in a quick hug, punctuated by a clap on the back. Kade could feel that wasn't the end of it, but it was a beginning of forgiveness.

"Can we go visit Miss Ashton, please?" Franklin said.

Jem took the kid's hand and started down the hallway, but stopped before he passed Kade.

"Thanks for bringing me back, by the way," Jem said.

Kade let Jem and Franklin continue on without saying a word. Despite how much Kade hated himself for his recent failures, he understood much of Jem's pain. Other people had given their lives for his—that was a burden that was hard for anyone to bear. It was harder to be a survivor than a casualty. As with all wounds, it would eventually scar over. His cohort would carry a lot of scars after this past week.

John and Grace had talked the entire time leading up to her coma like it wasn't about to happen. They talked about memories: the first Christmas of the Primal Age, when Grace had asked him who he thought would have won the Super Bowl, and he said the Yankees, she laughed at him.

Now she was asleep in his bed with her head resting on his chest.

He could hardly blink, let alone sleep. He would have been happy to finally have her with him if the reason for her being there were different. In every way John had tried to rationalize that the vaccine wasn't truly the Feline Flu vaccine, Damian had dashed his hopes.

Grace had made it most of the way into the night before the coma took hold, and now daylight had passed by and the moon was preparing for another round.

Around midnight, before she had succumbed, she had said, "I don't want you to take this as a goodbye, but I'm sorry I tested you so long. If I had a mulligan I'd have kissed you that first night on the roof."

John had leaned in and given her a kiss on the cheek. Testing her patience, he had taken another kiss, moving closer to her lips. Then he planted the third right on her lips. She had kissed him back, and he stayed with her lips to his as long as he could.

"We all slip up sometimes. We'll just start now," John had said.

A tear ran down his cheek as he tightened his arms around her. It was becoming harder and harder to feel her gentle breaths. He checked her pulse frequently because Damian had told him if she was heading for death it would slow; if she was going to make it out it would spike but then fall to a resting rate; if it spiked and didn't come back down she would turn. Her pulse had stayed steady through the day, giving him no indication of what would come.

Just before the coma had pulled her into its dark depths, she had said one last thing to John. He hadn't been sure if she meant to say it or not, since she wasn't responsive to anything he was saying at that point, but her last words had been, "I'm not ready to die."

Though the words had come out weakly, he hoped it had been her battle cry before plunging into unconsciousness. He kept telling himself she had the advantage of knowing what she was up against. Maybe there would be some way, somehow, like lucid dreaming, that she could control her path through to the other side.

Grace was tough—tougher than anyone. If any of them could make it through this, it would be her.

As night fell, her pulse spiked. He knew this had to happen sooner or later. He checked her pulse every ten minutes, and always found it remained elevated. Her breathing increased, and sweat ran down her brow in a steady stream. John held on tight, hoping that he could lend her some strength, that somehow his contact would see her through.

Another hour passed before anything else changed. Her eyes opened into the tiniest of slits. John's hope rose that she was coming out of the coma.

In a lightning-fast roll Grace was awake and on top of John. Her bloodshot eyes bore into him as her lips curled back.

She had made it through, but she was no longer Grace.

Red foam bubbled at the corners of her lips.

He couldn't believe this monster staring down at him was Grace just a few hours ago. The foamer hauled back and smashed a balled hand across John's face, then dove in for the kill. Her teeth bared as she attempted to chomp down on John's neck, but he got an arm under her chest to keep her at bay.

It was a foamer. It wasn't Grace. He knew he had to defend himself, but he couldn't bring himself to hurt her.

The bloodlike foam dripped onto John's face as the foamer pressed in toward John's neck. Her teeth snapped shut less than an inch from his face.

"Help," John called out.

The door flung open and Kade rushed in. He wrapped Grace up in a full nelson and took her to the floor. Damian was a step behind and injected her with something.

"You've done it! You created something to save foamers?" John cried out in joy.

Damian shook his head. "It's just a sedative."

John was on his feet. Tears ran down his face. His chest felt like it would explode. "I won't let you experiment on her."

"He's not. I'm going to take her to Alpha. We can't keep her in captivity but with Alpha she'll have a chance, and when Damian does find a cure she'll be the first one we change," Kade said as Grace's body went limp in his arms.

Dressed in her overalls, sandy-blonde hair spread out in a sweaty mess, she looked just like the dirt-covered grease monkey John had come to love.

"John, we have to move quick if we are going to get her to the ground before the sedative wears off. If you have anything you want to say to Grace, now's the time," Kade said, picking her limp body up in his arms like a groom carrying his bride across the threshold.

"I'll find a way back to you, Grace," John said as he collapsed onto the bed. He curled himself into the fetal position, and though he tried to wait until the Zerris brothers had left the room, he couldn't stop himself. He wept.

Kade drove the pickup through the slalom of parked vehicles as fast as he could, with Grace still unconscious in the passenger seat. He had donned his traditional gear of ballistic mask, katana, and Judges because he wanted to make sure Alpha would recognize him. One of the characteristics he hadn't been able to figure out about foamers was if they had a heightened sense of smell or if they were still fully human in that area.

Shooting a glance at Grace to make sure she was still out, he wondered how he could even get her under Alpha's protection. Unlike the first generation of foamers, she hadn't had the months to grow claws. He'd rather put her down himself than turn her over to be eaten.

The truck came to a stop along the tree line, and Kade hopped out. He took Grace into his arms and struggled to carry her into the area of woods where Alpha's pack roamed. Kade's body ached and itched from all the scrapes and wounds. Each step took its toll on him. With Grace so childlike in his arms, he had no choice but to continue on.

"I know you didn't want to say goodbyes, and this isn't goodbye. I'm going to find a way to bring you back." The corners of her mouth had taken on the red stain, making her look like a sleeping vampire.

"A million times out of a million, I'd choose to keep you. None of us would be here if it wasn't for you."

Her breath picked up, and Kade hoped he could find Alpha soon. The idea of wrestling with the foamer version of Grace didn't appeal to him. A growl came from behind him as a pair of arms wrapped around his legs. The impact knocked him to his knees and sent shivers of pain through this body. He rolled into his fall and gently placed Grace on the ground. He swiveled around, landing a fist into the foamer's face before it could sink its teeth into his legs.

Breaking away from the foamer, he set himself like a linebacker over Grace. He hadn't paid enough attention when his focus was on her—a pack of foamers had surrounded him among the trees. Most he recognized from Alpha's pack, but there were a few he hadn't seen, or perhaps noticed, before.

He spun in quick movements, trying to avoid exposing his flank, but with eight of them circling him it was only a matter of time before they struck. If he was lucky, whichever was the highest-ranking foamer would strike alone, claiming Kade's carcass for himself. In that situation Kade could just lay enough of a beating on the foamer to drive the others off. Lives would be lost if they all came at once. It would be the same as being dropped into a tank of piranhas.

Continuing his rotation, he kept his eyes focused on the closing group. The one place he wasn't looking was down. Teeth clamped on the bicep of his left arm. As Grace's teeth sank into his muscle, his support arm collapsed him on top of her.

The attack triggered the pacing foamers to charge on all fours, whopping and growling as they closed in. Kade had a clear line to land a knuckled fist into Grace's face, but he couldn't bring himself to harm her.

He wrapped his arm around her head and tucked it to his chest. Her teeth were still imbedded in his skin, but she couldn't get enough leverage to bite any harder. Kade rolled them both to the side and whipped his legs like an alligator's tail, knocking a foamer back. The first foamer to lay claws on him tore at his right arm as it struggled to get to his throat. Kade brought the creature closer and head-butted it with the ballistic mask, then slammed his elbow into its nose. The foamer howled in pain and retreated.

The next came straight at his head. Kade took the clawed hands to his protected face, then ducked forward and snapped his knee back into the creature before delivering a follow-up with the back of his skull.

Grace released her teeth from his arm, and a muffled scream roared from her trapped mouth. One of the foamers had gone for her legs without Kade noticing. With no other way to reach the threat, Kade barrel-rolled their bodies over the attacker, finishing with his knee on the creature's back.

Now in an upright position, with Grace still pressed tightly to his chest, there was no way he could defend himself hand to hand. Changing the game, he drew his katana and swung it in a wide arc around him. Striking out, he would just try to nip the foamers to cause enough pain for them to leave.

Slashing left, right, down, back, forward, the foamers kept coming at him. They took slow, deliberate steps while they circled just beyond his reach. Their eyes stayed locked on his flashing blade from under their overgrown hair. The only thing Kade had going for him was that Grace seemed disinterested in eating any more of his arm.

Branches and twigs snapped, a sign that something was charging the area. Without paying too much attention to the sound, so as not to create an opening for his attackers, he scanned the area quickly. The big hoss, Alpha, was barreling right for him. The gigantic creature that had been a monster of a man as an MMA fighter in the Old World was gaining speed. He looked like a demon right out of hell with his matted red hair and fight-scarred face.

Kade prepared to strike as Alpha closed in. The beast plowed shoulder-first through the pack of foamers, then skidded right past Kade, clearing a hole out the other side. Spinning to face the attacking pack, Alpha reared back and let out a holler while beating his chest.

Slamming his tree trunk–sized arms fist-first an inch into the ground he growled over his pack, and every foamer went down low, keeping their eyes to the ground and backing away from Kade and Grace.

Kade sheathed his katana, released Grace, and dropped to the ground in the same low bow as the foamers. Grace mimicked his pose beside him. The deep nasal breaths of Alpha let Kade know he was getting closer. Kade wondered if he could get to one of his Judges in time if this went south, but wasn't even sure if the pistol had enough punch to drop a creature the size of Alpha.

Alpha sniffed at the back of Kade's head, then slid over to inspect Grace. After a few sniffs he dropped his forehead to touch hers. She lifted her head and rose on all fours, but stayed where she was. Alpha moved back to Kade and let a low snarl reverberate from deep inside him.

Slowly, Kade pushed himself up to a height where he could see Alpha. He locked eyes with the monster that had its lip curled back. The moment he held Alpha's threatening gaze, the creature relaxed, and the hostility left his pose.

Waving a hand toward Grace, Kade patted his heart twice with an open palm. Alpha looked from Grace to Kade, then mimicked his motion. Kade nodded at Alpha, who tossed his head over his shoulder with a snuff.

Taking his cue to leave, Kade rose on two feet and walked past Alpha. He took one last look back at the Grace's blonde hair, calloused hands, and skin layered in perpetual dirt.

"Until next time, Grace," he said as he continued for the road. None of the foamers followed him.

When he returned to the truck, he sat in the passenger seat for a long time, unable to do anything. He was too overwhelmed to even know how to feel.

John sat on the roof by himself. With the depletion of healthy ranks, guard duty was now held by one person alone. This didn't bother him since he just wanted to be alone anyway. Grace wasn't dead, but she was gone. He felt like a person who'd just found out for the first time the world wasn't flat—only it was the exact opposite, since his world was closing in, not expanding.

He had done all the crying he could do. There wasn't a tear left he could shed unless he hydrated. Everything he wanted was gone.

In his fingers he twirled a solution. Each second that passed was a chance that he would lose Grace forever. Out there amongst the foamers, she had no guarantee of life. He stopped twirling the tube and looked at the vaccine in his hand.

If he injected himself, the odds were in his favor that he would turn into a foamer as well. Then he and Grace could live happily ever after. At least he could be with her in some way.

But he feared that as a foamer neither would have a recollection of the other. They had found, on too many occasions, people eaten by their own family members. If he couldn't remember her, the transformation would not be worth it.

The vaccine pinged off the rooftop, and John crushed it like a cigarette under his boot. There was one solution that had only one outcome. John went to the edge of the roof, listening to the dark whispers of the night. He placed his hands on the balustrade and climbed onto the ledge. The north point was the most beautiful view they had. It looked away from campus, over the creek and through a small patch of woods. On the other side of the trees was the prep school that John had been attending when Kade's group found him, where this had all begun. It seemed a fitting place for the end.

He closed his eyes and listened to the sounds of the creek, the soft caress of the wind, and the few animals that made the night their home. Gathering a deep breath in his lungs, he cleared his mind. On the empty slate he placed the only thing he wanted: his mental image of Grace. How she looked lying on the roof the first time they ever guarded together, when the moon made her hair look like a halo. Like an angel.

The door to the roof opened. John didn't open his eyes or turn around.

"Go back inside. Don't try to stop me," John said.

"If you are going to jump, hurry up. You're hogging the good corner," Kade said.

This caused John to open his eyes and stare at Kade. He thought Kade of all people would be the one to stop him. Kade crossed the roof and hopped up on the ledge with such agility it appeared the six-floor drop didn't faze him at all.

"What are you doing?" John asked.

Kade put his arms out and his head back as if he was about to swan dive. "Contemplating jumping."

"Stop screwing with me."

"Kid, do you have any idea how many times I have stood on this ledge and thought about how much easier learning to fly would be than actually going on living? And guess how many times in the Old World I was on the verge of doing the same?"

John would have liked nothing more than to shove Kade off at that moment. John was hurting. This was serious. Not some joke.

"This is your first."

Kade shot a sideways look at John and laughed. "More times than I am proud to admit. You know what kind of a week I just had. I screwed more pooches than there are breeds of dogs." Kade pointed toward the earth below. "Between kissing the dirt and living with myself, one of those options is far easier."

"Then why haven't you jumped?" John asked.

Kade took a deep breath. "Because it's the easy solution."

"Shouldn't that be more motivation?"

"If you want to take the easy way out, I understand. What no one ever tells you about life is that living comes with a price: pain. I tried to avoid the price for a long time. Then, the more I felt, the more I wanted out. I stand on this ledge and look down; the six floors give me perspective."

"What perspective is that?"

"If there's one thing in this world I can do, it's endure. The price I pay in pain is nothing compared to the moments of joy. I could throw myself off of this roof and never have to pay that price again. Or I could carry the pain of what I let happen to Grace and persevere, endure, to try to find a way to save her." Kade hopped back onto the roof and walked calmly toward the door.

John looked at ground beneath him. He weighed Kade's words. It would be an easy step to just let go. He wasn't as strong as the others. That had been clear from the first day. But he was still here. Still standing. Still breathing. His days of fighting weren't over yet.

John stepped back from the ledge, and when he turned around, Kade held a can of beer out to him. The only time John had tasted beer was when Kade had used it to cleanse his mouth after stuffing a sock in it. The memory almost made him gag.

John took the can from Kade and cracked it open. Kade held his beer up, and John tapped his can against it.

"For those we love. For those we fight for. We endure," Kade said.

"We endure," John repeated as they both took swigs from their cans.

John tried to swallow his mouthful, but the warm liquid tasted almost as bad as Kade's sock, and he spit it off the roof.

"How do you drink that crap?" John asked, wishing he had a sock to get the taste out of his mouth.

Kade took another long swig from his own can. "Endurance."

John took notice for the first time that Kade was bleeding from a number of scratches. "Shouldn't you get patched up?"

Kade smiled and took another swig. "To endurance."

Chapter XIII

Are We Not Invincible?

Kade had spent the night on the roof, and now his entire body felt stiff as a plank of wood. Sleep wasn't something he got much of, but with Tiny in the medbay, he figured it would be the safest place for him to avoid her.

He knew he had to talk to her, but there were two things he wanted to take care of first. When dawn took over the night, he set off to see his brother. Being careful to avoid any chance of being intercepted, he went through the dorm to escape over to the science center.

"You want to do what?" Damian asked him once Kade had entered the lab. Victoria had even stopped going through the papers she was organizing.

Kade looked at his brother's finger. He had lost it at the first knuckle, and the injury looked brutal. The fact that his brother was pushing on so soon made him proud to share the same blood.

"I want to help with the research," Kade said.

"Just to catch you up would take ages. And you have no scientific background at all," Damian said.

Kade clapped Damian on the shoulder and turned toward the door. "Just remember who outscored who on the SATs."

"I was under a lot more stress," Damian shouted after him, but Kade was already down the hallway.

Kade returned to Lambian, where he tracked down Mick, which wasn't too hard since Mick wasn't quite mobile yet. Mick's room, which was usually kept to a military level of cleanliness, was more disorganized than usual. Kade pulled the desk chair beside Mick, who was lying in bed reading over a medical textbook.

"Ready to pass judgment?" Mick asked.

Kade patted his friend on the shoulder. "I'm charging her to you. She's to be kept locked up until I say otherwise. If she becomes a threat to us in any way, I won't hesitate to kill her."

"I'm glad you said that, since I already had the girls patch her up. It would have been a bit mean to treat her just to kill her," Mick said.

"You did that without my permission?"

"Sorry, sir," Mick replied.

"Hell, don't be sorry. I'm proud of you. As far as treating goes, what did they have to say about you?" Kade said.

"I'm fine. Just need some time to recuperate. Did you know everyone already thought I was gay?" Mick asked.

Kade shrugged. "Is that so bad?"

"I just wish I'd have known," Mick replied.

The walkie on Kade's belt chimed, then X's voice followed. "*Kade, we need you on the quad.*"

Kade pulled the walkie off his belt. "What for?"

What sounded like a scuffle came through the receiver, then Ashton said, "*Just get down here.*"

"Do you know what this is about?" Kade asked Mick.

"I'd rather not lie to you," Mick said.

Kade stood up and left Lambian for the second time that morning. He made his way to the center of campus, to the quad. Coming around the corner of the first building, he saw the Little Bird helicopter that had been parked there since Jem had arrived before the winter.

Then he saw two field hockey goals set about half a football field apart. The makeshift field was cornered with soccer flags. The athletic field set between the buildings and beside a helicopter made him wish he had a camera to take a picture of the whole thing. Unless he counted scars, he hadn't collected many memories since setting off into the

Primal Age. Maybe he could place an order with X to find an old Polaroid camera on his next grocery run.

As Kade got closer, he saw that much of the cohort was on the field. X, Jem, Yuzuki, Franklin, Meredith, Emma, and Number Five were running around passing a ball around, while Ashton watched from the sidelines.

Kade walked up beside his sister, trying to make sense of whatever game was being played, but as far as he could tell there were no sanctioned rules—just a group of people running around, laughing and having fun.

"What is this?" Kade asked.

"A surprise. X and I were talking about his grocery runs, and we felt that it might be easier for him to stay put if we had more to do here besides training. He made the point that would be easier to train if we had a sport to play. We wanted to come up with something that everyone would be able to equally suck at, so primal ball was born," Ashton said.

Kade put his arm around his little sister, being careful with her broken arm, and let a smile spread across his face. Hearing the cohort laugh was a joy for which suffering pain was worthwhile

X, catching sight of Kade, came to the sideline. "Surprise."

"Good work," Kade said.

X tipped his hat. "You're good with it?"

"Why wouldn't I be?"

Wiping sweat from his forehead, X said, "Tiny said you'd kill me for proposing to Ashton."

"I didn't tell him yet!" Ashton shouted as she held up her hand to show off the ring.

Kade's smile stayed on his face. He couldn't have been happier for his sister. She'd landed the man of her dreams—even if, in the Old World, he was a thief.

"Same deal applies. You hurt her, I kill you," Kade said.

"I need a best man. You up for the job?" X asked.

X held out his arm, and Kade clasped with him at the elbow. "I'd be honored."

"Not sure where we're going to find strippers, but I know you'll come through for me," X said.

X's head went to the side as Ashton backhanded him. The diamond left a small gash on his cheek.

"I'm going to regret that ring," X said, shaking it off. "Anyway, primal ball would be a lot more fun with a goalie."

"I've gotta talk to Tiny," Kade said.

"We'll be here when you get back," X said.

"I'll walk you. These assholes are just making me jealous," Ashton said.

They walked side by side back toward the dorm, but didn't say anything to each other. The whole walk Ashton kept opening her mouth to speak, but would then would shut it again and just smile with her cheeks going red.

Kade grabbed the lowest rung of the ladder and hoisted himself up. "Thanks for the company."

"Kade," Ashton said, swallowing hard. She glanced sideways like she was making sure no one else was around. "I don't know if I've ever actually told you, but I love you."

He let go of the ladder and dropped to the ground. Gently, he gave his sister a hug, then lowered himself to give her a quick peck on the forehead. "When did you turn soft?"

"You're supposed to say, *I love you too*. That's how that works," Ashton said, pushing away from her brother.

"I love you too."

She smiled at him and headed back to the game. Kade climbed the ladder, not sure if he was ready to face what he had been avoiding.

The new one in the pack turned out to be stronger than any of them had thought she would be, since she still looked like an other. Alpha stayed close to her. Without the claws the rest of them had, she was at a disadvantage, so he kept an eye on her. Any of his pack could pose a threat to the one the interloper had charged him with, and he had communicated he would protect her.

Recently the pack had run down a deer, and Alpha was guarding Grace while she fed. Pepper nudged him in the ribs with her head, and Alpha did a pass to run alongside her before going back to watching over Grace.

There was a crashing through the trees, and the council of foamers led by Beta were upon them. Beta leapt headfirst through the air, smashing broadside into Pepper. He landed on top of her and slashed her face with a clawed hand. Before he could strike again, Alpha threw a shoulder into him, sending him sprawling across the ground.

Grace growled, locking arms with her attacker. Where her opponent's hands met her shoulder, the claws dug in, but Grace didn't give up her hold.

Alpha wanted to pursue Beta and finish the job, but there were three more foamers catapulting toward them. The nearest was heading for Pepper, who was still like a turtle on her back. Alpha stepped over Pepper and planted his weight in front of her.

The foamer leapt. Alpha didn't budge. He caught the creature's head in the air, letting his long claws pierce his opponent's eyes. Another foamer smashed into Alpha's side, knocking him to the ground. Alpha wrapped his attacker up and rolled before tossing him away. Rotating to all fours, Alpha braced for the next attack.

Pepper was back on her feet and went to Grace's aid. The two worked together to take her opponent to the ground, but the usurper fought frantically to keep them at bay.

Beta crashed into Alpha, who wrapped his arms around him. Letting Beta close was the last thing Alpha wanted to do. He had seen his second fight many times, and now he got to feel it. Beta struck rapidly with his knuckles into Alpha's ribs. Alpha tried to toss the smaller one away, but Beta had planted himself firmly.

Alpha let out a howl of pain as the other two rebelling foamers slammed into him. He landed on the fallen branches and rotting foliage. Beta stayed on top of Alpha, and instinctively Alpha protected his head, trying to toss Beta off him. Beta was going nowhere, squeezing tight to Alpha's sides with his quads. One foamer wrapped up Alpha's legs. The last one pounced for Alpha's throat. Alpha's left arm caught the attacker by the neck, holding him at bay.

Claws slashed and teeth snapped as the three foamers cut Alpha, but they were unable to deliver a kill shot. The two females were still locked in battle with the final foamer. Alpha had no help coming.

He reached out with his right arm, trying to find a hold he could use to pull himself away. His fingers curled around the thick branch of a fallen tree. Alpha pulled hard, trying to remove himself from the skirmish. The branch snapped off in his hands. He was about to drop the branch when a strange instinct came over him. The interloper had held something in his hand when he fought the pack. Instead of dropping the branch, he tightened his grip around it.

With a mighty swing, Alpha clocked Beta on the head with the branch. Beta rolled sideways off of Alpha. He was out cold. The next swing came down on the back of the head of the one holding his legs. The foamer loosened his grip, and Alpha stomped him off. Freeing his body, he kept his grip on the foamer's neck and slammed the weaker creature to the ground. Descending through a fury of slashes, Alpha bit hard on the neck artery and tore it open. The gush of blood covered his face as he turned to face the stunned attacker. The creature's head was held low while it stumbled about. Alpha brought the branch high, like an executioner's ax, and smashed in the mutineer's skull, snapping the branch in half. Alpha rushed to the two females, but arrived just in time to watch them finish off their aggressor.

Alpha sucked in deep breaths as blood dripped from a dozen small gashes across his body. Beta shook off his stun and found himself facing Alpha, Pepper, and Grace. Rearing back, Alpha beat his chest and let out a dominating roar.

Beta's eyes quickly accounted for the dead bodies around him. He backed away a step, but Alpha slammed down and closed the distance between them. Beta took the only option he had left and went to a low bow with his head to the ground.

Alpha wouldn't accept his submission and pinned Beta's head down with one of his large mitts, then drew his claws across Beta's neck in a quick jerk. While his former second bled out on the ground, Alpha lifted himself up on two legs and let out a series of hoots signaling to the rest of his pack that it was time to feed.

While the others came through the trees one by one, Alpha returned to the two females. Pepper nuzzled his face and let out a purring sound. Alpha reciprocated the nuzzle, then curled his fingers around one broken half of the branch. He picked it up and turned it over in his hand, watching the motions as if the hand didn't belong to him. Alpha stood as the proud patriarch and roared, lifting the branch high above his head, with Pepper on his right and Grace on his left.

Kade paced outside the door marked with a duct-taped *T*. He had been at it for more than a minute, but wasn't sure how to open the conversation.

"Either come in or go away," Tiny yelled from the other side of the door.

Kade opened the door and went in. Tiny was wearing a pair of athletic shorts and a black sports bra. The large purple bruise stood out against her milky skin, consuming most of her right side. She had dark circles under her eyes.

"Wondered when you'd finally show up. Did anyone treat your wounds?" Tiny asked.

"They're air drying," Kade said.

"You aren't funny. Mick told me about Zack." Tiny's gaze shifted to the floor. "I didn't think both of you could make it back. If it had to be one of you, I'm glad it's you."

Kade let out a deflated sigh. "He was right. Neither of us deserves you."

"I think you should have a seat. I need to tell you something."

On Kade's way to sit beside her, he said, "Zack made me promise I'd tell you he already broke the news before you could, so he knew he'd piss you off one last time. I know you're pregnant."

Tiny looked ready to murder, then her face softened and she let out a laugh. "That would be Zack. Seeing as you never wanted kids, how are you doing with the news?"

Kade sat beside Tiny, keeping his eyes forward. He ran a hand through his hair, then placed his sweaty palms on his legs. "I'd be lying if I said I was doing well, but I'm doing better than I was."

Tiny cupped Kade's face and turned it toward her. "I'm not going to try to sell you on the odds, but keep in mind, thirty is a long life expectancy these days. If we have a daughter, Huntington's will be the least of her worries."

Kade put his hand over hers. "I hate the idea of leaving you and a kid behind."

"I don't like the idea of you leaving any more now than I will then, but you've built a village. Neither of us will be on our own."

"I'm scared," Kade said, leaning his forehead against hers.

She gave him a gentle kiss. "Me too. But like everything else, we'll get through it together."

"There's no chance it isn't mine?" Kade asked hopefully.

"What!" Tiny said through gritted teeth.

"Just wishful thinking," Kade said with a smile that disarmed her rage. "I still can't figure out why you didn't take the box of Snickers."

"What Snickers?"

"When we stopped for Drew to use the bathroom. I came out of Sheetz with a box of Snickers. You were talking to Zack, then went into the store to get your own Snickers," Kade said.

Tiny's eyes went wide. "I never even noticed them. I'm sorry. That was the first I was able to talk to anyone about what I thought was going on, and he suggested I take a test. I wasn't looking for a Snickers. If the test hadn't been enough proof, that day in the woods when I puked solidified my suspicions."

"You could have told me sooner."

"There are few things you were ever absolutely certain of, and not having kids was one of them. I didn't know how you would take it, and on that trip it really wasn't the right time to bring it up."

He looked into her warm brown eyes. The woman he had always loved. He might not have ever wanted kids, but things didn't always go the way people planned. For once the derailing of his plans would actually create a life instead of destroy one. He was certain nothing was impossible for the two of them. Despite all the challenges that came with raising a child, especially during the Primal Age, if she was his partner, he would take his chances.

His fingers slid up her back and into her hair. He pressed his lips to hers, and they both forgot about their problems and their pains as he laid her back on the bed.

John burst through the door to the roof and hurried to the edge. He placed his hands on his ledge as his breaths caught in his throat. His chest felt like an elephant was sitting on it, and his vision was turning into tiny black tunnels. The last time he had a panic attack was when he was a kid, but this felt just like those days.

He had gone to Grace's room to see if he could figure out the project for which she had requested his help. There was no project. There was a clean room—something her room rarely was—with an end table sitting in the center. On top of the table were a bottle of wine, two glasses, and a candle.

It was so girly it didn't seem like it was possible he could be in her room. So he checked the door twice to be sure. It was her room. She had wanted to have him to herself. Finally, they would have been together.

John stared at the ground below, trying to remember Kade's words about carrying on, but he could only seem to recall the ones about the easiest step. He put his forehead to the ledge and closed his eyes, hoping to leash his spinning world back under his own control.

A small hand rubbed his back between his shoulder blades.

"Grace?" John asked as he spun around. He was face-to-face with Emma. All his hope and joy faded in that second.

"Just me. I'm sorry about Grace," Emma said.

John moved away from her. "You don't understand."

"I have no idea if my mum, dad, little sister, boyfriend, or anyone I ever knew is still alive. I do understand. This isn't something you have to deal with on your own," Emma said, watching John back away, but not pursuing him.

John waved his hands in front of his body, like a baby bird trying to fly. "I don't want help from you."

"All I'm trying to do is be your friend," Emma said.

"I don't think we can be friends."

Emma bit her bottom lip and turned her back to John. She didn't say a word as she left the room, and John wasn't sure, but he thought she may have been crying. The better man inside of John wanted to go after her and comfort her for what she was going through, but he couldn't bring himself to do anything but feel sorry for himself.

He leaned his forearms on the ledge and gazed in the direction he believed the pack of foamers—among them, Grace—were wandering.

The door opened behind him.

"I already told you, I don't want to be friends," John hissed.

"I never liked you much anyhow," Kade's voice replied.

John spun around to find his leader leaning in the doorway.

"Sorry, I thought you were . . . someone else," John said.

"Whoever that someone else is, you should probably reconsider being friends. There aren't many of us left. But I'm not here to lecture you. X told me you missed church. Tomorrow we can secure your old church and then, if you'd like, you can host a mass every week," Kade said.

John mulled the idea over. There were many doubts he had about the idea—like if he would even have an audience to address—but maybe if he spent time in church it would help fill that empty feeling.

"Thanks, Kade," John said.

"We all need to hold on to whatever gives us faith. Now come on, the rules have been finalized for primal ball," Kade said, waving John toward him.

John shook his head. "I really don't want to play games right now."

"Which is exactly why you should," Kade replied. "You can come by choice or force, and I'd rather not embarrass you."

John conceded with a nod and followed Kade.

Cunningham lay as still as she could. Her captors had treated most of her wounds, but they had not spared any painkillers, and just breathing was enough to make her want to pass out. Looking at the makeshift cast, she knew she would be stuck here a long time, but she wouldn't waste the opportunity.

The police officer seemed to think he could change her. She could simply play into his hopes until she had an opportunity to strike. She smiled to herself, thinking this was almost too easy.

She would be a spy without even having to try. By the time she left them, she would be able to provide the president with all the information he wanted. If she had known they were this stupid, she would have found a way to get captured a long time ago. For now, all she had to do was bide her time and tolerate some pain before her opportunity came.

The familiar feel of being alive came back to Kade while he stood between the two goal posts watching the ball work its way around the field. They had gotten everyone out to play, even the elusive Damian. Ashton jogged down the middle of the field, serving as their referee. The two horses grazed by the helicopter, while Fenris watched over Rex and Bristle. The cheetah and puppy were becoming quick friends.

Kade thought their unanimous involvement stemmed from the fact that, even though their most recent battles were behind them, all of them still had wars to fight. Each needed a brief respite from the reality of life, and this game of games was the best outlet they had.

In the Old World, Kade had loved being between the posts. It gave him clarity and silenced his thoughts. Watching each of his family members, blood and water alike, and knowing the struggles they each had made cleared his mind—a difficult task.

Jem hurled a ball past Kade, who fetched it from the goal and sent it back out for his team to restart at half. Kade had lost so much more than a point. Drew, Scott, Zack, and Grace were gone. He hoped one day they would be able to rehabilitate Grace, but he feared that day wouldn't come for a very long time. And though he hadn't really known him, Yuzuki's friend Anquan had died during one of Kade's plans as well.

Another goal blew by Kade, this one courtesy of John. Jem and Mick had spent days being tortured and drugged. Meredith had been violated by Wright and had to survive a bout with the Feline Flu vaccine. Damian had a finger shot off. Tiny had been shot. Ashton had her arm broken. Almost no one in the group had survived the past few days without an injury.

The next goal was delivered by Emma. Kade stood and watched the ball sitting in the net, wondering if he should even bother retrieving it. There was so little to be happy about. The battles had taken their toll. The cohort had gotten Victoria back, and added Yuzuki, Emma, Meredith, and Franklin. They had managed to retrieve Jem and Mick. Overall, it still felt like he was coming out in the negative.

Tiny walked past Kade and picked up the ball. She put a hand on his shoulder and looked him dead in the eye. "Goldfish."

A relic from Kade's past, *goldfish* was what his soccer coach used to tell the players when they needed to move on from their mistakes. A goldfish has a five-second memory, which never allows them to dwell on the good or bad. It was necessary for a goalie, and more importantly a leader, to always remember to keep moving forward. To move on.

Kade gave her a nod, and she returned to midfield to restart play.

He watched Tiny work her way up the field and couldn't help but grin. He was beyond terrified of being a father, but he knew anything was possible with her on his team.

As the ball worked its way back down to Kade's side of the field, he found the old goalie lying dormant within him and released him into a nirvana-like bliss. He focused on the laughter of his friends and believed for the remainder of the game that the only thing that mattered was the score.

Kade leaped to snatch the next shot that came his way. While he looked down field for a player to pass to, he noticed that the middle finger on his left hand was tapping on the ball. He hadn't told it to do that. After he made the pass down to Tiny, five seconds went by before his finger stop moving of its own accord. He tried not to think about it, and turned his focus back to the game and helping his team win, whatever the cost.

Eventually the game would end. The score wouldn't matter. And the Primal Age would come crashing back down on all of them. But for the next ninety minutes of their lives, the only thing that anyone cared about was winning.

ACKNOWLEDGMENTS

Thank you to the purchasers of the first book. Without you guys this series wouldn't have been able to continue. Cheers to two.

Kaylie Jones Books and Akashic Books for making this possible.

My first round of readers: Kristen Millar, Rachel Wiren, and Ryan McAninch.

My family for keeping me alive so I can keep writing.

The ten or so employers who keep spots for me whenever I need to work so I can keep my writing lifestyle.

Everyone who bounced ideas or was willing to tell me when I suck during the course of this project. Especially J. Patrick Redmond, author of *Some Go Hungry*, who offered advice on the development of a certain character.

Those closest to me who tolerated the difficulties of loving a writer.

And lastly, the Hi Life Diner in Mechanicsburg, Pennsylvania, for reserving the booth with the power outlet for me every day, keeping my coffee full, and letting me write for hours a day.

CPSIA information can be obtained at www.ICGtesting.com
Printed in the USA
LVOW08s0201060916

503281LV00013B/886/P